Sweet Sacrifices

by

Gloria Davidson Marlow

Sweet Sacrifices

Cover Art by *Nicola Martinez*

The Wild Rose Press
PO Box 706
Adams Basin, NY 14410-0706
Visit us at www.thewildrosepress.com

Publishing History
First Vintage Rose Edition, 2010
Print ISBN 1-60154-865-6

Published in the United States of America

Dedication

To Jason.

Prologue

Jacksonville, Florida
July 13, 1927

Kendall smoothed the secondhand dress over her knees and brushed a small speck of dirt from one shoe. She patted her hair gingerly, making certain the loose chignon still held. For the first time in her sixteen years of life, she felt almost pretty.

As soon as she'd opened the box of hand-me-downs Layton Christopher delivered to their door last month and saw the beige chiffon dress dotted with small burgundy flowers, she knew it was the one she would wear on her birthday. When she came upon the matching dress shoes at the bottom of the box, she actually squealed in delight. Like the glass slippers in the fairy tale her mother loved, the shoes were bright satin omens of her future.

Any minute, her father would come out of his house and walk towards her. This morning, she had no intention of letting him pass her by. She was going to speak to him today, and she needed to look like someone he would want to know.

A few blocks away the chiming of church bells announced the top of the hour, and her breath hitched in her chest. Her life was about to change forever.

As she focused her gaze back on the house, a startled gasp escaped her. Looking as if she had every right to be there, her mother marched through the wrought iron gate and straight up the pathway to the front door. Kendall surged to her feet,

1

intending to call out but rendered mute by surprise when her mother opened the door and let herself in.

Stunned, Kendall slowly lowered herself back to the bench, never taking her eyes from the door. A million questions danced through her head as she waited for her mother to emerge. In sixteen years, Kendall could never remember her mother speaking to her father. She barely spoke *of* him, as a matter of fact. Most of what Kendall knew of her father came from her own observations and conjectures.

The first gunshot echoed through the windows of her father's house and down the quiet, tree-lined street. The second came only moments later, followed by a seemingly endless scream.

"Mama!" Kendall jumped up, but this time the unfamiliar heels threw her off balance, and her ankle twisted painfully beneath her. She righted herself quickly and, ignoring the throbbing pain, stumbled into the street.

Arms caught her from behind, pinning her to a hard masculine chest as she fought wildly to get to her mother.

"Let me go!" she screeched.

"Shush, Kendall," he commanded as a car stopped beside them. He shoved her into the back seat and climbed in beside her.

"You know where to go," he told the driver. As the car turned the corner, he added, "No good can come of anyone knowing she was there."

Chapter One

August 1939

Kendall shifted uncomfortably on the hard wooden chair. The aches and pains associated with giving birth a little over two weeks ago made it almost impossible to get comfortable anywhere, much less on a chair at least two inches narrower than her hips. The sudden fullness of her breasts made her acutely aware of the time, and she glanced at the baby in the basket at her feet. Any minute now, his eyes would pop open and he would begin to cry. Like clockwork, her milk and his hunger came every two hours. When she left home at one o'clock, she planned to be back long before his next feeding, her teaching schedule for the year in hand. Instead, the receptionist had asked her to wait before finally leading her into the conference room where the board of directors held their monthly meetings. Today the room was empty except for Kendall, her child, and the two men seated behind the long, high tables.

"Miss James." Superintendent Daniels' normally warm voice was cool with what she recognized as condescension.

"Mrs. Templeton," she corrected as she ceased her wriggling and prayed for the baby to sleep just a few more minutes.

"Miss James," he repeated impatiently, "we have called you here today to discuss your request for a position in the coming term."

Choosing to ignore his blatant refusal to use her

married name, she pasted a smile on her face as she met his eyes. In the five years since she met him, she'd witnessed Edward Daniels stare down many people, students and adults alike. His pale blue eyes remained impassive even as he seemed to read their minds, delving into the darkest secrets they harbored. Although she found it intimidating, Kendall refused to look away. Let him read her mind. There weren't any secrets.

"We have thoroughly reviewed your request to teach at Chadsworth in the coming year. Unfortunately, we do not have any positions open at this time."

Her stomach dropped at his words, and she stared at him in surprise. Her eyes flew to Frank Howard, the principal and one of her closest friends. His kind blue gaze met hers briefly before he looked away from her silent plea.

"But I spoke to Ellen McDougal last week, and she said several teachers were leaving this year. I can teach anything." She hated the pleading note in her voice, but she desperately needed this job.

"Miss McDougal spoke out of turn, Miss James. She has no business telling anyone whether there are positions open at this school or not." Superintendent Daniels straightened the papers in front of him and stood up.

"Thank you for your time, Miss James," he said dismissively.

Fear clawed at her chest, and she placed a hand there as if she could stop the frantic pounding of her heart.

"Superintendent Daniels, please," she cried.

He turned toward her, pinning her with a cold stare.

"Miss James, it is my job to make sure Chadsworth lives up to its impeccable reputation. In order to maintain that reputation, our teachers' lives

4

need to be open books, above reproach. When we agreed to hire you several years ago, we overlooked your lack of breeding and appropriate history because of your association with Mr. Howard. You were an exemplary teacher, and we were quite pleased to have you. Now, however, your circumstances have changed, and there are several members of the board who think we would be doing the school and our students a grave disservice by allowing you to return. When we received your request, the board unanimously voted against it. Absolutely nothing you say will change that decision."

She remained seated as he exited the room.

"Come on, Ken," Frank said. "Let me walk you out."

"I don't understand," she told him as she picked the basket up and let him lead her out of the building.

Once they reached the cobblestone walkway that circled a large fountain before branching out to the educational buildings and dormitories, Frank stopped and turned toward her.

"Kendall, you're a woman alone with a baby. They don't think it's proper."

"I'm married, Frank."

He rubbed a hand over his prematurely bald head. She had met Frank after her mother's death, when he appeared on Mary Christopher's doorstep to retrieve her on behalf of the Christian Children's Society. After all these years, she recognized his nervousness.

"I'm married," she repeated.

"I know that, but they don't," Frank said. "You've spent your entire pregnancy alone. I believe you because I know you, Kendall. But anyone can buy a ring and say they're married. You wouldn't be the first girl to try it."

"That's crazy."

"Several of the board members took it upon themselves to look into the county records for your marriage certificate. I don't know whether they did it to prove you were married or to prove you weren't. They felt I was too personally involved to be objective, so they held the board meetings regarding your employment without me." He placed a hand on her shoulder and looked at her sadly. "There isn't a marriage certificate, Kendall."

She swatted his hand away impatiently. "That's ridiculous, Frank. I'm married, and you know it."

"Where is your husband, Kendall?" he asked. "He's been gone for months. He's been gone longer than he stuck around after your marriage. Longer than you knew him before you married him."

His voice softened. "You know I would help if I could, but my hands are tied. I can't go over their heads. I can't afford to lose my job."

What about me? I've lost it all, she wanted to scream. Instead, she nodded her head in feigned understanding and murmured an assurance.

Sunlight glittered on the water in the fountain's pool, and she thought of the countless girls who had sat on its edge, tossing in coins and making wishes. Over the years, she'd heard numerous claims of the fountain's mystical powers. Of course, she dismissed each and every one of them. Yet, when her own wishes seemed to come true, she was almost tempted to believe. She shook her head ruefully. Shouldn't she have learned long ago that a woman couldn't wish her way to happiness?

A bell announced the change of class and she forced her attention back to Frank.

"You're a wonderful teacher, and I would have been happy to take you back. I just can't do it." He pulled a paper from his coat pocket. "I wrote you a very good reference, and you can always have prospective employers contact me here at the school. I'll put in a good word for you. You should have another position in no time. Take care, Kendall."

Chattering school girls spilled from the buildings, and he gave her a quick fatherly peck on the cheek before hurrying back inside.

Aware of the curious glances from colleagues watching the students' progress from their doorways, Kendall practically ran down the path toward the parking area beyond the school grounds. Several students called out greetings to her as she pushed past them. Although she managed to return their greetings in a surprisingly normal voice, she never stopped moving, and made it to the edge of the cobblestones just as the tardy bell sounded behind her. With a cry of despair, she sank to the dusty ground of the parking lot, her legs no longer able to support her.

She buried her face in her hands, hearing Frank's words. *Where is your husband, Kendall? Why isn't he here?*

If only she knew the answers to those questions, her problems would be solved. She hadn't heard from him at all in six months and hadn't seen him in even longer. She didn't blame people for questioning his existence; sometimes she almost believed she imagined him.

The baby began to fuss, reminding her that somewhere out there she had a real flesh-and-blood husband.

****

Two weeks later, Kendall left the house she and Adam had rented after their marriage. She left the homemade kitchen curtains, the secondhand furniture, and the few whatnots she owned in their places and walked out. She placed the keys in the hand of the waiting sheriff's deputy. Then, with baby basket and suitcase in hand, she walked through the gate in the white picket fence for the last time. She forced herself to hold her head high, though she wanted to fall to her knees and beg for mercy. She knew as well as anyone that it wouldn't work. The landlord had done all he could to let her stay until after the baby was born, but times were hard for everyone, and he couldn't allow her to live there indefinitely without paying. Last month he had told her she needed to find another place to live.

After her meeting at Chadsworth, she desperately sought a job, but to no avail. The public school system didn't have any openings, at least not for a woman with a baby but no husband in sight. There were precious few jobs available anywhere, and in the long lines of applicants the mother of an infant held little attraction to any employer.

With nowhere else to go, she spent her last few dollars on a small hotel room near the bus station. She lay wide awake in bed, the baby close to her side as she planned her next move. She had no family, no friends, no past she cared to revisit, and no future beyond the one she'd planned to spend with Adam. There was nothing to hold her here, especially when all she dreamed of was somewhere else. Why would she stay? She came up with no good answer to the question. Why would she go? Adam. Love. Brady. She looked down at her son, and a small sigh escaped her. She wanted Brady to have a father, and she knew Adam well enough to know he wanted his son. No matter what, he would want to know his child. And hopefully, when he saw her again, he would know he wanted her, too.

Dawn was just breaking when Kendall slipped from the room and made her way to the nearest pawn shop. Her wedding ring was just a simple gold band, but the owner gave her enough money to purchase a one-way bus ticket. She suspected he knew he would never get his money out of the ring, but she was beyond pride at the moment, so she accepted his charity and took what he offered.

An hour later, she climbed onto the waiting bus and headed for the town postmarked on her husband's last letter.

As the sun began to sink into the horizon, she leaned her head wearily against the bus window, wrapping her arms around her waist in a halfhearted attempt to ward off the unseasonable chill seeping through her thin cotton dress. She knew the coolness should be a welcome sign that the long hot summer was coming to an end. Instead, it served as a frightening reminder that winter loomed before her while she had no place to call home.

The last vestiges of hope ravaged her heart on a daily basis. Even now, as she reached into her purse and drew out the single piece of worn paper and crumpled envelope, she prayed Adam was alive. She didn't want him dead, no matter if he chose a life without her. In her battered heart beat the faint hope that she would find him alive and well, with a logical reason for not coming back to her. In the rational part of her mind, however, she knew that hope ultimately led to a broken heart. That part of her mind said not to waste her time or energy on idle dreams and hopes for a happy ending. A woman must make her own ending, be it happy or sad.

The letter she unfolded and reread was different from his others. Each week for two months she had received a letter assuring her that his business ventures in Larrimore were going well and he would send for her as soon as he secured a place for them to live. Each of his letters contained a few dollars to see her through to the next week. Luckily, she had saved a portion of the money each week. Otherwise, she would have been on the street long before now.

Nearly three months after Adam left, the doctor confirmed her pregnancy. Longing to see his face when she told him the news, she wrote him, begging him to come home for a few days.

His reply was the last letter she ever received from him:

I miss you horribly. Things have taken a turn for the worse here. I don't know when I'll see you again. It may be a month. It may be longer. I may have to leave here. It's all very uncertain, but I will write you again as soon as I can. For now, know that I love you, and remember me kindly.

Certain he was in some sort of trouble, she wrote him back, this time telling him about the baby and promising that everything would be fine if he would just come home, but he never answered that letter at all. She wrote him a dozen more times but never received a reply.

She didn't know what to expect when she reached her destination. She wasn't even sure she would find Adam there. She could only pray she found the answers to her questions. In her darkest moments, she imagined standing at his gravesite, finally knowing why he had stopped answering her letters.

She could still hear his voice as clear as a bell, and the feel of his arms around her was a vivid memory she longed to forget during the endless lonely nights since he left. His face, however, came in fleeting little wisps. For a moment, she clearly recalled his features: the light, teasing eyes, the mouth that smiled so easily, the dark curling hair. She clung to the memory before it disappeared once again, like breath on a windowpane.

Beside her, the baby stretched and whimpered, and she pushed away the dark thoughts of Adam and turned to their son.

"Hi, Pumpkin," she cooed as she ran a finger gently around his face. "Are you hungry?"

He turned his head toward her finger, his tiny mouth open wide. When she pulled her finger away, he flailed his arms angrily and began to cry in earnest. With swift but gentle efficiency, she lifted him from his basket, placed a blanket over her shoulder, and opened her blouse. She smiled indulgently at the quiet piggy noises he made while he nursed.

She leaned back in the seat, welcoming the peacefulness that nursing Brady brought to her. It still surprised her that motherhood made her feel so complete. Her own mother had never seemed completed by it. Twelve years after her suicide, Lydia James remained an enigma to her daughter. As a child, Kendall had tried to solve the mystery of her mother's perpetual misery. She asked endless questions her mother refused to answer and, more often than not, after she peppered her mother with questions Kendall heard her crying in the night. Finally, she realized the questions were never going to be answered and, not wanting to cause her mother such pain, she quit asking them and came to her own conclusions about her mother's sad existence.

Through the years, she'd vowed to do everything differently and never make the same mistakes her mother made. Yet, here she was, alone with a newborn baby, barely a penny to her name, and no prospects of a brighter future.

Like mother, like daughter.

Chapter Two

Just as the baby drifted off to sleep, a few pitiful lights came into view ahead. Despite the burned-out bulbs in the signs, Kendall saw they announced the bus station, a hotel, and several bars disguised as restaurants along the waterfront. With a sinking heart, she placed Brady back in his basket and waited for the bus to come to a full stop before she stood. She grimaced a bit at the twinges of pain. Unsure if she could face what waited for her here in this sad little town, she was tempted to sink back to her seat and let the bus take her wherever it went next.

"Daddy!" a small voice cried from outside the bus window, and Kendall watched a soldier disembark from the bus and gather a tiny boy in his arms. With the other arm, he pulled a woman close.

Kendall straightened resolutely, lifted the basket, and moved out of her seat. Resolve strengthened her backbone as she slipped past the small family and walked toward the information booth of the bus station.

Soon, Brady would learn to talk, and she wanted him to be able to say "daddy" and have someone answer.

The man behind the counter of the information booth peered through his thick glasses at her.

"Can I help you, ma'am?" he asked, his eyes darting to the baby and back to her face several times.

"Could you tell me how to get to Hammond Street, please?"

"Hammond Street?" he repeated, puzzlement wrinkling his pudgy brow as he pushed the glasses farther back on his nose. "Who are you looking for?"

Kendall couldn't imagine what business that was of his, but before she could say so, he quickly offered an explanation.

"The roads around here might have proper names, but most of us just know them by who lives there. If you want directions on how to get to someone's house, you'll have to tell me who it is you're looking for."

"Oh," she said, looking around at the narrow street dotted with ramshackle buildings. "To be honest, I don't know where I'm trying to go. My husband is in town, um, he was in town, but I don't know if he still is. I was hoping to find him here, or at least find out where he was headed."

"What's his name, sweetheart?" the short, rotund man asked, his voice growing gentle. "Maybe I'll recognize it."

Kendall blushed at the understanding look in his eyes. He obviously mistook her for an unwed mother looking for the man responsible. She straightened to her full height and looked him right in the eye. She had no reason to be ashamed.

"Templeton. His name is Adam Templeton."

There was no mistaking the surprise and alarm on his reddening face as he repeated the name.

"Ma'am, I believe you'll find Mr. Templeton out at the Grove, but you don't want to try making it out there tonight. It's getting darker by the minute, and it's a ways down that road there." He motioned to a shadowed, winding road. "There won't be any traffic going that way tonight, but in the morning you'll be able to catch a ride for sure. Someone's always headed that way to make a delivery or pick up a load."

"How far is it?" Kendall asked, trying to curtail

the panic rushing through her at the thought of walking down that road in the dark.

"A few miles," he said, "but it ain't populated miles, just acres and acres of citrus trees."

"So, if I just head down the road, I'll get there?" she persisted.

"Yes ma'am," he said as he motioned to the baby, "but like I said, you shouldn't go out there tonight. Stay at the hotel. Nan Marvin will be happy to put you up. I'll call her myself and explain your situation. She can wait payment 'til you locate your man."

He picked up the phone, and she turned to follow the direction of his gaze. She shuddered at the sight of the hotel with its peeling paint and burned-out neon lights. Memories roared to life so quickly that they nearly sucked the breath out of her.

"No," she said, shaking her head. She wouldn't stay there for anything, not even to escape the darkness that stood between her and her destination. "I think I'll just head on out. Maybe I'll get lucky and run into someone."

She ignored his squawks of protest as she picked up her basket and suitcase and headed into the encroaching darkness.

Around her, the air smelled of something familiar yet foreign that tickled her senses with memories. Faces and voices floated about, shapeless and nameless in the dim light: dark memories of a lifetime ago.

Unable to face them tonight, she tried to conjure up a more pleasant memory. There were precious few happy memories of her childhood, so it didn't take her long to find one.

****

Dressed to the nines, her mother smiled like a movie star as she rested her hand against the hood of a black Packard. She wore a tailored gray dress suit trimmed in wide bands of black velvet. Her feet were encased in black high-heeled shoes, and a black cloche hat with a crimson ribbon rested jauntily on her dark curls.

A man stood off to the side, snapping pictures of her and the car. Kendall didn't remember exactly what he looked like, only that he seemed huge, like a big gruff bear.

"Beautiful," he praised as Lydia leaned a hip provocatively against the hood. "Ah, Lydie, you are still a beauty."

Her mother laughed, the sound of it a welcome reprieve from the weeping that overtook her in the night. Mesmerized by the sound and by her mother's beautiful transformation, six-year-old Kendall stepped closer. She wanted to memorize the way her mother looked, the way she moved, the way she smelled.

Although she tried to be quiet and stay out of the way like her mother had told her, her foot caught in a cord running from the lamps, and one of them teetered precariously as she tried to disentangle herself. The man ran to save it.

"Jesus, Lydia!" he roared. "I told you to leave her at home!"

"Go wait outside!" he ordered Kendall as his free hand shot out and caught her by the arm.

"I'm sorry," she whimpered as he opened the door. He gently patted her on the head as he motioned to the bench outside.

"Sit right there. Your mother will be out soon."

She sat there for what seemed like forever, listening to the hum of her mother's low conversation with the man. After a while, she curled up and fell asleep. The sun was setting when her mother, once again dressed in her ratty housedress and scuffed shoes, shook her awake.

Kendall saw the man press some money into her

mother's hand. "I'll let you know if I hear from anyone."

"No, thank you." Her mother tried to give the man his money back, and Kendall saw the tears in her eyes.

"Take it, Lydie," he insisted quietly. "Please. Take her to get some dinner or something. Consider it an advance. I'm sure Packard or someone will want to buy the pictures."

Lydia nodded silently and slipped the money in her pocket. "Come on, Kendall. It's time to go home."

"Will that man come see us, Mama?" she asked innocently as they walked the five miles to the rented rooms they called home.

"Of course not, sweetheart," her mother answered. "He's just a man who takes pictures. Why? Do you want him to visit?"

"I thought maybe he could be my daddy."

"He can't be your daddy, Kendall. You already have a daddy."

"I do?" Kendall asked, fascinated. "Why doesn't he come to see us?"

"He will one day," Lydia promised, and they once again grew silent.

****

Shoulders burning from the strain of carrying the suitcase and basket, Kendall stepped off the gravel road and sank onto the grass. She'd never dreamed how heavy a baby and suitcase would get or how long a few miles could seem. She pulled aside the blanket draped over the basket and peeked in at the baby. He was sleeping peacefully, and she smiled as his mouth turned up slightly in his sleep.

She stood at the sound of an approaching vehicle. Truck lights illuminated the road, showing only dense citrus trees as far as she could see on either side. She saw no evidence of a house in sight, and she wondered if the man at the bus station had sent her out on a wild goose chase. Suffused with uneasiness, she stood her ground as the truck approached her. She had no idea what else to do.

"Elmer called from the station. Said you might need a ride," the driver announced through the open window as he came to a stop beside her. He leaned down to the floorboard. "Just need to move these tools."

Her breath caught in her throat as the driver straightened and their eyes met in the dim glow of the overhead lamp.

"Adam," she breathed, joy shooting through her.

He stared at her, his face tight with emotion, before turning away.

"Get in," he ordered.

She fought a wave of pain and humiliation at his coldness. She had no choice but to do as he said. Turning back wasn't an option.

When she was in the truck, the baby basket between them, he shoved the gearshift into drive and the truck shot forward. He spared only a quick glance at the baby and never looked her way at all as he turned the truck back the way he had come.

When the silence got the best of her, she turned to face him. Even in the dim light she could see the anger that tightened his jaw.

"Adam," she began, but broke off with a cry as he jammed hard on the brakes. Instinctively, she reached for the basket, anger flooding through her as the baby began to cry.

"Why did you do that? You could have hurt him!"

His face softened almost imperceptibly as he looked down at the wailing infant.

"Is he okay?"

"He's fine," she snapped. With a sigh, she added, "I hoped to be there before he woke up."

Knowing he wouldn't hush until she fed him,

she lifted Brady from the basket and opened the top few buttons of her dress.

"What are you doing?" the man at the wheel demanded, sounding, if she wasn't mistaken, more than a little panicked.

"Feeding our son," she said without looking up from the baby.

"Put this over you." He tossed the baby's blanket at her.

Giving an exasperated sigh, she threw the blanket angrily over her shoulder and covered the baby so that only his feet were visible.

"For goodness' sake, Adam. You act like you've never seen my breasts before. What is wrong with you?" She lifted her eyes to his, her own blue gaze locking with his steel gray one.

"I'm not Adam."

"What?" Her voice was barely a whisper.

"You heard me. I'm not Adam."

"Of course you are," she said, touching his shoulder gently. Did he have amnesia? That explained so much. Surely, she hadn't really believed he left her on purpose. "Oh, Adam, what happened? Don't you remember anything?"

"I told you, I'm not Adam," he growled.

When their eyes met again, she knew the truth.

"Who are you?" she whispered. How could she mistake those deep angry eyes for Adam's clear, lighthearted gaze?

"Luke Templeton. I'm his twin."

"His twin?" she repeated, her mind numb with surprise.

"I gather my brother forgot to mention my existence?" He raised his eyebrows sardonically.

She nodded and quickly adjusted the blanket more carefully over her breast.

"Typical," he said as he started the truck and pulled back onto the road.

18

"Where are you taking us?"

"Home, of course. That's why you're here, isn't it? To see Adam? To demand that he acknowledge your baby and pay you what you want to go away? Or demand that my family does, if Adam refuses?"

"I'm his wife," she cried defensively. "We were married two years ago."

"Well, isn't that something? It seems he forgot to mention your existence, too."

Chapter Three

"Welcome to The Grove," Luke Templeton said as he pulled the truck to a stop in front of an immense antebellum mansion.

Kendall stared up at the house. What in the world were they doing here?

"Do you work here?" she asked, recalling the tools that littered the floorboard of the truck.

He gave a short bark of laughter. "You're kidding, right?"

At her denial, he rolled his eyes and jumped out.

"Why are we here?" she demanded as he walked around and opened the door for her.

Reaching into the bed of the truck and lifting her suitcase out, he looked at her with a smile that sent chills of foreboding racing down her spine.

"We live here, sugar. My daddy's granddaddy built this house a hundred years ago. We own everything for as far as your eyes can see. But I'm pretty sure you already knew that."

Speechless, she shook her head in denial of his assumption, but he already had his back to her as he marched up the large stone steps. Taking a deep breath to calm herself, she grabbed the baby and raced after him.

"Luke, darling. Where in the world have you been?" a feminine voice drawled just as they came through the etched glass doors. He stopped so quickly, Kendall nearly ran into him.

She looked toward the wide wooden staircase in the center of the hall and caught her breath at the woman descending them. Dressed in a long, flowing mauve dinner gown with a single strand of pearls adorning her neck, she moved forward with effortless grace. Her silver blonde hair was cut to curl fashionably about her face, and although she wasn't a beautiful woman, she was absolutely stunning.

The woman's eyes widened as Brady began to cry, and Luke turned toward Kendall.

"Mother, this is—I'm sorry. I don't think you told me your name." He searched her eyes for a moment as she fought for her voice.

"Kendall James Te—" She broke off when he narrowed his eyes in warning. "Kendall James. Most people call me Ken."

"Kendall, this is my mother, Delores Templeton. Most people call her Mrs. Templeton."

"Luke, don't tease the child," his mother scolded with a bewildered glance toward him. Quickly, she turned her attention back to Kendall. "You look ready to drop, dear. How old is your baby?"

"Four weeks." She smiled as she looked down at him.

"Why, he's not old enough to be out and about. Nor should you be out so soon after giving birth." She turned accusingly to her son. "Luke, you show this poor girl to the parlor right this minute, and make her sit down. I'll have some refreshments brought in."

Luke led the way to the room his mother indicated. Motioning to a sofa covered in flowered brocade, he lowered himself into a chair opposite it.

"Why didn't you want me to tell your mother my last name?"

"I thought it best if we tried to work this out calmly. If you just came right out and said you were Adam's wife, Mother would go nuts. When she comes in, I'll tell her. Then, you can explain everything to both of us."

Delores Templeton entered a moment later, followed by a young Spanish woman carrying a tray of drinks. The young woman's eyes widened at the sight of Kendall and the baby, before darting to Luke.

"Thank you, Juanita. That will be all," Delores said with a wave of her hand. When the woman left, she turned to Luke. "Why don't you tell me what's going on here, son?"

Before he could speak, a laughing couple strode into the room. They were dressed for dinner, he in a dark suit and she in an emerald green dress that enhanced the long straight line of her back and neck. Eyes only for each other, they made their way to the bar in the corner. The man leaned over and kissed the woman, who turned toward him with a smile. They didn't look toward the threesome already occupying the room until Delores cleared her throat in an effort to garner their attention.

"Oh, Mother," the man said with an embarrassed grin as he and the woman turned toward them. "I didn't see you sitting there. Or you, Luke."

He looked toward Luke, who in turn looked to Kendall sitting still and pale on the sofa.

The man followed the path of his brother's eyes, and his face drained of color.

She stood up slowly, her gaze never leaving Adam's. Her mind barely registered Luke standing and moving to her side. She wanted to beg him not to say anything, but her voice wouldn't come. From a distance, he spoke the most horrible words imaginable.

"Kendall James," he said, "I'd like to introduce you to my brother, Adam, and his wife, Margo."

His wife, his wife, his wife. The words beat like a drum in her head as her vision wavered and she felt herself sway unsteadily on her feet.

"Sit down before you fall down," Luke murmured for her ears only as he stepped in front of her, effectively blocking her view of Adam and Margo.

Her legs turned to liquid, and she sank obediently to the sofa.

Chapter Four

His mother shooed him away, and Luke quickly stepped back, letting her take over Kendall's care.

"I need to talk to you," he growled as he stalked past his brother and headed to the study down the hall.

As soon as the door closed behind them, Luke swung around.

"She says she's your wife. Says she has been for two years. But how can that be, Adam, when you've been married to Margo for eight?"

Adam glanced back over his shoulder, concern in his voice. "Do you think she's okay?"

"What do you care?" Luke couldn't remember ever in their lives wanting so badly to pummel his brother.

"I care for her, Luke. I came home to tell Margo I wanted a divorce, but as soon as I saw her again, I knew I couldn't do that to her. God, Luke, what am I going to do? I can't lose Margo. But I hate to hurt Kendall."

"I think you've already done that, Adam. Did you happen to notice the baby beside her?"

"What?" Adam's face lit with joy. "A baby? Mine?"

"Well, that's what Kendall seems to believe. Do you?"

"It would have to be. I'm the only guy she's ever been with."

"What about since you?"

"Kendall? Are you kidding? She thinks we're married. She's not the cheating type."

"She seemed completely floored by the fact that you lived here. She actually asked me if you worked here. Apparently, she's quite an accomplished actress."

"I never told her about the family. She doesn't know we're rich."

Luke could hardly believe his ears.

"So, you're telling me that you seduced a virgin, a—how old is she?—twenty-something-year-old virgin, pretended to marry her, and left her?"

"Don't lecture me, Luke," Adam said with a wave of his hand. "I don't know if it was all that bad. Maybe she did know I had money. I mean, maybe I let it slip somehow."

Luke stared hard at Adam, trying to gauge the truth of what he said. He'd known his brother was irresponsible and somewhat flippant, but he'd never known him to be cruel. He could imagine Adam seducing a woman, but he couldn't believe he would manipulate one into marrying him or abandon his own child. Refusing to allow himself to even consider the possibility that what Kendall claimed was true, he turned his attention back to Adam.

"I need to get back in there before she spills the beans. We'll talk it over later." As he strode down the hall, Luke knew that nothing good could possibly come of any of this. Adam had screwed up big time and there would be hell to pay.

****

"See what I mean?" Delores clucked as she lifted Kendall's feet onto the sofa. "You girls are absolutely killing yourselves these days. Carrying a baby and giving birth is not as easy as men seem to think it is. Don't let them tell you it's all right to be up and about, traipsing all over the place, just because it's convenient for them."

"I'm fine, Mrs. Templeton," Kendall protested when the woman tried to make her lie back.

The woman Luke had introduced as Adam's wife still stood by the bar, drink in hand. Though her stance and her dress bespoke worldly sophistication, childlike confusion marred her beautiful face.

When Adam and Luke reappeared at the door, she hurried to Adam's side. He pulled her against him protectively, his mouth moving against her hair as he murmured soothing words. Within seconds, her eyes cleared and she relaxed against him.

Kendall swallowed the lump in her throat and turned to Luke, who now stood beside his mother. His eyes burned into hers, but mixed with the anger she detected a hint of sympathy.

"Luke, you help Kendall up to the guest room near the nursery," his mother commanded. "Adam, you and Margo do whatever it was you were planning to do before supper. I'll see you then. For now, I want this poor young woman and her baby made comfortable."

With that, Delores picked up the basket with the sleeping infant inside and left the room.

"I can walk," Kendall protested as Luke bent to lift her from the sofa.

"I'll carry you."

"I'll walk," she said and pushed herself to her feet. The near faint was embarrassing enough; she certainly refused to let him carry her up the stairs.

Luke walked beside her, his arm at the small of her back, as she made her way out of the room. She felt Adam's eyes on her as she climbed the stairs, and she fought the urge to turn back to him. As if he could read her mind, Luke's hand pressed firmly against her back, compelling her forward.

"What's your name, honey?" Delores cooed to the baby as they entered the room.

"Brady," Kendall answered wearily as she dropped to the edge of the bed.

"He's my grandson, isn't he?" Delores asked.

"Yes," Kendall whispered in a voice thick with grief.

"What's his full name?" Delores ran her thumb across the tiny fingers curled around her own.

"Brady Adam Templeton."

"So, he's Adam's?" she asked quietly.

"Yes."

"I so hoped he was Luke's." Silence stretched between them as Delores simply stared at Brady. Kendall wondered if she even realized she'd spoken the thought out loud. Finally, she raised her eyes to Kendall's and spoke again, "Why did you come here?"

"I wanted him to know his daddy."

"Didn't you know Adam was married when you got pregnant?"

"Yes, ma'am, I thought he was married to me."

"You thought you were married?" Her eyes widened in disbelief.

"We had a wedding. It was small, but we had one. We rented a house. We lived there together."

"Kendall, I know you're hurt, more than hurt, but Margo and Adam have been married for eight years. His marriage to you was a sham. I'm very sorry. I don't know what possessed him to do such a thing."

"Adam loves me," she declared. Almost unbearable pain overcame her, leaving her sick and weak, when she thought of Adam's duplicity. How could their life together be a lie? They had been totally absorbed in each other, spending as much time as possible in each other's arms. They built a home together. They made a son. And all along, he had another wife. She wondered if he had other children, as well. She hadn't seen any sign of children, but she hadn't been here long, and it was a huge house. He might have a dozen children somewhere, and one baby boy would make little

27

difference to him after all. Then, Brady would just be the unwanted, illegitimate child of a rich man. It broke her heart to think of her son knowing the same pain and loneliness that had haunted her own childhood.

She looked at him, lying so peacefully in his grandmother's arms. The possessive look on the woman's face frightened her, and Kendall held her arms out for him. Delores met her eyes, and Kendall knew instantly that the older woman wouldn't give up her grandchild easily.

"I won't let you take him away," Delores said calmly as she placed him in Kendall's arms.

"He's my child, Mrs. Templeton. If Luke doesn't mind taking us back into town, we'll be leaving. Adam knows about his son now. If he decides he wants to be a part of Brady's life, he knows where to find me."

She picked up her suitcase and turned toward the door.

"Don't be silly, child. It's late, and you don't even know if there's a bus to take you home. You can't very well stay the night in the bus station."

"I'll get a hotel."

"There aren't any." Luke stood at the open door.

"I saw one. I'll stay there. I know it's small, but still..." She tried not to remember the nights she'd spent in similar hotels as a child.

"Kendall, what Luke means is there aren't any acceptable establishments in town. All of them are old and rundown."

"And rented by the hour," Luke added with a slightly mocking smile.

"Luke, don't be crude." Delores moved to her side and grasped the handle of the suitcase Kendall held. Tugging gently, she took it from Kendall's hand and carried it to the bed. "You will not take my grandchild into one of those places. You can stay here. Give Adam the chance to talk to you. Maybe he can explain. If nothing else, he can arrange support for the baby."

What else could she do? She didn't have the money for a room, and she might not be allowed to sit in the hotel lobby all night. She forced away the question of what would happen after tonight and nodded.

"Thank you."

"All I ask is that you are discreet with any dealings you have with Adam. I don't want Margo to get wind of this."

"Of course." Kendall couldn't help the sarcasm and bitterness that tinged her voice. Tall, blonde, beautiful Margo embodied everything Kendall had longed to be since she was a short plump child with limp brown hair and freckles.

"Naturally, you won't be joining us for supper," Delores informed with a dismissive glance from Kendall's crumpled dress to her dusty shoes. "I'll have Juanita prepare a tray and bring it up to you."

"You don't have to bother," Kendall protested. "I'm not hungry."

In truth, she was famished, but she didn't want these people to know she couldn't even afford to feed herself. If they did, they would know how very precarious her position was, and she was certain they would use that knowledge to keep Brady here.

"Still, I'll have a plate sent up to you in case you change your mind," Delores promised. "I'll also have some of the men bring a cradle down from the attic and set it up in here for you."

"Yes, ma'am," Kendall agreed shakily. "Thank you."

With a gentle hand, Delores touched Kendall's cheek. "We'll work this out somehow. Just give me a chance to recover my wits."

Once the door shut behind Luke and his mother,

Kendall got up and locked it. She clutched Brady to her chest and lay back on the bed. Tears flowed down her cheeks, and she fought to control the sobs that racked her body.

Chapter Five

When Kendall woke the next morning, her breasts ached and milk soaked the front of her gown. She'd nursed Brady at two, but he always woke again around four. According to the clock on the night table, it was six, and he still wasn't crying to be fed.

Bounding from the bed, she hurried to the cradle, only to find it empty. With a horrified cry, she rushed from the room, oblivious to the fact that she wore only a sodden nightgown.

"Brady?" she cried as she ran down the hallway, frantically pushing open doors without caring who might be behind them.

The door at the end of the hallway stood partially open, and she heard muffled noises coming from inside. Without knocking she rushed into the room, slamming into a solid wall of a man.

"What the...?" Luke exclaimed as she backed away from his damp, bare chest. Her gaze searched the room frantically.

"What is it?" he demanded catching her by the arm.

"My baby's gone!" she cried.

"Gone?"

She nodded before turning to the door.

His hand tightened around her arm, preventing her escape. "Mother must have him. Follow me."

As they entered his mother's room, Delores set the baby bottle on the table beside her and held Brady against her shoulder, patting him gently.

She looked in surprise from Luke to Kendall.

"What are you doing?" Kendall panted. Weak with relief at the sight of her son, she leaned against a small writing desk for support.

"Feeding him. You were sleeping so soundly, I sent Juanita into town for some milk and a bottle."

"Mother, you should have woken Kendall. You almost scared her to death," Luke said.

His mother was silent as she looked pointedly at the towel around his waist.

"Do you mind telling me why you are running around in nothing but a towel?" she asked disapproval evident in her voice.

"Kendall came to my room frantic. I brought her down to you."

"And neither of you noticed how indecent you look?"

Kendall, much calmer now that Brady was in her sight, turned toward Luke. For the first time, she realized he wore a soft blue towel and nothing else.

She watched his eyes rake over her and was suddenly aware of the soft wet cotton clinging to her breasts and the front of her body. She shivered as the cool morning air wafted through the open door behind Delores.

"I have to get back to my room. I have to change into something dry," she stammered as she walked over to Delores and held her arms out for her child.

"Luke, go get some clothes on. Close the door on your way out," Delores commanded, and Kendall heard the door click behind her.

"Sit down, Kendall."

"I'd prefer to stand, Mrs. Templeton." Her chin lifted defiantly, willing her knees to stop trembling.

"Suit yourself."

Delores stood and began to pace the room with the baby in her arms.

"I've been up all night, Kendall. I can't help but

wonder what you expected to happen when you showed up on Adam's doorstep. Didn't it occur to you that had he wanted to see you, he would have come back to you?"

"Yes, ma'am. That thought did occur to me."

"But you still decided to force yourself into his life?"

"No, ma'am. I decided to force his son into his life."

"And you had no idea he was married?"

"I told you, Mrs. Templeton. Adam and I went through a very real ceremony. I thought we were married."

"Why did you marry my son, Kendall?"

Kendall stared at the woman. Was she completely mad? What could this possibly be leading to? She'd answered these same questions last night. She thought for a moment of just grabbing the baby and running, but the idea of wrestling for him frightened her. What if they dropped him, or she hurt the older woman?

"I love your son, Mrs. Templeton. He is a kind, considerate and handsome man. I fell in love with him the moment we met." Of course, kind, considerate men didn't trick women into marrying them and then abandon them, but she forced that fact away so she could concentrate on Delores' questions.

"Because he's rich?"

Kendall drew in a quick breath at the harshness of the words.

"No," she whispered in denial.

"His money had nothing to do with it?"

"I didn't know he had any money."

"How did you think he ate, or paid for your home, or drove that expensive car of his around?"

"He told me he was a salesman. We rented a very modest home. He didn't drive an expensive car.

He took the city bus every morning." She added the last defensively, as if this cleared her of the woman's suspicions.

"Kendall, my son drives a brand-new Alfa Romeo. There are also a Rolls Royce, a Bentley and a Cadillac limousine in our garage, all of which Adam drives on occasion."

Stunned at the extent of Adam's deceit, Kendall sat heavily on the ottoman in front of Delores. He'd left her to live on barely enough to keep herself alive, give birth alone, and get evicted from their very modest home. All while he lived in this mansion, drove an expensive sports car, and dressed to the nines for dinner with his real wife.

"You truly didn't know?" the older woman asked quietly.

She shook her head miserably.

"Kendall, I don't know what you expected to find when you got here. But I am sure it wasn't this." Delores waved her well manicured hand around the room. "I don't know what kind of reception you expected from a man who hasn't gotten in touch with you for almost a year, but I suspect you're telling the truth when you say you came so Brady could know his father."

Humiliation burned inside of her. Desperate not to repeat her mother's mistakes, certain her son should never face a life without a father, she had chased Adam down only to realize that he'd played her for an absolute fool.

"I have a proposition for you," Delores said. She glanced at the door as if assuring herself it was closed against listening ears. "I know your financial situation. I know you don't have a job, and there are no jobs to be had anywhere right now. I know you lost the house you and Adam shared. I know you have no place to go and no way to survive. I can't imagine what Adam was thinking, how he could be so irresponsible."

"How?" Kendall demanded. "How do you know all those things about me?"

"Before I went to bed last night, I contacted a friend who checked into your background. And I mean all of your background, Kendall. Make no mistake. I know exactly where you come from."

Kendall felt her face grow pale at the images the woman's words brought to mind. Images of dark, smelly hotel rooms, with her mother and men she didn't know, swirled through her head. The smell of smoke and liquor seemed to fill her nostrils as she remembered the nights spent huddled on her pallet listening to the noises coming from the bed beside her.

How could someone dig up her past so easily? How long would being her mother's daughter haunt her?

"Kendall, I can tell just by looking at you that you want better for your son. You wouldn't have come here if you didn't at least want him to have a father. Because you know how it feels not to have one, don't you?"

Kendall nodded, silently. Yes, she knew. It was hard not to have a daddy when every other little girl she knew had one. They told stories of their daddies taking them to the zoo, bringing them candy at the end of the day, and putting toys under the Christmas tree. Even the few children in her class whose fathers were dead had memories to share. She, on the other hand, had nothing at all.

Oh no, that isn't true, she thought bitterly. She had memories of her father.

****

She still remembered the first time she saw him. Her mother had borrowed a car from the man who owned their boarding house and announced they were going for a drive. Seven-year-old Kendall didn't even know her mother could drive. She was absolutely amazed at the sight of her mother sitting there behind the steering wheel, dressed like every other mother, in a flowered dress with a sash, driving gloves and a hat perched on her head. Kendall knew she would never forget that day. They rode for hours, it seemed, before turning onto a tree-lined street in a neighborhood filled with stately mansions.

"That's where your daddy lives, Kendall," Lydia announced as she pulled to a stop in front of a huge brick house with white columns. Flowering trees and shrubs sprinkled the lush green carpet of grass, and a brick pathway led from the front door, across the wide circular driveway, and through an ornate gate in the wrought iron fence.

As Kendall leaned her head out the car window, a tall handsome man came down the steps, holding the hand of a small blonde girl.

"Is that him, Mama?" Kendall glanced at her mother, who nodded mutely. Even at her young age, Kendall recognized the adoration on her mother's face. She also recognized the agony.

"Who's that girl, Mama?" she asked.

"That's his daughter, Kendall," her mother said sadly. "That's the daughter he chose."

She still remembered the sharp sting of pain that had followed her mother's words, though only a dull ache still lingered.

****

"Kendall, don't you want better for Brady?" Delores pressed, bringing her back to the present, to this beautiful room that smelled of expensive perfume and orange blossoms.

"Yes, of course I do." She wanted him to have a father and a mother. She wanted him to be a part of the warm, loving picture everyone else could paint of their families. She wanted him to feel safe and loved.

She never wanted him to be hungry, never wanted him to live in some rat-infested hotel room. Mostly, she never wanted him to have to listen to his mama give her body to a man in exchange for a quart of milk and a pack of cigarettes.

"Well, then, hear me out. I have a plan to give my first grandchild the life he deserves." Delores smiled down at the baby she still held firmly but gently in her arms. "Adam will stay married to Margo, no matter what. I will not have him cause a scandal by divorcing her. Nor will I lose the friendship and business relationship our families have enjoyed for years. I would prefer to keep this strictly between us. Not a breath of this can ever reach Margo's ears. She must never know that Brady is Adam's son."

"Mrs. Templeton, I don't see how you can have it both ways. Either you accept Brady as Adam's son and welcome him into your family, or you let me take him away and forget you ever met us. I think if you just speak to Adam you'll see that this is all a mistake that he'll make right."

"You're wrong, Kendall. I can and will welcome him into my family. He is my grandson, and he will have all the privileges that entails. But it can never be known that he is Adam's son."

"And whose will you say he is?"

"Mine." The terse reply came from behind her, and Kendall swung around. Luke Templeton lounged casually against the doorframe, his arms folded across his chest and a look of utter boredom on his handsome face.

"You're kidding, right?" Her gaze swung from Luke to his mother. "I refuse to have my child grow up as some rich man's bastard."

"Why? That was good enough for you, wasn't it?" Luke inquired.

Kendall opened her mouth to say something vile

and hateful, but quickly snapped it shut again. Some instinct told her she must strive not to antagonize Delores Templeton, strive not to say or do anything that would cause the woman to make good on her veiled threats. She answered Luke with the soft, reasonable voice she used with especially rebellious students.

"I want better for my son. I truly believed your brother and I were married. I wouldn't have gotten pregnant without the benefit of marriage if Adam hadn't lied to me. Brady deserves better. He deserves a father's name."

"Didn't you give him our name?" Luke demanded.

Kendall glared at him.

"Yes," she ground out. With a wave of her hands, she turned back toward Delores. "I want him to be acknowledged as legitimate, but the name isn't enough. A child needs more than just a name. I came here because I want him to have what I never did. I want him to know his father. I want him to feel his father's love."

"We can give Brady a father," Delores promised softly. "He'll be acknowledged and raised as a Templeton. No one will ever know about the cruel trick Adam played on you. No one need ever know what a fool you were, or where you came from."

"How?"

"You'll marry Luke. He'll claim Brady as his own, and no one will ever be the wiser."

"Are you both crazy?" Kendall cried.

"It's the perfect solution, Kendall. A solution, I might add, that will benefit both you and your son immeasurably."

"And what if I refuse to go along with this asinine scheme?" Kendall met Delores's cool gray gaze. She shook her head in denial at the answers she saw there.

"I've already contacted my attorney, Kendall. He's drawing up papers as we speak. I'll take you to court, and I'll tell the world where you came from, what kind of mother you had, and your steps down the same road she took. I will leave no stone unturned, and when I'm through, when I've proven beyond a doubt that you are unfit to raise my grandchild, I doubt many school systems will think you fit to teach their children, either."

"Mother..." Luke's voice held a soft note of disapproval, and Delores cast a cold glance his way.

"Don't chastise me, Luke. I want to be very sure Kendall understands her choices. There are only two, dear." She turned her gaze once more to Kendall. "Which will it be?"

The fear Kendall had managed to control since arriving here threatened to overwhelm her as she stared at the woman. She didn't doubt every word Delores said was true. Even if the court overlooked all the Templetons could give Brady and all she couldn't give him, once they brought her mother into it, the court wouldn't hesitate to take her child. Her mother had murdered Kendall's father and then killed herself. That coupled with her unwed state would convince any jury she was unfit. After all, there was no guarantee she wasn't afflicted with the same passions and insanity as her mother.

Still, could she marry a man she didn't know and certainly didn't love, a man almost identical to the one she did love? Now that she knew how wonderful love felt, could she face a life without it?

The baby began to cry, and milk flowed through her breasts in response. With a soft cry of her own, she held out her arms.

"Give him to me," she begged.

"Make your choice now, Kendall," Delores urged, ignoring Kendall's outstretched arms. "Will you marry my son?"

"Yes," she cried desperately. "Yes."

Silently, Delores placed Brady in Kendall's arms.

He rooted greedily at her breast, and without a glance at Luke Templeton, who still stood in the doorway, or Delores, who watched from her place in the rocking chair, Kendall freed one of her breasts from her gown and sat down. If it offended them, so be it, she thought as he nursed.

As soon as possible, she intended to find Adam. He would realize the insanity of his mother's plan. Surely, he wouldn't want her here any more than she wanted to be here. She refused to think about the possibility that he wouldn't care one way or the other.

Luke stood in the doorway, his eyes glued to Kendall. She wasn't drop-dead gorgeous like Margo, but he saw what had drawn his brother to her. She had a sort of ethereal beauty that was quite at odds with the earthy promise of her curvaceous body and temptingly full lips.

"He's not hungry, Kendall," his mother said imperatively. "I just fed him. Go to your room and get dressed. We'll join the rest of the family for breakfast on the patio as soon as you're ready."

"In a minute," Kendall's face was a mask of tranquility as stared down at her baby.

"Breakfast won't wait."

"Go ahead without me. I can find my way once I'm dressed."

Luke fought back a smile at her softly spoken rebellion. Brady's mouth slackened in sleep and her rosy nipple slipped from its grasp. Kendall looked up at his mother with a smile.

"I'll be ready in a few minutes."

"Very well." His mother's eyes were sharp with disapproval as Kendall buttoned her gown and hoisted the baby over her shoulder.

"Will Adam be at breakfast?" Kendall asked, the hope in her voice making Luke's stomach tighten. Surely she couldn't still expect things would work out between them. His mother had made it abundantly clear that she was to have no such aspirations. Her future rested with him and him alone. Adam was off limits.

"Yes," his mother was saying. "Adam and Margo will be at breakfast. I can see on your face that you still have hopes that you will win him over to your side, but I assure you it won't happen. Adam doesn't love you. He never loved you. And he doesn't want to be the father of your child."

For a moment, he felt sorry for the blue-eyed woman standing stock still in front of his mother. Although he could hardly fathom the possibility, it appeared she might really believe she was in love with his brother. If money were her only objective, he and Adam should be interchangeable. After all, they were almost indistinguishable. She'd thought he was Adam on the road, hadn't she? He was just as rich as Adam, actually more so, as he'd made several investments on his own that increased his personal wealth substantially. So if all she was after was a life of luxury for herself and her child, why did she look so devastated by his mother's cruel words? And why did he find himself doubting what he knew to be the truth?

His mother had spoken to him last night about her plan for him to marry Kendall. He'd argued, of course, but in the end, he agreed. Standing outside the door of his mother's room this morning, he'd heard most of their conversation. He knew what Kendall claimed to have hoped for when she came here, and he knew her history.

Although desperation at her plight as an unwed mother seemed a reasonable enough reason, he realized with a start of disbelief that he was beginning to doubt either money or desperation was her only impetus in coming here. Could she really still harbor a stubborn belief that everything would work out right in the end?

Had she honestly believed there was an acceptable reason for Adam's abandonment, and once she found him they would live happily ever after with their tiny son?

With a muttered curse, he turned and stomped from the room. What was his mother thinking? What was he thinking, agreeing to this crazy scheme? How could he even think of marrying a girl who loved his brother, was the mother of his brother's child, and came here thinking she was his brother's wife?

As he strode through the doors leading to the pool and patio, he barely noticed Margo and Adam sitting at the table.

"Luke, join us. As always, Adam had Rosie cook enough to feed an army. And, Lord knows, he doesn't need to eat all of this." Margo reached over and teasingly patted Adam's belly.

Luke's mind immediately went to Kendall and her child. Here at The Grove they were sheltered from the misery the rest of the country was enduring, but they weren't ignorant of it. How did Adam sit here day after day not knowing or caring if Kendall had enough to eat or a place to sleep?

Adam raised an eyebrow quizzically as Luke glared at him.

"Do join us, Luke. Where is Mother this morning? I haven't laid eyes on her. Generally, she's up swimming laps before daylight."

Taking a seat at the table, Luke accepted the plate of pancakes and bacon Margo passed him.

"Mother is in her room with Kendall and the baby," he said, watching Adam closely. Except for a tiny twitching of Adam's mouth, he showed no reaction whatsoever.

"Oh, yes, how is our little guest this morning?" Margo inquired. "Feeling better after a good night's sleep, I hope."

"She seems much better this morning."

"And the child?" Adam asked eagerly.

"Fine."

"Who is she, Luke?" Margo asked, oblivious to the tension crackling between the brothers.

Luke's eyes never left Adam's face as he answered her.

"She's my fiancée."

"Your what?" Adam's fork clattered to the table.

"You heard me, Adam. She's my fiancée. We'll be married as soon as Mother makes the arrangements."

Adam surged to his feet, almost upsetting the table.

"You can't marry her!"

"Adam!" Margo cried, reaching for the carafe of juice teetering too near the edge of the table.

"Adam," Luke warned quietly.

"What in heaven's name is going on here?" Delores effectively cut off Adam's protests as she glided through the doors.

Kendall walked sedately behind her, dressed now in a black, high-collared dress, her head bowed and the baby cradled protectively in her arms.

"Adam, do sit down, darling. Whatever is wrong with you?" Delores narrowed her eyes in warning.

"Luke has just told us the most extraordinary news," Margo said excitedly.

"Yes, absolutely extraordinary," Adam drawled as he sat down once again.

Delores sat in the chair beside Adam and patted the one between herself and Luke.

"Sit down, Kendall dear," she instructed. "It isn't good for you to be standing long."

Obediently, Kendall lowered herself into the

chair Delores indicated.

"Can I please hold him?" Margo whispered as she eyed the baby in awe.

Bitter anger swept through Kendall in a violent rush, and she opened her mouth to refuse. Before she could speak, however, she caught the longing in Margo's eyes, and her heart softened. This poor woman was just as much a victim of Adam's duplicity as she was. Noting once again the absence of children, Kendall's anger was replaced by pity. At least she had Brady to soothe the pain of betrayal. Leaning across Luke, she placed the baby in Margo's arms.

"He's beautiful," Margo breathed. "Hi, pretty man, I'm your aunt."

Brady gazed quizzically up at her as she babbled at him, and his mouth turned up ever so slightly.

"Look, Adam. Oh, look at him. He's smiling at me." She looked up at Kendall, a soft smile on her face. Then she held him out to her husband. "Hold him, Adam. Feel how tiny he is."

Kendall swallowed the lump in her throat as Adam held his son for the first time.

"What's his name?" Margo asked, removing one of his booties to study his tiny toes.

"Brady," Kendall said through a tear-clogged throat.

Luke's large warm hand covered hers where it clenched tightly on the arm of the chair, and she dared a glance at him. His eyes were warm with approval as he looked at her, and she attempted a watery smile.

"Hello there, big guy," Adam's voice boomed, and she looked back at him. "You certainly are a handsome little fellow."

His eyes quickly darted to Luke, then back to Brady.

"Why I believe you look just like your daddy,

don't you?" He brushed one long finger gently across the baby's cheek. "Just like your daddy."

A soft sound of distress escaped Kendall, and Delores quickly reached for the baby.

"Give him back to his mother, Adam. You're making her nervous." Delores turned to place Brady in Kendall's arms. Her voice softened almost imperceptibly as she spoke to Kendall. "Don't worry, dear. All new mothers are nervous about their babies. You'll both be just fine."

Luke brushed his hand across the back of her head gently as he moved his arm to the back of her chair, and Kendall closed her eyes for a moment.

Was she so desperate for kindness that the touch of a stranger would comfort her so? Aware of eyes on her, Kendall opened her eyes and met Adam's angry glare across the table. With a false show of bravado, Kendall gave him a small smile and looked toward Margo, who silently and intently buttered a piece of toast.

"We've been trying to have a baby for years," Margo said quietly, her voice thick with tears. After a moment of silence, she looked up from her toast and smiled brightly, feverish excitement sparkling in her eyes. "I can't believe it! Luke, of all people! How could you be so secretive, planning a wedding and not telling a soul? So, when is it? Where will it be? How many people are you inviting?"

Suddenly panicked, Kendall's eyes shot to Delores, then to Luke.

"I—I'm-not sure," she stammered as Margo continued to toss questions at her.

"Margo, let us answer one question before you throw out another," Luke reproved his sister-in-law gently.

"I'm sorry," she laughed. "I get carried away sometimes."

"The wedding will be tomorrow afternoon,"

Delores said. "I've already made the arrangements."

"Tomorrow?" Margo cried in consternation. "But that doesn't give us time to plan anything!"

"There's no need to plan anything elaborate, Margo. It will be a very quiet, private ceremony. As I'm sure you can understand, we don't want a lot of attention called to the date of our marriage, given the date of Brady's birth."

"Oh, of course, Luke," she agreed as understanding dawned in her eyes. "I didn't even think of that."

"Now isn't this a nice family picture?" said a dry feminine voice.

"Avery, darling, come join us," Delores called out to the young woman coming through the gate from the pasture. Waving toward the table on the other side of the pool, Delores glanced at Adam. "Adam, get your sister a chair."

Kendall studied the short, lean young woman striding toward the table, the muscles in her legs bunching beneath the tan riding pants she wore.

A thick mass of black hair hung around her face and shoulders. Despite her strong resemblance to her brothers, Kendall saw her exquisite loveliness as she bent to kiss her mother softly on the cheek.

"Good morning, Mother," she said as she straightened. "Adam, do hurry up with that chair!"

As she plopped into the chair Adam brought her, she studied Kendall curiously. With a small taunting smile, she turned toward Margo.

"So, Margo, what have you done, finally bought yourself a baby?"

Tears sprang to Margo's eyes and color stained her cheeks as she shook her head and quietly excused herself from the table.

Kendall looked at Adam, waiting for him to say something in his wife's defense, but it was Luke who spoke.

"That was unnecessarily cruel, Avery." He glanced sharply at his sister.

Avery glared at him before she thrust her chin out in defiance.

"What is unnecessarily cruel is for me to come to breakfast and find my chair usurped by a stranger."

"Well, I guess we should have introduced you," Luke said indulgently. "Avery, this is Kendall. Kendall, this is Avery, my baby sister."

Kendall held her hand out, but dropped it when the girl pointedly ignored it.

"And, would it be terribly rude of me to ask why she's here?" Avery asked.

"Kendall and Luke are getting married," Adam said, watching his sister closely.

Nothing could have prepared Kendall for Avery's reaction.

Leaping up from the table, her face white with fury, Avery cursed vehemently.

"Married? You're marrying *her*? Who is she? Where did she come from? And who the hell's baby is that?"

"The baby is mine." The lie flowed so easily from Luke's lips that both Kendall and Adam stared at him, dumbfounded for a moment.

"How do you know? It could be anyone's. Maybe she just picked you as the father because you're rich. You're a Templeton, for Pete's sake! And God knows what she is!"

Suddenly too angry to sit still and quiet any longer, Kendall stood. With as much control as she could manage, she faced the screeching girl in front of her.

"Listen to me," she said softly, deceptively calm. "I'm not a Templeton nor am I rich, but by God from what I've seen of both here, I'd rather be exactly what I am than one of you any day."

Avery Templeton opened her mouth in

47

astonishment, but it snapped closed as Kendall held out her hand once more.

"I'd like to thank you," Kendall said. "You've just kept me from making another huge mistake."

Avery simply stared at her hand and, after a moment, Kendall shrugged and turned toward Delores.

"Mrs. Templeton, thank you for your hospitality. I will leave the address of friends. You can contact me through them. As I said before, you are more than welcome to visit Brady." She ignored Luke, Adam and Avery as she headed for the door leading into the house.

"Kendall." Delores' voice stopped her with her hand on the doorknob. "My lawyer will be contacting you. As I said before, I will not allow my grandson to be deprived of the lifestyle to which he is entitled."

Unconsciously, Kendall's arms tightened around Brady, but she willed the trembling from her voice.

"That's fine, Mrs. Templeton. He can contact me at the same address." The strength of her voice belied the shaking of her hands as she fought to open the door.

"You've made your point, Ken. Come sit down," Luke drawled from close behind her. In a sterner voice, he commanded his sister to be quiet.

"Come on, sweetheart," he said jovially as he caught her shaking hand in his. "I won't let Avery hurt your feelings anymore."

He leaned down and kissed her softly.

"You don't want to do this," he murmured against her lips.

"Oh, for Pete's sake," Avery groaned.

"Give me the baby," he said as he straightened, one arm already firmly wedged between her and Brady. One look in his eyes told her that he wouldn't take no for an answer.

With a defeated sigh, she let him take Brady

and lead her back to her seat at the table.

"You wouldn't really have left, would you?" Avery leaned eagerly toward her.

"Come with me, Avery. I need your opinion on furniture for the guest rooms." Delores stood and motioned for her daughter.

"You want my opinion on furniture? Right, Mother," she said grudgingly, but stood and followed her mother inside.

Without a word, Adam stood and followed them. Kendall watched him go. There were so many questions she needed him to answer.

"Adam?" she called softly.

He stopped for only a moment without turning. Then, with a slight shake of his head, he went into the house.

She drew a ragged breath and willed herself not to cry.

"I know Avery's difficult, but give her a chance. She can be a real sweetheart," Luke said.

Kendall looked at him doubtfully.

He laughed softly at the expression on her face.

"It's true. She's had a hard time of it since Dad died. She was his princess, and ours, too. Spoiled rotten, yes, but you'll like her once you get to know her."

"How old was she when your dad died?"

"Twelve."

"And now?"

"Sixteen," he said and grinned at the astonished look on her face.

"I know. Mother lets her have too much freedom. She seems much older than she is."

"I would have been much more patient with her if I had known she was so young," Kendall said worriedly.

"Don't worry about it. Avery needs someone who will stand up to her. You should have seen her face when you were walking away. She was astounded, but impressed, too. She's still young enough to think money can buy everything. She's in awe of anyone who thinks they can live without it."

Kendall shrugged and grinned up at him.

"She'll really be impressed when she finds out that I don't just think I can live without it. I've actually done it for years."

"Well, that's all changed now. Money isn't something you'll have to worry about as my wife."

"Why are you agreeing to marry me and say you're Brady's father?"

His eyes grew cold as they met hers.

"Templetons take care of our own. And, like it or not, your child is a Templeton." His voice matched the ice in his eyes.

"Don't you have a life apart from being a Templeton? Don't you have anyone or anything you don't want to give up?"

"Do you mean a woman, Kendall?" he asked softly. "Is that what you want to know?"

At her nod, his mouth twisted into a painful grimace.

"As a matter of fact, I was engaged until this morning. However, whatever assets Rebecca has, she doesn't already have the first child of the next generation of Templetons."

"But don't you love her?"

Anger melted the ice in his eyes, and he waved his hand toward her.

"Look, you're the one who came here. You're the one who forced yourself and your child into our lives. I understand why. But now that we know the child exists, we can't just ignore him. Things must be done to protect him, to give him the life he deserves as Adam's son. Nothing else matters. What I wanted yesterday or last week or last year is no longer important. What is important is Brady."

She nodded in agreement as she looked at the baby, still cradled in Luke's arms. As it always did when she looked at him, love swelled inside of her, making her willing to concede to any sacrifice required of her in order to give him a better life.

"There's something you should know right up front, Kendall. It will make all of our lives easier if you remember it."

She lifted her face and looked at him expectantly. Once again, his eyes and voice were cold.

"Love has nothing to do with anything here. In the grand scheme of things, it only gets in the way."

She couldn't imagine how a person could come to such a heartbreaking conclusion.

"What a very sad way to live," she observed quietly before plucking Brady from his arms and turning away.

In all the years she'd dreamed of having a father, it never occurred to her she could have one without being loved by him. Yet Brady might know the heartbreak of having a father who didn't love him. She imagined him being raised here without her, learning that love was a bother, an emotion that got in the way of things. The thought broke her heart, and she sighed in resignation. Marrying Luke was the only way for Brady to have the best future possible. It would give Brady a father and legitimate name, and she would love him and teach him how to love in return.

****

Luke watched Kendall's retreating form. He couldn't mistake the pity in her huge blue eyes before she turned away.

Shouldn't she be just a bit jaded by this whole ordeal? Shouldn't her own life have dispelled any idealized notions of love she harbored? Shouldn't she realize that love obviously had led her astray just as it had her mother? How could she still believe love was a good thing, not something that wreaked havoc on one's life?

An old longing lodged in his chest, and he swore aloud as he strode toward the garage.

Chapter Six

"So, did you and Luke have a fight?" Avery taunted from the doorway.

"No," Kendall said as she laid the baby in the crib.

"No?" Avery repeated with a mocking laugh. "Then why did my brother, who is notorious for driving like an old woman, just fly down the drive like a bat out of hell?"

Kendall looked at her reprovingly.

"You should watch your language," she said.

"And just who would you be to tell me to watch my language?" Avery asked menacingly, taking a step toward Kendall.

"It was merely a suggestion. If you want to present yourself to people in such an odious fashion, that's your prerogative. Excuse me, please." Kendall attempted to brush past the girl.

Avery refused to move so Kendall could pass, but Kendall waited patiently until the girl stepped aside with a confused frown.

"What are you anyway? A teacher?" Avery sneered. At Kendall's nod, she burst out laughing.

"Oh, my Lord, you're serious. You really are a teacher? That's why you use words like 'odious' and 'prerogative' in that absolutely condescending way? This is priceless. Luke is marrying a teacher?"

"What is so funny about that?" Kendall asked sternly as she glared down at the girl holding her sides and rolling around on the bed laughing.

"Oh, it's an old family joke," Avery said, her eyes shining with mischief. "He loved school and was such a bookworm that Daddy and Adam used to tease him that he should just marry a teacher so he could be in school twenty-four hours a day."

Kendall turned and began to take the baby's clothes from the bag on the bureau. She had the distinct feeling Avery didn't find the situation nearly so funny but was exaggerating her reaction in order to irritate her.

When Kendall continued to ignore it, Avery's laughter quieted and she grew still, her arms flung out on the bed.

"So, how'd you two meet?" she asked.

Never much good at lying, Kendall decided she'd best stick to the facts as they related to her and Adam. She ignored the bitter taste of betrayal as she spoke, substituting Luke's name for Adam's.

"We met in court. I was crossing the hall to go into the courtroom, and Luke came around the corner. We ran right into each other." Adam's strong hands had instantly grabbed and steadied. Attraction swept over her in a wave, and she smiled up at him even as she told herself not to waste her time. He would never look twice at a mousy thing like her. Now, she knew why she had instantly pictured him with a beautiful, fit blonde.

"Why were you in court?" Avery brought her back to the present.

"I saw a car accident."

"Was anyone hurt?"

"Yes, yes. Someone was hurt." Kendall wondered if she wasn't the one hurt most of all.

****

Luke stared out at the water as he sat on the deck of Barnacle's, the bar he found when he reached the ocean. The beer in his hand did little to ease his worries as he thought of his impending marriage.

If Rebecca were in town, he'd go to her tonight

54

and explain things, but she was in New York on a photo shoot and then doing a gallery exhibition. She wouldn't be back for a month. He could call her hotel, of course, but it seemed cruel to tell her something like this over the telephone. It would be crueler, however, to let her find out from someone else. He would call her in the next few days and tell her, but even she couldn't know the whole truth.

He couldn't really call what he and Rebecca felt for each other love in the romantic sense of the word. It was more like they'd fallen in affection with each other. They'd known each other their whole lives, had been playmates, best friends, and, finally, part-time lovers.

He asked her to marry him four years ago just because it seemed to be what everyone expected them to do. She agreed but didn't want to rush into it. Neither of them made any move to plan a wedding and actually seemed to avoid discussing it whenever possible. They jokingly told each other they'd start planning when they were thirty-five.

He took the last long sip of his beer and motioned for the waitress to bring another.

Even Rebecca wouldn't understand his agreement with his mother's plan. No one ever really understood how it was in their house, how desperate he was to make his mother happy. Of course, as an adult he realized it was totally fruitless and beyond stupid to continue to try to gain his mother's approval, but that didn't change the fact that he tried.

Adam had been the golden child from the day they were born. When he told people that, they thought he was crazy. After all, to most people twins were interchangeable. How could one be favored and not the other? The truth wasn't that simple, however. In reality, they were separate individuals, as different in temperament as night and day. While

Adam was outgoing and charming, Luke had always been more taciturn and withdrawn. It wasn't that he didn't like people, but he didn't show them the open affection Adam did. That the affection he did show was genuine while Adam's was usually an act meant to get his way wasn't important to anyone but Luke.

Luke had loved school, loved books, and strove for high grades and praise from teachers. Adam generally did barely satisfactory work in school and passed because the teachers liked him rather than because he deserved it. A star athlete, Adam was his father's pride and joy, often toasted at the country club and discussed on the golf course. Luke, on the other hand, was left to his own devices. He learned the business end of their estate quietly, without either of his parents really realizing it, and when his father died of a heart attack, he was ready to take over. Since then his mother had leaned on him more and more, relying on him to keep their lives running as smoothly as they always had. It was part of his duties to clean up Adam's occasional messes.

Though Kendall wasn't the first woman Adam dallied with, Luke had never seen Adam go to such extraordinary lengths to bed a woman. Of course, Adam was always determined to have his way and get what he wanted. If Kendall denied him, it was only natural he would attempt to remedy whatever problem prevented him from obtaining his goal. Although Luke couldn't condone it, he understood his brother well enough to realize that to Adam's mind what he did to Kendall was necessary.

Typically, once he had what he was after, he didn't want it as badly as he thought he did. Now, it was up to Luke to make it right. Of course, he'd argued with his mother, trying to make her see that this plan of hers was crazy, but she'd pleaded and cajoled until he agreed. Now, he felt as if he'd sacrificed his soul for his mother's approval.

Chapter Seven

A knock at her bedroom door brought Kendall awake. Moonlight streamed through the window, and, sitting up, she glanced into the cradle where Brady lay on his belly, sleeping peacefully.

"Yes?" she called cautiously after another soft rap at the door.

"Let me in, Kendall."

The familiar sound of Adam's voice sent her hurrying to open the door. Her hands shook with anticipation as she turned the lock and let him slip inside. Pushing the door closed, she turned to him, ready to launch herself into his arms.

But he didn't reach for her. His arms remained crossed over his chest, and she forced herself to remain where she stood.

"You cannot marry my brother," he announced, aloof and disapproving.

She silently agreed, but out loud she asked, "Why not?"

"Because you're mine."

The words felt cold and foreign as they settled in her heart. He offered no professions of undying love, no promises that he would be there for her and her child. All he was doing was staking his claim.

"You already have a wife."

"But I really do care for you, Kendall."

"Then, why did you leave me?"

"I already have a wife," he quipped, using her own words.

Anger and impatience spiraled through her. She refused to stand here playing games with him. She wanted to know exactly what his intentions were.

"Are you going to support your son?" she demanded.

"No."

"If I take you to court, you'll have to."

"If you take me to court, my mother will sue you for custody of him."

"You would have to acknowledge him."

He shook his head. "No, Luke would have to acknowledge him."

"Luke isn't his father," she cried.

"He's the only one willing to claim him."

She took a step back. "You wouldn't?"

"No." He paused only a moment before explaining his answer. "It would kill Margo if she knew I'd fathered a child that wasn't hers."

Kendall felt herself pale, and her voice quivered with rage.

"Get out," she said quietly, not trusting herself to speak any louder.

"Tell me you aren't going to marry Luke," he demanded as he backed toward the door.

Trembling with fury, she pushed at him. "Go."

"Kendall?" Luke's voice came from the other side of the door. "Are you okay?"

He entered the room before she could answer and moved toward his brother.

"Get the hell out of here," he growled at Adam. "Margo's up looking for you."

"You remember what I said, Kendall," Adam said before hurrying from the room.

"What was that all about?" Luke turned his icy glare on her.

"He doesn't think it's a good idea that we marry."

"Would he be willing to make things right? Would he claim Brady as his own?"

"No," she answered honestly. "He couldn't care

less about me or Brady."

"Have you changed your mind about marrying me?"

She looked away from those eyes that seemed to penetrate her soul.

"Has your mother changed her mind about trying to take Brady from me?"

"Of course not," he said.

"Then I haven't changed my mind about marrying you."

****

Kendall stood in the doorway that led from the great room to the lawn at the side of the house. The lawn sloped gently toward a huge lake dotted with Canadian geese and large white swans. A white linen runner lined with luminaries ran from the steps to a flowered arch under which Luke stood in a black suit.

"Do you like the way I decorated?" Margo asked from beside her. "I know you and Luke both said not to go to any trouble, but you only get one wedding. It's not much, but I wanted it to be a little special. I wish you had agreed to a new dress."

"It's very nice. Thank you. This dress is fine." Kendall smoothed down the gray jumper. She knew it and the white blouse underneath weren't a typical wedding ensemble, but this hardly constituted a typical wedding.

"I'm so happy for you and Luke. I hope everything works out well for you. Luke is such a good man." The wedding march began playing softly, and Margo clasped her hands together excitedly. "Oh, there's your song."

Taking a deep breath, Kendall stepped onto the lighted path. When her eyes met Luke's, she pasted what she hoped passed as a convincing smile on her face.

As his bride walked toward him dressed in a

dove gray jumper and a white high-collared shirt, Luke bit back a sardonic chuckle. She looked just like the teacher she was. Oh, how his father would like that ironic little twist.

She bravely attempted a smile he couldn't help but answer with one of his own, and when she reached him he took her trembling hand and placed it in the crook of his arm while the preacher began the ceremony.

She began to cry as they exchanged vows, and he wanted nothing more than to run from the sadness in her eyes and voice.

When the preacher pronounced them husband and wife and gave him permission to kiss her, Luke leaned toward her. "There's no other way," he whispered against her lips.

She nodded in silent acknowledgement and let him kiss her softly.

****

She was married. Again. This time apparently it was legal and binding, and as she sat at the dining room table with Avery, Delores and Margo, Kendall wondered wildly what had possessed her to do such a thing. Shortly after the ceremony, Luke disappeared in the direction of the stables, leaving her in his mother's care. If Avery or Margo thought it strange that Kendall spent her wedding night in their company, neither said anything.

"Kendall," Delores said, "I've contacted my physician, and he will be coming by in the morning to check on both you and Brady."

"Why would your doctor need to check us?" Kendall asked.

"You just had a baby. It's important that both of you have proper care. I would just like to make sure that you are recuperating as you should be, especially after the excitement of the last few days. He tells me that babies should be checked at about

Brady's age, just to make sure they're progressing as they should."

"Brady saw a doctor back home," she said defensively.

"Of course, dear, but this is home now, and it's very important for Dr. Landon to become established as his physician in case there is ever an emergency."

Conceding to her mother-in-law's point, Kendall offered her thanks.

"When I spoke to Dr. Landon, he told me you should have a few more days of bed rest, especially after your trip and your fainting spell the day you arrived."

"I feel fine, Mrs. Templeton."

"Well, that's wonderful, dear, but there is no reason for you to do anything but relax and take care of yourself."

Kendall nodded, knowing it was useless to argue over it. She wasn't exactly sure what else she would do anyway. She was virtually certain she wouldn't be allowed to take a teaching position, and the house seemed to run just fine without her help.

"I have also scheduled an appointment with my dressmaker, Janine Perkins. She can help you with your wardrobe."

"What wardrobe?" This was really too much.

"The wardrobe you will need now that you are Luke's wife."

"I already have a wardrobe."

"You brought one suitcase, Kendall. You need a wardrobe."

"One suitcase?" Margo seemed awed by that information.

"Yes, but I have everything I need," Kendall said, matching Delores' haughtiness with her own. "Mrs. Templeton, I do not need a wardrobe."

"You *will* have a new wardrobe, Kendall, no matter what you think of it."

"Oh please, Mother, let her alone," Avery said wickedly. "Are your dresses all respectfully gray, Kendall?"

Kendall thought of the dresses hanging in the closet upstairs, two gray and two a nice appropriate navy blue.

"No," she told Avery, her eyes meeting the girl's. "Two of them are dark blue."

Avery burst out laughing.

"For goodness sake, Kendall, are you serious?" Margo asked in astonishment.

"I was a schoolteacher at Chadsworth School for Girls. Those were the accepted colors."

"Chadsworth?" Margo exclaimed. "I graduated from Chadsworth."

"Those clothes are no longer acceptable, Kendall," Delores broke in before Kendall could comment on Margo's revelation. "There are quite a few social events in the coming months, and you must have clothes for them. My housekeeper, Cora, will keep the baby."

"I'd prefer to take him with me," Kendall said.

"No," Delores said. "Not yet. We will introduce Brady to the people closest to us first and work our way outward. My dressmaker will not be the first person outside of this household to know about him."

Kendall wanted to protest further, but Delores held up a hand.

"Cora has raised five children of her own and had a large hand in raising my children, as well. She is quite excited about helping you with Brady whenever you need her. In the future, we will hire a professional nanny to tend to him, of course. For now, I can assure you Brady will be fine in Cora's care for a few hours on the day of our appointment."

Kendall sighed in defeat. Delores would not be swayed tonight, and she really didn't have the energy left to argue with her.

"What are you all in such deep conversation about?" Adam stood in the doorway, a drink in his hand.

"Clothes," Avery said.

"So, Kendall," he sneered, "have they won you over to their side? Would you sell your firstborn for a bit of silk and satin?"

"Adam, for heaven's sake," his mother said, "go back to your study."

"Not yet, Mother. I'm waiting for my answer. What would it take for a woman like Kendall, a prim and proper schoolmarm with a child a month older than her marriage, to abandon her principles?"

Kendall remained silent while Margo stood up and moved to Adam's side.

"Adam, darling, let's go to our room." Margo placed a hand on his arm, but he quickly shook it off and came to lean against the table. Anger blazed in his eyes as he thrust his head toward Kendall.

"No. Not until Kendall answers me. What does it take, Ken? Money? Clothes? What?"

"What the hell's going on here?" Luke's voice came as a welcome relief.

Adam swung around to face him.

"I'm just trying to figure out why a girl like Kendall would come to a place like this and marry a guy like you."

"You're drunk," Luke said in disgust. "Get out of here."

The two men stared each other down, before Adam gave a mock bow.

"As you wish, brother dear. I wouldn't get an honest answer anyway, would I?"

He left with Margo in his wake, and Luke lowered himself into the empty chair.

"What's wrong with him?" Avery asked, looking from face to face.

"He's drunk and stupid," Luke said, pouring

himself a glass of iced tea.

"It's been an exciting few days. Two days ago, none of us had any idea that the new generation of Templetons had already been born." Delores offered in excuse for her son's behavior.

"Luke knew," Avery observed. "Didn't you?"

"Of course," he said easily.

"So, why didn't you tell any of us?"

"Mother's right. It has been a rather exhausting day. Why don't we all turn in?"

"Does Rebecca know?" Avery wasn't to be deterred.

"No, she doesn't, and I'd appreciate it if you waited until I've told her before you do."

"Well, you'd better tell her by the time she gets back, or someone else will."

"Don't worry, Ave. I'll make sure I've spoken to Rebecca before she hears it from someone else."

"You should make sure you've spoken to Kendall, too. She's making a real fuss about Mother ordering her a new wardrobe. It's bad enough she got married in that hideous thing, but she sure can't wear it to the Citrus Ball."

"Kendall knows what's appropriate for a formal occasion," he said patiently.

"How in the world do you know what Kendall knows? You two couldn't have known each other for all that long. You're practically strangers."

"How long we've known each other is none of your business, Ave."

"Well," she corrected herself derisively, "I suppose you've known each other at least nine months."

Luke's face tightened and his voice was cold with fury when he spoke.

"Brady is my son, and Kendall is my wife. Don't you ever call attention to the chronology of it again."

Avery's gaze slid from his, and she nodded

without speaking a word.

****

"You've got to get it together, Kendall," Luke said when she opened her bedroom door to his knock later that night. "You can't freeze up every time someone asks you a question about us."

"I'm sorry, Luke. I've never been any good at lying."

"Then you'd better get good at it, Sweetheart, because you're going to be lying for a long, long time."

She went cold at the realization that she had agreed to a never-ending lie. She hadn't let herself think about how long the lies would continue. Brady would grow up with Luke as his father, and she would go to her grave with the secret she harbored. If the truth ever came out, Luke would look like a fool, cuckolded by his twin brother and his own wife. The magnitude of what she'd done hit her hard and she dropped to the edge of the bed.

"You never even thought of that, did you?" Luke asked. "What did you think, Kendall? That this would be a convenient solution to all your woes? Did you think it was a temporary thing?"

"I didn't really think about it. I mean, I realized it would be a lie, but I didn't think about it being forever."

He knelt in front of her, his eyes boring into hers.

"Don't think I'll let you leave, Kendall. You're my wife. I've accepted your child as mine. That means, in the eyes of the law, you're entitled to a part of everything I own if we divorce. So hear this, Sweetheart. If you ever leave me, if you ever even attempt to divorce me, I'll make damn sure you won't leave with *our* son."

Anger, once such a rare emotion to her, engulfed her.

"I don't know how many times I have to tell you that I'm not interested in anything you own. The only thing I'm interested in is my son."

"Spare me."

"I realize that you won't ever accept the fact that a poor little bastard could look at what you have and not want it, but I swear it's true. I wanted it once. I used to stand in front of my father's huge brick home and watch him and his legitimate daughter, and I wanted so badly to be part of their world, part of what they had."

"But you don't anymore?" he prodded.

"I watched my mother die wanting what she couldn't have, and I swore to myself that I wouldn't do the same."

****

Her quiet confession rendered him speechless as he imagined her standing in front of her father's house, longing to be on the other side of the fence, accepted instead of rejected.

"Get some sleep," he said quietly and slipped from the room.

Chapter Eight

From her bedroom window, Kendall watched Luke talk to Dr. Landon in the driveway. Though both she and his mother had tried to make him go, he refused to leave the house until he spoke to the doctor himself.

"The doctor says you're both right as rain," he said when he came into her room a few minutes later.

"I tried to tell your mother that."

"I know, but she wanted to make sure."

"Well, I appreciate it, and it is good to know that there is a doctor available if Brady should need him."

"The doctor says it's really important that you eat enough while you're nursing the baby. When you and Brady were alone, and when you were pregnant, did you have enough to eat?"

"We had enough," she told him, touched by the concern that darkened his eyes.

"I still can't believe Adam left you there without any means of support."

"He said he didn't know I was pregnant," she said quickly.

"Of course not," he agreed, but his eyes darkened even more at her hasty defense of his brother.

Remarkably, Kendall found she was able to sleep for the better part of three days. She got up to feed Brady and eat, and then fell right back to sleep.

On the fourth morning, she felt so well rested she found it difficult to stay in bed, but Delores still insisted she not do anything remotely strenuous.

Finally, she decided to pass the time reading. Slipping on her robe, and hoping not to run into anyone, she went downstairs to the small library that adjoined Delores' study and the office Adam and Luke shared. She perused the shelves, trying to decide if she wanted to read for fun or for edification before settling on a romance novel and a book about historical landmarks in the area.

"What are you doing down here?" Luke scolded as she exited the library. He stood in the office doorway, and with the morning light streaming through the foyer windows, it was impossible not to see how handsome he was.

She waved the books in front of her. "Finding something to exercise my mind."

"*Flames of Desire*?" He laughed. "That should do it."

She blushed and hid the novel behind the thicker tome.

"Ah, that's more like it, Mrs. Templeton. That should bore you to tears."

"Yes, well, I'm already bored to tears, Mr. Templeton."

"When did Mother say you can stop resting?"

"Saturday."

"Well, that's only one more day."

"These should keep me busy until then."

"Kendall!" Delores' voice came from behind her. "What are you doing?"

"Going back to bed," she grumbled and waved the books over her head. Luke's low laughter followed her up the stairs.

Chapter Nine

Kendall stood in the center of the spacious master bedroom. At the opposite end of the hallway from the small bedroom where she and Brady slept, this beautifully decorated room contained a huge bed covered in green brocade. Realizing exactly what the bed meant, Kendall stared at it in trepidation.

"You can change it if you'd like," Delores told her, obviously mistaking her look for distaste. "It's been like this for ages. Luke's father and I used this suite when his grandparents owned the house. I haven't redecorated since we moved into their wing."

"Oh, no, I won't change anything. It's beautiful. I'll just wait to decorate when Luke and I get our own home."

As she followed Delores through rooms that once served as the nursery and other rooms for growing children, Kendall realized that she and Luke wouldn't be getting their own home. This entire wing of the house was theirs, while Adam and Margo had their own wing. All of them were expected to live here together, sharing meals and daily life forever. She could barely hide her dismay at the thought of living the rest of her life under the same roof as Adam.

****

"I can hardly stand to look at Adam right now. I imagine you feel the same," Luke said as he followed her into their new room after a dinner punctuated by Adam's random snide comments.

He was right, of course, but she was sure their reasons were different. Every time she looked at

Adam, she was afraid everything she felt for him showed on her face.

"What are you doing?" she cried when Luke kicked off his shoes and began unbuttoning his shirt.

"Getting comfortable." He pulled the shirt off, leaving only a white undershirt tucked into his trousers. The shirt hugged his broad chest and muscled arms, and Kendall looked away.

Panic made her breath come in shallow gasps as he moved toward the bed, and she realized that as her husband he expected to sleep here with her. She quickly placed Brady on the bed, hoping that the baby would be some deterrent to Luke's sexual desires.

He chuckled softly and shook his head as he sat with his back against the headboard. With a gentle hand, he ran his fingers over Brady's head.

"I'm not staying here tonight, Ken," he promised.

"You're not?"

"Of course not. Eventually I will, but not tonight."

She sank onto the chaise lounge in the corner.

"Would you like to know why?" he asked.

She nodded, though she really didn't care why. She was just glad to know he didn't intend to stay.

"Number one, even though we're married, we don't know each other at all. Number two, you love my brother. Number three, you just gave birth and haven't had time to heal completely."

She blushed and looked away.

"It will take a while for us to get to know each other and for your body to heal. So, we'll take it slowly. I'm your husband and you're my wife. There will come a time when we make love, but when we do, you'll be ready, physically and emotionally."

She couldn't imagine ever being emotionally ready, but she held her silence.

"For now, I'm just letting the rest of the house get to bed so we don't raise any suspicions. Once everyone's turned in, I'll go to my own room. In the meantime, I thought this would be a good opportunity for us to get to know each other."

"Where do we begin?"

"How did we meet?"

"I really am a terrible liar. So I thought it would be easier and more convincing if I just told the truth about how I met Adam."

When he nodded in understanding, she told him what she'd told Avery.

"So, we were in the same courthouse, but how did we meet?" he inquired.

"You were running late, and you almost knocked me over when you came around a corner. You apologized and hurried away."

"So, how did we end up married?"

"When I finished testifying, you were waiting in the corridor outside the courtroom. You asked me to dinner."

"Ah, our first date. Where did we go?"

"Charlie's Diner."

"So, when did you fall in love with me?"

"The minute I saw you," she said, unable to hide the wistfulness in her voice.

"Well, I think that's enough for tonight," he announced as he stood. He picked Brady up, kissed him softly on the head and laid him in the crib next to the bed. He turned to Kendall, "Maybe you can get some sleep before he wakes up again."

Chapter Ten

"Jeeze, Kendall, you've got the biggest boobs I've ever seen." Avery tugged at the blouse.

"Avery!" her mother scolded from just outside the fitting room. "That is not appropriate."

"But it's true, Mother. Look at her." Avery flung open the door.

Kendall cried out in protest when both Delores and Margo crowded the doorway.

"That is the most hideous thing I've ever seen," Delores sniffed. "Take it off this instant."

Sighing, Kendall removed the offending garment. When they'd arrived at the dressmaker's boutique, Kendall picked out four outfits. As she tried them on, Delores summarily dismissed each and every one of them.

"Kendall, maybe you should find something with a bit more color, or at least something in a more flattering style," Margo suggested hopefully.

"These are all different colors," Kendall defended her choices.

"Beige, brown and tan?" Avery said skeptically.

"Those are different colors."

"No, Ken, those are different shades of the same color. Just like black and gray. They don't count as variety."

"Janine, you simply must find Kendall more appropriate clothing to try," Delores called imperatively.

"Yes, Mrs. Templeton," agreed the petite, middle-aged woman who darted around them. She quickly moved to the dressing room and studied

Kendall from head to toe. "I know just what you need."

She disappeared for a few minutes and returned carrying an armload of clothing. In a flash, she replaced Kendall's choices with her own and left the dressing room.

"Would you get out of here?" Kendall asked Avery.

"Nope," Avery said. "What do you want to try first?"

"Let me in, too," Margo said and pushed her way inside the room.

"I don't care what I try on. You pick something, Avery."

"Fine. This one first. Close your eyes."

Kendall obeyed without argument, and Avery slipped the dress over her head. She kept her eyes closed while Avery and Margo hurriedly buttoned and fluffed, only opening them when the others stepped back to survey her.

"Oh, yes," Margo clasped her hands to her chest in ecstasy.

"Mother, look!" Avery cried and pushed the door open again.

"Perfect," Delores said, and Kendall finally looked in the floor-length mirror.

"Oh, my goodness," she breathed.

Perfect didn't begin to describe the beautiful light coral dress accented with a cream collar, cuffs, and belt. Janine was hurrying toward them with a pair of cream heels and a coral hat.

By the time they left the shop, Kendall owned six dresses with matching purses, gloves, and hats, as well as new undergarments and nightgowns.

"You look like a movie star," Avery announced as they were leaving the store. "Luke's not going to believe it."

"If he thought you were beautiful before, just

wait until he sees you now," Margo agreed.

Would he think she was beautiful? What about Adam? Would he regret that she wasn't his wife? So far, he'd barely shown any sign of remembering her at all.

For lunch, they stopped at a trendy café, making Kendall glad she was still wearing the coral-and-cream outfit.

"Oh my," she said when she saw the prices on the menu.

"You are a Templeton now, dear," Delores reminded her. "You don't look at the prices. You simply order."

"I'm sorry," she said, but she couldn't keep her eyes from straying to the prices. "They're just so exorbitant."

"That's why we eat here," Delores said shortly.

Kendall wondered if that really made sense to anyone. She thought of the dozens of men and women she'd joined in the lines in Jacksonville, all vying for the dozen or so available jobs. She remembered one woman quite distinctly. She'd been dressed in a well-cut dress suit, a flowered hat and a fur stole. As they waited, the woman told Kendall how her husband lost his high-paying job, they were losing their home, and she was searching for work so she didn't have to send her children to live with relatives in the country. She'd sold everything they had that was of any value except for the suit and the stole she wore. She hoped being well-dressed would boost her chances of getting a job. She was called in ahead of Kendall and after a few moments she emerged, crestfallen and without her stole. "I didn't get the job," she told Kendall, "but the boss bought my stole for his wife." It was impossible to ignore the tears that clogged her voice.

Standing there under the brutal Florida sun, Kendall had never dreamed that within weeks she would be in a position where she wasn't worrying where the next meal would come from, much less wasn't supposed to notice these kinds of prices for one meal. It was hard for her to fathom that there were still people who didn't worry about money.

As they finished their meal, Kendall felt a hand on her shoulder and turned to find an elderly woman standing behind her.

"How are you, dear?" the woman asked.

"I'm fine," she answered uncertainly.

"And your mother? How is she?"

"I think you have me confused with someone else," Kendall told her.

"Oh, no," the woman said, shaking her white head vigorously. "I'd know you anywhere. You're Louisa's girl!"

"I'm sorry," Kendall said, "I'm not."

The old woman glanced around, a bewildered expression on her face.

"Mother, come on, now." A younger woman came from the direction of the restroom and gently took the old woman's arm. "I told you to wait for me."

"I wanted to come over and say hi to that young lady," the old woman said. "I knew her mother when we were in school."

The other woman looked at Kendall questioningly.

"I'm sorry," she said when Kendall shook her head. "She gets confused."

"It was no problem at all," Kendall assured her.

"You tell Louisa that Miriam Rogers said hi," the old woman said, patting Kendall's hand.

"I will, Mrs. Rogers. It was very good seeing you." Kendall offered the woman a warm smile as her daughter led her away. It certainly wouldn't do any good to tell her again that she didn't know Louisa.

"How very sad," Margo said. "She was certainly

sure she knew you, wasn't she?"

"I probably remind her of someone she knew ages ago."

"Are you girls ready?" Delores asked, ignoring the whole episode.

"I bet none of your students would recognize you," Margo told Kendall on the ride home.

"No, I'm sure they wouldn't."

"It's just like a fairy tale," Avery said with a romantic gleam in her eyes. "There you were destined to be an old maid, dressed in nothing but dreary clothes. Then the handsome knight showed up, rescued you, and brought you to his castle, where you'll live happily ever after."

Kendall fought the bitter laughter that threatened, as Delores quickly turned the topic to other matters.

Chapter Eleven

"I'm going to go up and lie down," Kendall said once they were home.

"Are you ill?" Delores asked her.

"No. I'm just a little tired."

"Well, that's to be expected. I'll have Cora wake you before dinner."

"Thank you," she said, but the thought of sitting at the dinner table with Adam made her stomach do nervous somersaults.

Cora got up from the chair by the window and put a finger to her lips as Kendall entered the bedroom and tiptoed to the crib.

"He just drank a bottle. He's only been asleep a few minutes, so he should sleep a while." Cora whispered.

"Thank you, Cora." Kendall laid her hat on the dresser and began removing the pins from her hair.

"It was no problem, Miss Kendall. He's an angel just like his daddy. Mr. Luke was so perfect, he never caused a problem. Not like Mr. Adam. He was always one to be in trouble."

Kendall pinched the bridge of her nose in an effort to stem the headache beating behind her eyes.

"You're tired," Cora announced, peering up at her. "You rest for a while. I'll wake you before dinner time."

"Thank you," Kendall murmured, desperately wanting to lie down.

When Cora left, she pulled the curtains shut, slipped off her dress, and lay down on the bed. She took a ragged breath as the tears began to flow. Not wanting to wake the baby, she cried silently, fighting the sobs that threatened to overtake her.

How many nights had she lain awake in bed, listening to her mother's sobs? How many times did she vow to herself that her life would be different? Her mother's obsession with the man she loved destroyed her. It kept Lydia holding on, hoping that things would be different. Did she actually go to his house that morning thinking she could change what happened between them? Did she hope to turn back the clock and make him love her again? Or did she simply want to punish him for the years of sorrow he'd caused her?

Was she herself headed toward such misery? Kendall wondered. Had she already put her own destruction into motion?

****

Luke stepped into the darkened room and stared down at her. She wore only a slip, and he took a soft cotton blanket from the closet and gently spread it over her. Tear marks tracked her cheeks, and even in her sleep she took a shuddering breath once in a while. He wished he could comfort her, but he didn't even know where to begin.

Brady began to move restlessly, and she immediately turned toward the sound. With a soft reprimand for her to stay still, Luke quietly lifted him from his crib and laid him beside her.

"What are you doing?" she mumbled as she rolled to her side and pulled the baby close to her breast.

"Mother told me you were resting. I just wanted to check on you and make sure you weren't ill."

"I'm fine."

He rested his hand on her arm.

"If you need anything, let me know," he said.

She nodded, tears once again clogging her throat. *I need your brother to acknowledge me and our child,* she wanted to cry. *I need to be his wife, not yours.*

He slipped out of the room without another word, and Kendall closed her eyes against the emptiness around her.

Chapter Twelve

Kendall dozed again while Brady nursed, waking only when Cora tapped lightly on the door and put her head in to say dinner would be ready in an hour.

She turned on the shower, letting the water run as she went to her closet. She knew everyone expected her to wear one of her new dresses to dinner, but she pushed them away to look longingly at her old familiar ones.

The gray jumper she wore to her wedding was the first dress she'd bought when she started teaching. Next to the new dresses, it looked worn and dowdy. Still, she wished she could slip into its comforting folds. In it, she could be the same old Kendall, able to sit quietly unnoticed at the table. The new dresses turned her into someone she barely recognized, someone who would not go unnoticed. When she and Adam were married, she dressed carefully each night before he came home, wanting him to think she was beautiful. Tonight, she just wanted him to ignore her and not make her the target of his anger.

She came out of the shower a few minutes later, dressed in a soft cotton slip, and found Luke sitting on the bed holding Brady. With a startled exclamation, she rushed into the closet. Then, reminding herself he'd seen her in only her slip earlier, she came back out.

"What are you doing here?"

"I came to make sure you were up. Brady was making some noise, so I thought I'd sit with him."

"He certainly doesn't lack for attention," she observed.

"He likes it, don't you, little man?"

She went back into the closet and pulled out the cherry-red sleeveless dress Margo had picked for her. From the other room, Luke let out a cry of delight.

"He smiled at me, Ken. There he goes again! Look at that!"

She wondered if her husband realized how close he was to falling in love with the child he held.

"Wow!" he exclaimed when he looked up at her. "You look absolutely gorgeous."

She looked longingly back toward the closet, eyeing the reliable grays.

"Mother would be furious," he warned, reading her mind.

"I didn't want new clothes," she told him.

"I know," he said. "You'll be glad of it when you have to go somewhere."

She nodded in agreement. "We went to lunch at Gabrielle's today. I was glad then."

He smiled at her admission, and she took Brady out of his arms. They continued talking as she changed the baby's diaper and got him dressed.

"Avery told me you ruffled Mother's feathers about the prices."

"Have you eaten there? I know I'm not used to places like that. But those prices were ridiculous."

He chuckled. "Yes, I have eaten there. Once. I refuse to pay such prices for food that is almost inedible. Mother hates the food, too. She just goes there to see who else is there. She must have wanted to show you off. Did you meet any of her friends?"

"No. There weren't many people there. The only person we talked to was a little old lady who thought I was her friend's daughter."

"Really?"

"It was sad. She just kept insisting she knew me, even when I told her she didn't. I'm supposed to tell my mother, Louisa, that Miriam Rogers said hello."

"Are you ready to go down to dinner?" he asked.

Something had changed in the last two minutes, and she missed the easy camaraderie of moments before.

"Oh, I almost forgot," he said, pulling an envelope from his jacket. "You have mail."

She handed him the baby in exchange for the envelope. She searched in vain for a return address or any clue to where it came from, before opening it and pulling out two pictures. One was of seven-year-old Kendall standing under a neon Vacancy sign while the school bus pulled to a stop in front of her. The other was of her mother sitting on a barstool, one hand wrapped around a glass and a cigarette in her other. She stared toward the camera, not at it, her face ravaged with sadness.

"Kendall?" Luke touched her arm, and she lifted her face to his. "Are you okay?"

"Yes, I'm fine." She stuck the pictures back into the envelope before he saw them and crammed it into the drawer with her nylons. She smiled at Luke. "Let's go."

She spoke little at supper, her mind on the pictures in her room upstairs. Few people knew who her mother was. She had never discussed it with anyone, including Adam. Her conversation with Delores her first morning here was the closest she'd ever come to discussing it with anyone. Even then no names were mentioned, no specifics given. Did Delores know who her mother and father were? Even if she did, where would she have gotten those pictures, and what would she gain by sending them to Kendall?

No one she knew had any reason at all to either

have pictures of her and her mother or send them to her.

****

"You were quiet tonight," Luke observed when they entered their room later.

"I'm still tired." She began taking the pins from her hair, and he put his hand on her arm.

"Are you sure nothing's wrong?"

"I said there's nothing wrong, Luke. Please, just leave me alone."

He looked as if he were about to protest, but shrugged and sat down on the bed like he did every night.

"So, why don't you tell me about growing up," he said.

Though she suspected the request was innocent, coupled with the pictures it was too much. She went to her drawer, grabbed the pictures, and flung them on his lap.

"There, look at those closely. They'll tell you all you want to know."

She slammed the bathroom door behind her, hoping he'd be gone by the time she came back out.

She took much longer than necessary to change into her nightgown and perform her usual nightly routine, but when she came out, he still sat where she left him.

"Who sent these to you?" he demanded.

"I don't know. There was no return address, no note."

"This is you?"

"Yes."

"And your mother?"

She nodded miserably.

"These are candid shots. It doesn't appear that either of you knew your picture was being taken."

"I'm sure we didn't."

"Why weren't you going to tell me about this?"

83

"It's bad enough to have you know what my life was like growing up. I didn't want you to see the proof. Pictures make it all too real."

"You don't have any idea who could have sent them?"

"No."

"They're not threatening, so I don't think the police would do anything."

Horrified, she grabbed the pictures from him. "We are not calling the police. Nor are we telling anyone else about this."

"We won't tell anyone for now, but people don't do things like this for no reason, Kendall. Promise me you'll tell me if you get any more pictures or if anyone contacts you."

It occurred to her then what he was thinking.

"You think someone will try to blackmail me? As in, they won't tell anyone about my past if I pay them?"

"Does anyone you knew as a child, anyone your mother knew, know where you are now?"

"No."

"If you think of anyone, let me know. Okay?"

Brady began to cry and Kendall went to get him.

"Let's get some sleep, Luke," she said.

He gave Brady the usual kiss on the head and brushed his lips gently across Kendall's cheek before leaving the room.

Chapter Thirteen

As summer gave way to fall, Kendall spent each day in much the same way as the one before, caring for Brady and getting to know her sisters-in-law. Every day she watched the mail nervously, but nothing else came.

Each night after dinner, Luke came to her room as he'd promised to do, and Kendall found herself looking forward to their time together.

As she learned more about him, she began to understand the man who vowed that love had nothing to do with life here.

On Halloween night, Avery went out with friends, and Luke volunteered to stay up and make sure she got home. After she bathed and dressed in her nightgown, Kendall slipped on her robe and went back downstairs to wait with him.

"I thought you might like some company," Kendall said when she found him heading out to the patio.

"I'd love some company. Do you mind if we sit outside?" he asked, and Kendall readily agreed.

It was a beautiful night. The moon was full and hung so low it seemed they could touch it. A warm breeze was blowing, compliments of a tropical storm brewing somewhere offshore, and the scent of citrus blossoms infused the air, compliments of the oil Cora bottled each year and burned in imported glass oil lamps like the one on the poolside table.

She followed him to a small alcove in the corner of the patio where rattan furniture formed a semi-circle lit only by the soft glow of the moon.

"Comfy?" He teased as she kicked off her slippers and sat down in one of the chairs, bringing her feet onto the pastel cushion beneath her robe.

"Very." She looked up at the sky. "I love this time of year."

"And why is that?"

He lowered himself into the chair opposite hers, listening with rapt attention as she reminisced about how mischievous her students became this time of year.

"You liked teaching, didn't you?" he asked when she grew quiet.

"I loved it."

"Do you miss it?"

"At times, but I enjoy being with Brady."

"Maybe when he's older you could teach again."

"You wouldn't mind?" She couldn't keep the excitement out of her voice, as she leaned forward in her chair.

"No. Why would I?"

"Your mother said it wouldn't be appropriate."

"It wouldn't be my mother's decision. I've never known how she and Margo just wander around the house all day."

"They both do charity work," she defended.

"I know, but if you would rather teach, why not do it?"

"I *have* wondered what I'm supposed to do with the rest of my life. I mean, I appreciate being able to be with Brady, but he'll go to school before we know it."

"Maybe you'll have another baby by then."

She looked at him in surprise. It had never entered her mind that he might want children of his own.

"I always wanted a sister or brother. I would love for Brady to grow up with siblings," she admitted.

"I love Brady, and if he's the only child we ever have, I'll be okay with that, but I keep thinking of a little girl with dark hair and violet eyes."

Without thinking, she rushed over and threw her arms around him, elated that he wanted to be the daddy to her little girl.

In an instant, his arms closed around her, and he pulled her onto his lap. Desire curled through her when he caught her mouth with his own, and her hands moved of their own accord, glancing over the light stubble on his jaw and coming to rest in the soft dark hair at the base of his skull.

Car lights lit up the drive, and they heard Avery telling her friends good-bye.

"Avery's home," she said against his lips.

"Mm-hm," he hummed as he kissed her again.

"Good night!" Avery called from the open doorway.

"Night, Ave," he yelled back, barely lifting his lips from Kendall's.

"I need to get back to the baby, Luke," Kendall said, pulling back from him.

He made no move to get up, and she looked at him questioningly.

"Are you coming up?"

"Are you inviting me?"

She felt her face turn red.

"Good night, Ken," he said with a soft chuckle.

Chapter Fourteen

"This is exactly what Kendall needs for the Citrus Ball, Mother." Avery jabbed her finger at the magazine on the bed.

"Oh, yes," Margo cried, peering over Avery's shoulder. "That's exactly it."

"Well, it must be quite a creation if the two of you can agree on it," Delores said and held out her hand for the magazine. "Let me see."

She nodded her elegant head in approval.

"Janine, can you do this?"

Janine stopped pinning the hem of Kendall's dress and peered at the book.

"Yes, and I agree it is perfect."

"Same color, but a shade darker," Delores said decisively, and the seamstress nodded as she began working again.

Kendall tried to see the dress they were all agreeing to, but Delores happily slapped the book shut and shoved it in Janine's bag.

"Don't I get a say-so?" Kendall asked.

"No," the other four women said at the same time.

Kendall stared at them. She didn't want to argue with them, but she did want to know what they intended for her.

"Kendall, I don't want to hurt your feelings," Margo said hesitantly, as if trying to decide how to say what needed to be said as delicately as possible.

"Oh, just say it, Margo," Avery said in exasperation. "Kendall, you have the worst fashion sense of anyone I've ever known."

"Avery, that's not nice," Margo chided her.

"No, but it's true."

"Girls," Delores said, and Kendall wondered whether Margo ever minded being lumped in with a sixteen-year-old. "Kendall, trust me. The dress is beautiful. It will suit you perfectly, and it is a wonderful choice for the ball."

"All right, Miss Kendall, you can step out of it now," Janine said, unzipping the dress and letting it pool around Kendall's ankles.

"Miss Kendall," Margo repeated in a soft, stunned voice as she stared at Kendall.

Avery couldn't contain a startled gasp.

"Margo, dear, I think I hear Brady crying. Run fetch him while Kendall gets dressed," Delores said smoothly.

Margo's beautiful face lit with delight and she hurried from the room.

Avery, however, wasn't so easily distracted.

"Kendall?" Her voice held a million questions.

"Avery," Delores warned, and the girl paled.

"Oh, hell," she whispered and disappeared through the door before either her mother or Kendall could reprimand her.

The dressmaker looked completely confused, and Kendall felt certain she looked the same way.

"What's going on?" she demanded of her mother-in-law.

"Both my daughter and Margo are extremely high-strung, Kendall. Certainly you've realized that by now. It's almost impossible to determine what set them off."

****

Luke lay stretched out on the bed playing with Brady as Kendall sat at her dressing table. She studied him in the mirror while she pulled the brush through her dark hair. His dress shirt was cast over the rocking chair in the corner, and he wore only an undershirt and trousers. His hair was rumpled where he'd gently rubbed it across Brady's belly, and she felt a sudden urge to run her fingers through the soft waves. It had been a week since Halloween, and she still felt his kiss on her lips. So far, he hadn't tried to kiss her again. She was almost certain she wanted him to try it again. When she caught herself running her tongue over her lips, she forced herself to turn her attention to something else.

"The strangest thing happened today," she told him.

"What's that?" he asked as he shook a rattle in front of Brady's face.

"Janine was fitting me for a dress and something, I don't really know what, but it may have been Janine calling me Miss Kendall, caused both Margo and Avery to have the oddest reaction."

"Margo and Avery have a lot of strange reactions. Hell, Avery throws a fit at the drop of a hat, and Margo spends half her time in la-la land."

"That's what your mother said." Sometimes their words were so similar, she found herself wondering if they all practiced their lines before she got up in the morning.

"Kendall, really, I don't know what you want me to say. Margo was probably fine in a minute, wasn't she?"

"Well, yes," Kendall admitted, thinking of Margo returning with Brady.

She turned back to the mirror. In the reflection, she watched Luke run a long tanned finger across the baby's palm. A bond had already formed between the two of them, and Kendall grew more certain every day that she'd done the right thing in giving her son a father.

"He's something else," Luke murmured, grinning when Brady's fingers closed around his. "You've got quite a grip there, Little Man."

Oh Adam, you don't even know what you're missing," she thought.

Had her father ever missed knowing her?

****

She was ten the first time she caught the streetcar that stopped a few blocks from her father's house. Once there, she found a bench across the street and sat looking at his home, watching the people come and go, and wondering why her father didn't want her to live there with him. She could tell it had plenty of room for her.

After a while, he came out of the house, looking like a movie star as he crossed the street holding the hand of his pretty blonde daughter.

Kendall's heart fluttered with excitement as they walked toward her.

"Here they come," she thought. "They know who I am."

As they came nearer, Kendall scooted a little closer to the edge of the bench, ready to leap from the bench and run to him. Neither of them even looked her way as they walked past her and disappeared around the corner.

"Where shall we go today, Princess?" Kendall heard him ask. She barely heard the girl's reply as she fought the scalding tears that filled her eyes.

When she got back to the dank room she shared with her mother, she stared at herself in the cracked mirror that hung askew on the bathroom wall. Why, oh, why couldn't her daddy love her the way he loved his other little girl?

As she glared at her reflection, she knew. His chosen daughter had soft blonde curls that shimmered in the sunlight and bounced when she walked. No matter how hard Kendall brushed her own brown hair trying to make it do something beautiful, it just hung there.

His chosen daughter always wore ruffled lacy

dresses that could belong to a fairy princess, while Kendall always wore whatever was in the boxes Mary Christopher sent over every spring and every fall. Mary had two girls who were older than Kendall, and she always sent her their hand-me-downs. The only problem was that their hand-me-downs were someone else's hand-me-downs. By the time they got to Kendall, they were practically worn out and hopelessly out of style.

Before that day, Kendall was always excited when she saw Mary's son Layton coming down the sidewalk with a big box on his shoulders. After seeing her father and his other daughter, however, just the thought of those old, worn-out clothes made her cry.

****

Tonight Luke didn't wait for her to finish nursing the baby before he sat on the bed. He lay on his side beside them and watched her. She didn't say a word. She just finished feeding the baby, and moved to her dressing table, leaving him and Brady alone on the bed. Though he had every intention of focusing his attention on Kendall, Luke couldn't seem to resist the wrinkled-up little face and bright gray eyes that stared at him as if trying to memorize what they were seeing. No one had ever looked at him like Brady did. Maybe it was a hazard of being a twin, but from birth it seemed no one ever saw only him. Brady was different. He looked at Luke and saw no one else.

Thank God Kendall had chosen to stay here and marry him. When his mother came up with the idea, he'd thought it was crazy, but even then he couldn't bear to think of Kendall and Brady being homeless, penniless.

Now, the thought of Kendall turning to the kind of life her mother had lived made his stomach turn. He imagined her old before her time, the hope wiped from her beautiful eyes by harsh reality, her lush body pawed by the grubby hands of strangers so she could feed her child.

He fervently wished he had met her first, before she gave her heart to his brother.

He and Adam grew farther apart each day. He simply didn't understand Adam anymore. He couldn't understand a man who would trick a woman so cruelly, then leave her and his child alone and defenseless against the world.

The baby's fingers tightened around his own again, and he smiled.

At least this good came out of it, he thought. Kendall's son. Adam's son. *My* son.

Chapter Fifteen

Kendall woke with a start as lightning lit the room, followed by a clap of thunder. When a scream echoed through the house, she jumped from the bed and ran into the hallway, where she found Luke rushing toward the staircase.

"It's Margo," he said, waving her back into the room. "She's petrified of storms."

Another crash of thunder brought another scream, followed by a quick succession of thunder and screams. Each scream seemed to grow more hysterical than the one before.

Wanting to help, Kendall peeked out at the open door. Margo ran toward the nursery, Adam close on her heels.

"Close the door, Kendall!" Luke roared. He was there in an instant, pulling the door closed. As he did so, their eyes met and his voice was soft but firm when he spoke. "Lock it and keep it locked until I come back."

"You can't be serious," she argued, but let go of the door when Margo began to wail.

"I told you to let me save him! Baby! Baby!"

Margo's voice took on a scared, little-girl quality as she began to beat on the doors along the hallway.

Kendall locked the door and huddled in her bed with Brady while the storm raged outside and Margo raged inside.

She jumped when Margo's fist struck her bedroom door. "Baby! Are you in there?"

Brady began to wail, and the hallway grew strangely quiet.

"He's in there," Margo said in a loud whisper. "He's crying. See, he's afraid. He needs me."

"It's okay, Margo." The gentle assurance came from Adam. "Luke has the key."

The sound of the key in the lock sent shivers of apprehension down Kendall's spine.

The door swung open just as Adam handed Luke an empty syringe and then lifted his unconscious wife in his arms.

Kendall sighed with relief once Luke sat on the bed and gathered her against his chest.

"Why didn't any of you tell me that Margo was so ill?" she whispered.

"She's fine for such long periods of time. Adam always believes she's better, or at least he wants to believe that. So, we all pretend she's just a little ditzy instead of really ill. It's not right, but it's the way she and Adam want it."

For the first time, she felt sorry for Adam.

****

The sun broke through later in the day, and behind the rain came cooler temperatures. It seemed a perfect day for a walk around the lake, and Kendall bundled Brady in a warm blanket and set out. As they were returning from their stroll, Avery came out of the house waving a large envelope. Kendall's stomach dropped when Avery placed it in her hands, her curiosity about its contents almost palpable.

"Aren't you going to open it?" Avery asked when Kendall took it from her but kept moving toward the house.

"Not yet. I'm going to put Brady down for a nap."

Ignoring Avery's sighs and eye rolling, Kendall took the envelope to her room. Once there, she took her time bathing Brady, feeding him, and putting him down for a nap.

Finally, with shaking hands she tore open the

envelope.

These pictures were larger and more personal.

Her mother, long limp hair hanging around her face, sat on the short wall of a flower bed in front of a hotel. She looked tired, but a small smile played about her mouth as she looked toward the nearby child wearing a too-small dress and a diaper.

In the other, twelve-year-old Kendall perched on the edge of a park bench, staring across the street with an expectant look on her face.

"Waiting on Thomas," scrawled across the top of each.

She ran a finger across the picture of her mother. Waiting on Thomas. She was so young in the picture, but already waiting for him. She waited the rest of her life, until she couldn't wait anymore.

Chapter Sixteen

"So, Kendall, how are you?" Adam asked as he entered the parlor the next night.

She looked toward the door, expecting Margo to be with him.

"Margo isn't feeling well. She won't be down tonight."

"Will she be all right?" Kendall asked in concern.

He shrugged and walked to the bar, where he poured himself a glass of brandy.

"There are times when her headaches are debilitating, but this one doesn't seem to be so bad. Still, I thought it would be better if she rested instead of joining us for supper."

"Has she seen a doctor?"

"Of course. Dr. Landon seems to think a lot of it's in her head. She seems to get them frequently during stressful times."

Kendall felt a slight twinge of guilt that her coming here may have added to Margo's illness.

"She gets depressed. I don't think Brady being here helps."

"Of course not," Kendall said. "I'm sorry."

"Are you really?" he said in a bored tone. "I'd never guess it."

Her hand shook slightly as she lifted her glass to her lips. He appeared lost in thought as he swirled his drink.

"Why did you marry me, Ken?" He didn't lift his eyes from his glass when he asked the question.

She set her drink down quickly, afraid that the shaking in her hands would cause her to drop it.

"I loved you," she said in answer to his question.

"Did you know I was rich?"

A harsh laugh escaped her, and she leaned back against the sofa.

"What is it with you people? Is money the only reason any of you do anything? How in the world would I have known you were rich? Why would I have doubted you were what you said you were?"

"You're way too trusting," he observed.

"No kidding," she retorted. "I think I probably realized that about the time I lost my job and the house."

He had the good grace to look ashamed, but he quickly resumed his usual detached demeanor.

"So, if you loved me so much, why'd you marry my brother?"

"I wanted a father for my son." She refused to let him put her on the defensive.

"*I'm* his father."

"No, Adam, you aren't."

"Do you love Luke?"

The question set her back a bit. Did she love Luke? She was attached to him, fond of him, even, but she wasn't sure she loved him.

"I barely know him. I married him to give Brady a stable home, a stable father."

"I want you to leave."

"I'm aware of that."

"I mean it, Ken. You had no business coming here."

"What else was I to do, Adam?"

"There were other choices."

"What were they?" she asked, wondering if he really believed that. "If you had left me a list of my other choices, or if you'd bothered to just come back and tell me what they were, maybe I'd have decided to go with one of them. Instead, you left me alone and pregnant."

"I didn't know you were pregnant," he said defensively.

"That doesn't change the fact that I was. It doesn't change what you did to me."

"Oh, give me a break, Kendall. Look at yourself. Look where you came from and where you are now. I did you a favor."

"What?" Certainly she misunderstood his words.

"I did you a favor," he taunted. "I led you here. Like your fairy godmother, I gave you a better life. I gave you a chance to become a Templeton. That's nothing to sneeze at."

She didn't trust herself to speak, nor did she trust herself not to knock that smug, self-satisfied smirk off his face. So, she stood and hurried into the hallway. Intent on escaping, she pushed past Luke, who was coming down the hall, and continued toward the door.

"What's going on?" he called.

"Nothing," She couldn't hide the tears that choked her. "I just need some air."

She heard his footsteps behind her as she rushed into the cool night air. He caught up with her before she rounded the outside corner of the house, heading for the lake.

"What just happened in there?"

"Your brother's a jerk," she said angrily.

"Did that just occur to you today?"

She shook her head, afraid to speak. He didn't say a word when she began to cry, just stepped closer and turned her to face him. He wrapped his arms around her as she fell against his chest with a sob.

When her sobs subsided, she stepped back and looked up at him. "I'm sorry."

"It's okay. I wish I could do more to help," he said, running a hand over her hair.

"You've already done more than anyone else I

know would have."

"Are you ready to try going to supper now?" he asked.

She told herself it was just for strength that she grasped his hand and held onto it for dear life.

Chapter Seventeen

Kendall sat on the stone wall separating the lawn from the pasture, shading her eyes against the bright November sun. Luke sat astride a large gray stallion, Brady held firmly in his arms as the horse walked slowly across the field.

She could see Luke's mouth moving, and she wondered what he was saying. His voice didn't quite carry this far, but she heard the gentle cadence of it as he talked to the baby.

She could have done much, much worse than Luke Templeton. There was no denying he was handsome. Adam was handsome, but there was something so much more so about Luke. Maybe it was the warmth in his eyes. She realized now that Adam's were often cold and calculating. Luke was kind to her, gentle with Brady. She knew he had a temper, she had seen and heard it, but he was never cruel, although cruelty seemed to be a common trait in both his brother and sister. She could tell Brady loved him. When Luke held him, Brady couldn't take his eyes off Luke's face. When she nursed him, anyone else could come in and Brady wouldn't even notice, but as soon as Luke entered the room, he stopped nursing and tried to see around the blanket that covered him. To him, Luke was Daddy and always would be.

The closest she'd ever come to having a daddy was Marty Raymond, a fisherman who lived near the Wayside Inn. He was her mother's most regular boyfriend. One night, she overheard him propose to her mother, and they had a fight so big that her mother left. Marty stayed there with Kendall because he didn't want to leave her alone and didn't know what else to do with her. When her mother came back three days later, Marty left. After that, he came around less and less. Finally, he stopped coming altogether. Kendall knew Marty really cared for them. Most of the men her mother brought through their doors never spared Kendall a second glance, but Marty was different. He tried, really tried, to fit into their lives, but her mother steadfastly refused to let him. Why hadn't Lydia seen the difference it would make for her daughter to have that steadiness instead of the intermittent parade of men who came through their lives?

****

"Were you worried?" Luke teased as he brought the horse to a stop in front of her.

"Yes," she said, sliding from the wall and holding her arms up for the baby.

"I told you I wouldn't let anything happen to him," he said and handed Brady down to her before dismounting.

"He seemed to like it."

"In a few months, he'll love it."

The horse nuzzled her, and she patted it gingerly.

"Would you like to ride?"

"No," she shook her head quickly, and he laughed.

"Ever ride before?"

"No."

"Stay right there." He took the baby from her and strode to the kitchen door.

"We won't be gone long," she heard him promise Cora before bounding across the lawn.

He swung himself onto the horse and held out his hand to Kendall.

"Come on."

"I can't," she said, terrified.

"Sure you can. Listen, Bard's big, but he's gentle. I wouldn't have taken Brady out on a horse I didn't trust."

"Bard?" she asked.

"Yeah, like Shakespeare. The Bard. You do know who that is, right?"

She laughed, and he took that moment to grab her hand and pull her onto the horse.

Scared to move for fear the animal would begin to run, she held her breath and waited.

"Loosen up," he breathed in her ear.

"I don't think I can," she whispered.

"Don't act afraid," he warned with a chuckle. "He can sense your fear."

She tried to convince her body to relax and her mind not to be afraid, but it was no use. She was petrified. Her joints felt locked in place, and her insides quivered with nervousness.

With a flip of his wrist, Luke sent the horse moving at what she assumed was a sedate pace but which had her clutching his arms for balance.

"It's okay," he murmured. "Just loosen up. Let your body move with the horse."

"He's a very tall horse," she said, looking at the ground.

"Close your eyes," he commanded.

"Why?"

"Do it, Ken."

She let her eyes close.

"Now, just lean back against me, loosen your body, and let it move with the horse." His voice was a husky whisper.

She obeyed without question, and was almost instantly lost in sensation. Overwhelmed by the feeling of Luke's hard chest against her back and his strong arm around her waist, she barely felt the horse beneath her. Keeping her eyes closed, she let her body move with the rhythm of the horse's movements as Luke's breath ruffled her hair.

When the horse came to a stop, she opened her eyes. They were at the other end of the lake, where they could see the house from a distance.

"Do you see that, Ken?"

"The house?" She hoped she didn't sound as disappointed as she felt that they had stopped moving.

"Everything," he said as he bent down to kiss her neck.

"Yes," she said.

"It's all yours."

"I don't want it," she said. Why did he want to ruin such a pleasant moment with more talk about his family's possessions?

"It doesn't matter if you want it or not. It's yours."

"What does that mean?"

"It means when you married me, it became yours. The same as it would have if your marriage to Adam was real."

"I didn't know he was rich," she said for what seemed like the hundredth time.

"I know that," he said, "but it doesn't change it."

"So, why are you showing me this?" she asked, frustration edging her voice.

"Because I want you to understand that there are people who would kill for what you see there."

"I'm not one of them."

He kissed the top of her head and laughed softly.

"Just remember it, okay?"

She nodded, confused and disappointed by their conversation.

"We'd best get back," he said and set the horse in motion once more.

Chapter Eighteen

Kendall was sitting at her dressing table in her brassiere, panties and slip when he walked in. Her breasts threatened to spill out of their moorings as she lifted her arms over her head to secure her dark tresses into a topknot, and his breath caught in his throat.

Her eyes met his in the mirror, and in the reflection he saw the blush that stole over her face.

"I have something for you."

Letting his fingers trail over her skin, he encircled her throat with a strand of gold holding an oval sapphire surrounded by diamonds. His hands rested on her shoulders as she looked at it in the mirror and ran her fingers over it in disbelief.

"Beautiful," he murmured, placing a soft kiss on her neck.

Their eyes met once more in the mirror.

"You're my wife," he said.

"Yes," she answered.

"I want you."

Silently, she stared into his eyes.

"Do you want me?" he asked.

"Yes."

With a sigh, she let her head fall back against his chest, exposing her throat to his mouth. His tongue and lips traced the path of her jugular from the pulse point at the bottom of her throat to her jaw line. She turned her face to his and their mouths met as his hand skimmed across her breast. Heat suffused her as he gently caught her silk-covered nipple between his fingers.

"Luke," she whispered against his mouth, and his kiss deepened.

She turned so her body pressed against his, front to front, and pulled his shirt free from his waistband to run her hands eagerly inside and across his bare back.

"Kendall?" he asked.

She heard the question and remembered his promise that he wouldn't make love to her until she was completely ready.

"Yes," she whispered.

The word seemed to set them free, and he quickly disrobed her, leaving her naked except for the necklace, and lifted her against him.

He laid her back against the bed, his hands touching and stroking, setting her afire with every touch. She met him touch for touch until they were consumed with passion and released into satiated oblivion.

****

As Luke came back to himself, he ran his hand over the soft swell of her belly, and she made a noise that sounded suspiciously like a purr. She turned toward him with a smile.

He let out a breath he hadn't realized he held as he admitted to himself that he'd half expected to see Adam's ghost in the violet depths of her eyes.

Seeing her look at him with passion-dazed eyes, feeling the soft touch of her hand on his chest as she leaned toward him, and knowing the gentleness of her kiss, all left him wondering anew how his brother could have held something so pure and beautiful and heedlessly crushed it beneath his heels. A wave of anger followed the realization that even now thoughts of Adam intruded on them.

An hour later, he stood at the bottom of the grand staircase and watched her descend. A midnight blue dress skimmed her torso like a glove before fanning out from her hips. It sparkled with opalescent fire as she moved, reflecting the light in her eyes and the stone at her throat.

"I knew that dress would be perfect for her," Margo said from beside him.

He looked at Margo, whose own dress of fawn-colored silk showcased her beauty and, for a moment, he almost understood Adam's dilemma. Tonight, Margo's eyes were clear and showed no sign of her illness. Hoping for the best, he tried to ignore the frenzied energy radiating from her.

"She really is stunning," Adam said as Kendall came closer.

"I'm lucky she's mine," he retorted and led her away from Adam and Margo to the waiting car.

****

Kendall was fairly miserable. A group of men had stolen Luke away as soon as they walked into the ballroom of the Delacroix mansion, and the rest of the family migrated to their own cliques, leaving her to fend for herself.

A hand touched her arm, and she turned to find an attractive man standing beside her.

"You're Luke's wife, I presume?" His blue eyes sparkled with obvious interest as he studied her, and she felt a blush creep across her face. He slicked his hand over his blond hair and nodded in approval. "Can't believe it was Luke who snagged you. I never knew he had such fine taste."

"Douglas, I do hope you aren't filling my daughter-in-law's head full of nonsense." Delores' sharp voice came from just behind her, and the man lifted his eyes from Kendall to her mother-in-law.

"No, of course not," he said with an easy smile and turned away.

Kendall watched him go. At the door, he turned back toward her, and she was struck by an inexplicable sense of recognition.

"Who is he?" she asked Delores.

"Douglas Martin. Now, come with me, Kendall," Delores commanded. "There's someone I'd like you to meet."

Dismissing the thought that she knew him from somewhere, she followed Delores to the side of a stunning blonde chatting animatedly with a group of older women.

"Julianne," Delores said when the woman stopped for a breath and turned toward them with a gracious smile. "I'd like you to meet my daughter-in-law."

The smile seemed to melt from the woman's face, leaving her pale and not nearly as attractive as she appeared moments before. She swayed slightly before quickly recovering, her previous reaction rewinding until the smile once again settled into place.

"You must be Kendall," she said, shaking Kendall's hand half-heartedly.

"Kendall, I'd like to introduce you to Julianne Delacroix, Margo's mother."

As she did when standing near the daughter, Kendall felt woefully inadequate before the mother. She reminded herself that Luke seemed to find her somewhat attractive, and she tried to picture how she'd looked in front of the mirror this evening. Still, she felt as if she were shrinking into herself as Julianne studied her.

"Where are you from, Kendall? Who are your parents?" Julianne asked in a rather loud voice. The women gathered around them seemed to lean forward, anxiously awaiting her answer.

As often as she'd fielded similar questions at Chadsworth, she should have a universally acceptable answer by now, but of course she didn't. So, she stood mute, trying to decide how best to answer.

"I'm sorry, ladies, but I'm stealing my wife away from you," Luke apologized as he appeared at her side.

She breathed a sigh of relief, as he led her to the dance floor.

"You looked like you needed rescuing," he said, placing a hand on her waist and turning her into a waltz.

"Thank you," she said. "I have to warn you, though, that being my rescuer could keep you very busy."

"I have a lifetime."

Quick tears sprang to her eyes as his simple words hit her heart. She covered them with a laugh as she inadvertently stomped his toe.

"You'll be sorry you chose dancing as your means of rescuing me. My mother tried to teach me how to dance, but I am pathetically uncoordinated."

Kendall smiled wistfully as she remembered the nights her mother came home alone but still wound up. Pulling Kendall from her bed or the sofa or wherever she slept, Lydia would twirl around the room, dodging furniture while she laughingly instructed Kendall to move to the beat of an invisible orchestra.

"Just follow my lead," Luke said and pulled her closer. The memories went back into hiding as she concentrated on not smashing his toes.

When the music died, he led her into the dining room. Avery, beautiful in a light pink gown that exhibited her age and her beauty in equal measure, appeared to be holding court in one corner. Several young men lingered nearby, but Avery seemed completely oblivious to all of them save a handsome boy with auburn hair and green eyes.

"It looks like your little sister's got quite the following," Kendall said.

"Avery's a doll. You've been really good with her.

She needs a friend at home. Adam and I don't have much time for her, and Mother's too overbearing. That's left Margo, and she and Avery have loud and frequent disagreements. Having you here has helped immensely."

She smiled up at him, and he leaned down and gave her a quick kiss.

"Lucas," his mother reprimanded as they took their seats. "You know how I feel about public displays of affection."

"Mother, don't start," he admonished her. "I'm a grown man. I'll kiss my wife whenever I want."

Chapter Nineteen

Kendall was in search of a nice quiet place to hide. After dinner, Luke had left her in his mother's care while he, Adam, and several other men retired to the billiard room down the hall where they could discuss politics and the imminent war in Europe without distressing the ladies.

After a round of introductions, Delores became engrossed in a conversation with several women regarding a benefit they were organizing. Kendall slipped out of their circle without their even realizing it.

She let herself into what appeared to be a den. The trophy animals mounted on every wall gave her the eerie feeling that she was being watched. Still, she preferred the glass eyes of the animals over the prying, judging eyes of the partygoers outside the room. She wandered through the room, stroking fur and feathers.

"Do you hunt?"

Kendall jumped and swung around at the sound of the voice behind her. Douglas Martin sat in one of the large leather chairs, an amused look on his face.

She tried to catch her breath as he watched her expectantly.

"Do you hunt?" he repeated.

"Me? No," she answered. "Do you?"

"No," he said with a shudder. "I think it's a vulgar sport, but I suppose we all have our little trophies."

He absently twisted his wedding ring, and she thought of the buxom black-haired beauty she'd seen him dancing with earlier.

"I'm sorry," she said. "I don't think we've been introduced. I'm Kendall Templeton."

She held out her hand, and he took it in his own. He stroked his fingers across her skin, as his eyes met hers.

"Douglas Martin. Margo's uncle," he said, his fingers continuing their soft movements against her skin.

Suddenly, his grip tightened around her hand and his eyes darkened. "People don't willingly give up their trophies, Kendall."

She had no idea what he was talking about, but she grew increasingly uneasy about being alone with him.

"Excuse me, Mr. Martin. I think I'll go find my husband." She sincerely hoped her grimace passed as a polite smile, and she tried to pull her hand from his, but he held tightly.

"Don't you want to know whose trophies these are?"

"I assume they're Mr. Delacroix's since this is his den."

"Assume nothing, sweetheart. This is *Mrs.* Delacroix's den. The trophies are hers and Margo's."

"Margo's?" she repeated. Sweet, crazy Margo shot some of these animals?

He gave a not-so-pleasant bark of laughter as the door opened behind her. He let go of her hand, and she quickly stepped back.

"Margo's what?" asked Avery as she came in.

"Margo's trophies," Douglas said, with a grand flourish of his arm. "She's an amazing hunter. And you should see the maniacal gleam in her eyes just before she pops one."

"Yuck," the girl said her eyes moving over the display. Then, with a dismissive flip of her head, "Mother's looking for you, Kendall."

Grateful for the excuse to escape the room and its occupant, even if it meant she was to be in Delores' custody once again, Kendall hurried behind Avery.

Chapter Twenty

Luke had hoped to avoid being alone with Rebecca. He knew it was cowardly, but he hadn't spoken to her since she learned of his engagement, and although she took the news with her usual dignity, he didn't want to be in a position where she might expect a more detailed explanation. As luck would have it, however, they now faced each other in the wide hallway that led away from the ballroom.

"Luke!" she exclaimed as she pressed her body against his in greeting. He supposed she meant it to be a hug, but with a cigarette in one hand and a glass of champagne in the other, she couldn't use her arms, so it didn't pass as one. "How are you?"

"Wonderful," he said and tried to push past her. He could tell by her voice and movements that this was far from her first glass of champagne.

"And how is your little wife? Avery told me she's a schoolteacher. Can you imagine my surprise? I thought we were an item, Luke. And you dumped me. Of course, I wasn't dumb enough to get knocked up, was I? Or was I not clever enough? Had I known you were such a man of honor, I may have done things differently. Or is that a man of so little honor?"

"Rebecca, you know how sorry I am. You also know that you and I weren't quite an item. We never would have worked out as husband and wife. There's no passion between us." His mind suddenly filled with the memory of Kendall's pliant body pressed against his.

She raised her eyebrows.

"Passion, Luke? I never knew that was your cup of tea."

"Neither did I," he admitted.

"Kiss me one last time. Just to make sure there isn't any passion."

"Good night, Rebecca," he said.

As he moved past her, she stepped closer, swaying precariously. Instinctively, he reached to steady her and set her away, but she leaned forward, her lips landing on his.

"Jesus, Luke," Avery said from over Rebecca's shoulder.

Both his sister and his wife stood in the hallway staring at him. Avery's glare was hot enough to scorch him, but it was Kendall's stone-cold pallor that seemed to burn holes through him.

Rebecca stood straighter and with an indulgent smile, staggered past the other women.

"Kendall," he began, but she turned and hurried through the door leading to a wide veranda.

She sucked in deep breaths of cool night air. Her hand came to her chest and she felt the hard smooth face of the sapphire he'd placed around her neck earlier. She felt ill with self-loathing as she remembered the moments afterward and knew with shattering certainty she was her mother's daughter.

"Ken," Avery said from behind her. "Are you okay? Should I get Mother?"

Kendall could hear the worry in the girl's voice, and she shook her head.

"No, of course not. I'm fine. I just need a minute."

"He says it wasn't what it looked like," Avery offered hopefully.

"It never is," Kendall said. She felt old and burdened. "My mama used to tell me that no matter what lie you catch a man in, it's never what it looks like. I can't believe I keep making the same mistakes she made."

"Kendall," Luke said as he came up behind her. "I promise I wasn't kissing her. She was trying to kiss me."

"You didn't appear to be fighting her off very hard," Avery accused.

"Avery shut up and go inside," he snarled.

"You're an ass, Luke. I can't believe you did this."

"Please go inside, Avery," Kendall said. She refused to let this child fight her battles for her.

With a sound of dismay, Avery fled through the doors, and Kendall looked Luke in the eye, the dark pain of disillusionment straightening her backbone and forcing her to face the truth..

"You're not being fair, Ken. You know I care about you. I wouldn't jeopardize what I've found with you and Brady for anything or anyone."

"You were honest with me when I first came here, Luke. You told me there was someone else. I should have expected that you would keep seeing her. After all, our marriage is just as big a farce as my first one. The only difference is that I entered it with my eyes wide open. I can't believe I wasn't any more prepared this time around."

"You're wrong, Kendall. Our marriage may have started out that way, but it's changed. We both know that. It's real now. We're real. Don't say we aren't."

"What I know is what I just saw, Luke. Regardless of what I believed earlier tonight, our marriage is still a lie." She placed a trembling hand to her throat, running her fingers over the sapphire. "And I'm still a whore."

"Don't ever say that again," he ground out, lifting his hand to the necklace at her throat.

Her eyes grew huge as his palm closed around the stone and he gave it an angry tug. The chain gave way and he pulled it from her neck. He held it up to her, furious at her words and her conclusions. "This was a gift for my wife, damn it. Not payment for her sexual favors."

When she continued to stare at him, he cupped her head in his hands gently.

"Listen to me, Ken. Hear what I'm saying. Believe me when I say what you saw in there was good-bye."

He saw the glint of hope before she doused it and tried to pull away.

"I swear," he murmured as he pulled her closer and lowered his mouth to hers.

She softened beneath his touch and relief swept through him.

"Lucas!" His mother's voice jerked them apart.

She came around the shrubs that hid them from view just as he released Kendall.

"What in heaven's name is going on? Avery is in a panic, saying you've broken Kendall's heart and ruined everything."

"It was a misunderstanding, Mother. It's all right now." He could hardly drag his eyes away from Kendall's as he turned toward Delores.

"Then you should both come back in. As newlyweds you're allowed a little more freedom to disappear now and then, but people will begin to talk if you stay gone too long."

She led them back to the ballroom, where Avery came rushing toward them. She ignored Luke completely but threw her arms around Kendall.

"I'm so glad you came back."

Margo and Adam followed at a more leisurely pace, but in mere seconds Kendall found herself surrounded on all sides by Templetons.

Whether to make her feel safe or to make certain she didn't escape, for the rest of the night she was accompanied by at least one of them at all times.

Chapter Twenty-One

The next afternoon, Kendall sat by the pool while Brady played on a blanket beside her. Though Luke still maintained his innocence in what she had witnessed, it nagged at her. Between it and her moments in Douglas Martin's company, she'd found it impossible to fall into a peaceful sleep last night.

"Hello!" a voice called from across the yard.

She shaded her eyes and watched the tall redhead stride toward her. Jealousy knifed through her at the thought of those tinted lips against Luke's.

"I hope I'm not disturbing you," Rebecca said when she stood beside Kendall's chair.

"Not at all," Kendall assured her through clenched teeth as an uncharacteristically violent imagination reared its ugly head. Perhaps she was her mother's daughter in more ways than one.

The woman lowered her long frame into the chair on the other side of Brady.

"I'm Rebecca Houston." She wore huge sunglasses and still shaded her eyes against the sun's glare with her hand. Kendall, wondering if she was suffering from a hangover, felt childish for hoping it was a massive one.

"Kendall Ja—" Kendall said, then corrected herself, "Templeton."

"Listen, I came to apologize for last night." Rebecca smiled sheepishly. "To tell you the truth, I don't fully remember it, but Avery was kind enough to fill in the blanks. I know you saw me kissing Luke. I just wanted you to know that he wasn't kissing me back. That I *do* remember."

Kendall felt a growing respect for the woman as she continued to speak.

"I've known Luke all my life. He's a man of his word. You won't go wrong if you believe what he says."

"Thank you," Kendall said, her anger dissipating at the woman's obvious sincerity. "I know it must have been hard for you to come here."

Rebecca laughed and leaned back in the chair.

"You have no idea," she admitted. "I'm never at my best when I drink. I usually avoid it, but I saw you come in with him last night, and you were nothing like I expected. I know it's horrible, but I expected some calculating bitch that lured him into bed and got pregnant to force him to stay. I expected someone much trashier than you. I could tell right away that you weren't like that. I saw the way the two of you looked at each other, and I knew I'd lost him. Not that I ever really had him. But I knew there wasn't a chance in hell that he was coming back."

Kendall felt a twinge of guilt that her coming here irreparably changed Rebecca's life. She wouldn't blame Rebecca if she hated her, and she certainly couldn't blame her for hoping Luke would come back to her.

"Like I said, we've known each other all our lives," Rebecca continued. "Our parents were close friends and we naturally saw each other a lot. We connected right from the start. I have three overbearing older brothers. So, I spent a lot of time alone. Luke was born into the wrong family, so he spent a lot of time alone. You haven't known them long enough to realize it or to even know what I mean by it, but Adam is Delores' son through and through. Luke never quite fit in with the rest of them. He never gained the approval or acceptance that Adam did. No matter what he did, they overlooked it in favor of Adam's accomplishment. Luke was smarter, but Adam was more athletic. Luke was sweeter and more caring, but Adam had that outgoing, devil-may-care attitude that drew them to him. I used to be so angry at them for not seeing how great Luke was. All their talk was about Adam, how he'd done this or that, won this event, while Luke read like crazy, observed everything, soaked it all up and learned to run this place while no one was looking.

"Anyway, Luke and I, we just kind of grew together. When my family came to visit, he always set his book down, and we would set off on the grandest adventures. When we were older, my parents sent me to boarding school and Luke stayed here. Adam was the oldest by a few minutes, but Luke was the one who shouldered the responsibility when their father died and someone needed to take over. Adam's a playboy by nature, but to be fair, he has Margo to contend with, and she can be more trying than a dozen businesses."

"When we were in college, Luke and I started dating casually. Of course, there was never really any grand passion between us. It was more that neither of us found anyone we liked more. We joked that if neither of us found someone else by the time we were thirty-five we'd marry each other. Last night, I guess I realized he'd found someone else."

From his blanket, Brady cooed loudly and Rebecca scooped him up. He giggled as she smiled at him.

"He's a beauty," she said to Kendall. "He looks a lot like you, but those eyes are all Luke, aren't they?"

Kendall nodded in agreement. Though it surprised her, she was rather glad that somehow Brady inherited Luke's eyes instead of Adam's.

"Listen," Rebecca said, bouncing Brady on her knees. "Avery doesn't often find people she can get close to, but she feels very close to you. She's very concerned about you."

"Why?" Kendall asked, startled.

"Rebecca!" Delores Templeton exclaimed as she came out of the house. "I certainly hope you've come to clean up your mess."

"Of course, Delores. I couldn't let Luke take the blame for my silliness, could I?"

Rebecca put Brady down on the blanket and stood up as Delores came to embrace her.

"I knew you would do the right thing," the older woman said as they both sat down. "You've always been such a good, honest girl."

Rebecca's smile was strained while Delores peppered her with questions about her parents and other mundane things.

"Well, I guess I should be going," Rebecca said finally. "It was very nice to really meet you, Kendall. And it was a pleasure seeing you, Delores."

Rebecca embraced Delores quickly, then did the same to Kendall.

"Watch out for Margo," she murmured against Kendall's ear.

"I'll see you at supper, Kendall," Delores said as Rebecca hurried away.

"Yes, I'll see you then," Kendall agreed, shocked and confused by Rebecca's warning.

Chapter Twenty-Two

The third set of pictures came in the mail a week later.

The first one caught a young woman, not much more than a girl really, with long dark hair and huge eyes. The swell of her pregnant belly stretched the dress she wore to its limits. She looked tired and scared but at the same time so much younger and more hopeful than Kendall could ever remember her mother looking. *Like Mother* was scrawled across the top of the picture.

The next one had a similar scrawl saying *Like Daughter*, and it caught a very pregnant Kendall checking the mailbox in front of the house she and Adam had shared. She wore the same expectant look as the picture of her sitting in front of her father's house, as if she were still waiting for something wonderful to happen.

The realization that someone secretly photographed her when she was pregnant frightened her much more than someone having pictures of her childhood.

She put them in the drawer with the others. When Luke came to her room tonight, she would show them to him. He would be mad about the ones she hadn't shown him, but he needed to know that someone knew about her life with Adam.

****

"Let's be late for supper tonight," Luke said with a leer as she passed him on her way to the closet.

Smiling, she shook her head.

"I don't think your mother would approve of

that."

He followed her into the closet, his hands closed around her upper arms, and he lowered his mouth to hers. Her body responded instantly, and she ran her fingers through his hair as their kiss deepened.

Finally, she pulled away and slipped back into the bedroom.

"I really need to get ready."

"Remember where we left off," he said with a wink and pulled the door closed behind him.

How could her body react so quickly to him? In the last few weeks, he had completely obliterated Adam from her body's memory. Her heart still remembered the love she'd shared with Adam, although Luke's presence in her life overshadowed Adam's more and more each day. Her body, however, had erased everyone but Luke the very first time he kissed her.

It still shocked her when she thought of what Adam had done to her, but the utter heartbreak of her first few weeks here was gone, and she was surprised at her increasing ability to act normally around him.

She dressed carefully in a long copper dinner dress, then secured her hair in a matching snood. With a little makeup, she was ready, and after a quick glance in the nursery at Brady, she went downstairs.

"Ah, my brother's beautiful bride," Adam observed when she entered the parlor and went to stand beside Luke. "How's married life treating you, Ken? Is it everything you always dreamed it would be?"

Kendall looked to where Margo sat on the sofa, staring into her martini. A definite pattern had emerged in the last few weeks. She just wasn't sure which came first, Adam's spiteful sniping or Margo's spells. Did one cause the other? Certain Margo wasn't paying attention to either of them, Kendall met his eyes across the room. She made no attempt to hide the innuendo in her words.

"It's better than anything I've ever known, anything I've ever dreamed." As a last hurtful afterthought she added, "Brady and I are so lucky to have Luke."

"Careful," Luke murmured, his arm tightening around her waist when his brother's eyes flashed with anger.

"You and Luke are the lucky ones," Margo said her voice thick with tears. "I'd do anything for a baby like Brady."

"Good God, Margo. Not tonight," Adam spat at her.

"Go to hell, Adam," she cried and rushed from the room.

"I suppose you love that, don't you, Kendall? Does it satisfy your need for revenge?" he asked bitterly.

"I didn't come here for revenge. I came here so my child would know his father. I came here because I hoped everything would work out for the best."

"And has it?"

"Yes," she told him truthfully. "Now go to your wife. She needs you."

After supper, Avery went out with friends again, and the rest of the family gathered in the parlor.

Delores, Adam and Luke were discussing a new addition to the stable. Margo was holding Brady, who was fascinated by the gold buttons on her dress. Kendall sat in a chair reading, her bare feet tucked beneath her so Delores wouldn't scold her for having kicked off her shoes. Rebecca's vague warning still echoed through her head, making it hard to concentrate, but as she watched Margo with Brady it was impossible to imagine there was anything to fear. She might be ill, but she didn't seem dangerous.

"Do you have parents, Kendall?" Margo asked from out of nowhere.

"What?"

"Do you have parents? Does Brady have any grandparents besides Delores?"

Kendall fought the sense of panic that lying always gave her.

"No. Well, of course, I did, but both of them are dead."

"How sad. My father's gone, but luckily I still have Mother."

Without another word, she turned her attention fully on Brady once again.

Kendall looked up at the others and felt a deep sense of unease at the worry on every face.

Slowly, they resumed talking, and Kendall picked up her book.

"Oh, my God! He's choking!"

Margo jumped up and thrust the baby toward her.

Kendall grabbed Brady as chaos broke loose around her. Before she could do anything, Luke snatched him out of her hands, draped Brady over his arm, and smacked him firmly on the back several times. Kendall dropped to her knees so she could peer up into Brady's large frightened eyes as she murmured assurances that he would be fine.

She could hear Adam yelling into the telephone as Luke continued his attempts to dislodge the object.

"What in the world did he swallow, Margo?" Delores exclaimed from behind her.

"I don't know," Margo wailed. "He was just sitting there playing with my buttons."

Kendall felt weak with relief when a bright button popped from Brady's mouth and he began to wail.

Luke had him upright and in her arms before she was completely to her feet.

"He's okay," he whispered. As if his legs could no longer support him, he fell into the chair behind him and pulled her down onto his lap. The last vestiges of fear smoldered in the gray pools of his eyes, and his face was pale beneath his tan.

Holding the baby against her chest, she leaned against Luke and let him hold them both as tears of relief spilled down her cheeks.

When she looked at Adam, he looked as pale and shaken as his brother.

"Adam, take your wife upstairs." Delores' voice was tight with emotion.

Adam grasped Margo's arm roughly and pulled her out of the room.

As Margo's soft protests faded down the hall, Kendall had the fleeting thought that something was going on she didn't understand. At the moment, however, she was too shaken to care what it might be.

Chapter Twenty-Three

Avery came to Kendall and Luke's room at daylight, bending over the crib in the half-light of dawn. Kendall opened her eyes and peered at her sister-in-law.

"What are you doing?"

"I'm making sure he's okay," Avery said. "Mother told me what happened last night."

"He's fine, Avery. The doctor came and checked him."

"Yeah, I know. I just wanted to see for myself."

Kendall smiled to herself at Avery's gradual transformation from a spoiled brat to a sweet, caring young woman.

"Avery, Rebecca says you're worried about me. Why is that?"

"She didn't tell you?"

"No, she didn't get a chance." Leery of Rebecca's warning about Margo, she chose not to mention it yet.

Avery opened her mouth, but before she could speak the bathroom door opened and Luke appeared, clad in a black silk bathrobe, his hair damp from the shower.

"I've got to get dressed, kiddo, so you'd best get out of here," he said.

He reached for the belt of his robe, and Avery scurried from the room.

"Works every time," he murmured as he bent down and kissed Kendall.

"Luke, Rebecca says Avery's worried about me. Do you know why?"

"I don't have a clue. Why don't you ask Avery?"

"I did, but you chased her away before I got an answer."

She slipped from the bed and padded across the floor.

"I'm going to take a bath."

As hot water filled the bathtub and she brushed her teeth at the sink, Luke came to stand behind her, his hands caressing her back and waist. She turned into his arms and he lifted her to the counter, pressing his body to hers.

Without a word, he opened her gown and lowered his head to her breasts. Her fingers dug into his back, forcing him closer, deeper, riding the wave of desire as his body shuddered and she buried her face against his neck.

He lifted her effortlessly, and she wrapped her legs around him as they sank into the steaming tub. He lathered a washcloth and washed her from head to toe. She leaned her head back against the tub and closed her eyes as he let the water run from the cloth, rinsing her with a delicious stream of warmth.

I've never known anything like you before," he whispered, stroking her leg.

She smiled softly, and sighed, "I love you."

Before he could answer, Brady cried out from the other room, and she sprang from the tub, leaving him sitting there in wonder.

****

"Luke! Thank God you're here. I need you to ride to the hardware store with me." Adam came into the kitchen where Luke was finishing up his breakfast. "There's some stuff Josef needs for the stable, and I'll be damned if I know what he's talking about. He wrote it all down here, but I can't read it."

"It wouldn't hurt you to learn a little Spanish," Luke said as he took the list.

"Well, I don't see that happening. You're the

twin gifted in languages, not me. Hell, I don't know what I'm gifted in."

"You have a special talent for screwing things up." Luke grinned wryly.

"Guess what that means, Bro? It means I'm the one having fun, and you're the one who's not."

Luke thought of Kendall, wet and glowing in the steam. He'd call that fun. He cursed silently as he realized his brother may have seen her the exact same way.

"What?" Adam asked.

"Nothing." Luke stalked toward the truck.

"Talk about a mood swing. What the hell's wrong with you?"

"I said nothing. Now leave me alone about it."

"Are you jealous?"

"Of what?"

"Me. Are you jealous that you're the fix-it twin, and I'm the fun twin?"

"Go to hell, Adam."

"That's becoming quite the catch phrase around here," Adam observed dryly. "My feelings are bound to be hurt eventually."

"Maybe you should stop pissing people off."

"Maybe I would if I could figure out what I did to you."

"Maybe you should start with what you did to Kendall," Luke retorted.

Adam was silent, and Luke turned around to find him standing stock still, staring at him with a bemused expression.

"You're in love with her."

"Love has nothing to do with it."

"Really? It's been months, Luke. You didn't suddenly get angry at me about what I did to her. Which I feel very badly about, by the way."

"Whatever," Luke said and started walking again.

"You're jealous, aren't you?"

Luke scrubbed his hand across his face. "Did you love her?"

"No," Adam admitted. "I cared for her, still care for her, but I didn't love her the way you mean."

"You pretended to marry her. You made a child with her."

"Aha," Adam said as if a light had suddenly come on in his head. "This is all about sex, isn't it?"

"Never mind, Adam. Forget I mentioned it." Luke suddenly realized he didn't want to have this discussion. He didn't want to know all the details of his wife's relationship with his brother.

"She wasn't at all what I was used to," Adam admitted. "You know the type of woman I like, Luke. Mother was always certain I'd marry some burlesque dancer. That's why she's put up with Margo all these years. Margo may be a little touched, but at least she isn't wild white trash."

"Are you saying Kendall is?" Luke swung around with fists clenched at his sides, suddenly aching for an excuse to beat the living daylights out of his brother.

"No! I'd hoped she was. And with her mother being who she was, I expected it, if you must know. But Kendall's the opposite of everything I expected. She held out on me until the honeymoon. Imagine my surprise when I realized she was a virgin. I don't think she really even liked sex."

Luke stared at him. Were they talking about the same woman? Kendall came alive at the merest touch. He loved the way she melted against him one minute, then turned to fire the next. He stifled a groan at the thought of her ready responses to him.

"Let's go," he said. The sooner he went, the sooner he'd be back and could find Kendall.

****

The phone rang just as Kendall left the dining

room.

"It's for you, Miss Kendall," Cora said. "It's Miss Rebecca."

"I really need to talk to you, Kendall," Rebecca said. "But I don't want to do it there. Would you meet me in town in an hour?"

She agreed quickly, as much for an excuse to get out of the house as to hear what Rebecca had to say.

As Juan, the Templetons' driver, pulled the car into the parking place, Kendall glanced toward the restaurant where she and Rebecca planned to meet. Through the window, Rebecca smiled and lifted a hand in greeting, but the smile left her face at the same moment a shadow fell beside Kendall's car.

"What are you doing here?"

Kendall jumped at the sound of Adam's voice so close to her.

"Meeting Rebecca for lunch," she said.

"Rebecca? Houston?" Kendall almost laughed at the look of surprise on his face. "Why?"

"Why not?" she countered.

"Aren't you jealous of her?" Adam asked.

"No."

Adam appeared to be completely speechless.

"Isn't Luke with you?"

"He's in the hardware store. I was waiting outside. I saw the car pull up and thought I'd come see if you were here for a reason."

"Well, tell him to pop in when he's done."

Although she expected Adam to leave once she was inside, he followed her to the table.

"Hello, Rebecca," he said, sliding into a chair.

"Hello, Adam," she said, turning a questioning glance to Kendall.

Kendall shrugged in answer as she too sat at the table.

The three of them made small talk while they ordered and ate.

131

"So when is your next assignment?" Adam asked.

"Next week. I'll be gone a week or so. The New York Municipal Airport opens for business in December, and Daddy wants pictures of it and Mayor LaGuardia for the December issue."

Kendall's blood ran cold. "You're a photographer?"

"Rebecca's family owns *Gala* magazine," Adam answered. "Have you heard of it? She's their best photographer. She also does photographs for some other illustrious and intellectual publications."

Rebecca checked her watch and stood quickly.

"Oh, my goodness, look at the time. I've really got to run. Kendall, thanks so much for meeting me. I'll talk to you later." She gave Kendall a quick hug and turned to Adam. "You, too, Adam. It was great seeing you."

She was gone before Kendall could say a word. Had Rebecca taken the picture she received a few days ago?

After all that happened that same evening and her worry about Brady, the pictures had slipped her mind. Now, learning of Rebecca's photography, she remembered them and wondered if Rebecca could have had anything to do with them.

"Ken?" Adam's concerned voice brought her gaze to him. "Are you okay?"

"I'm fine," she lied as she stood up. "I'm going home."

Halfway home, she realized Rebecca had never told her the reason for their meeting.

Chapter Twenty-Four

"Come here! I have to show you something." At the sound of Margo's frantic voice, Kendall looked up from rolling out a pie crust. It was the day before Thanksgiving, and she'd cajoled Cora into letting her contribute to the feast by baking. She wasn't very skilled in the kitchen, but she made a fine pecan pie.

"I can't. I've got flour all over me," she argued, holding up her hands as evidence.

"It will only take a minute," Margo insisted, grabbing Kendall's arm. She barely gave Kendall a chance to wash the flour from her hands before she pulled her down the hall.

Kendall caught her breath at the sight of the ransacked office. Drawers were pulled out and emptied. The cushions from the leather sofa were thrown on the floor, and the contents of the file cabinets were strewn about, torn and crumpled.

"What happened?" she asked Margo.

"I don't know." She shrugged and walked to the desk.

"Who could have done this?"

"I don't know," she said nonchalantly, as if the condition of the room weren't of any concern at all. "*This* is what I wanted to show you."

She held out two pictures. Certain Margo would notice how badly her hands shook as she reached for the pictures, Kendall looked up at her. Margo's eyes weren't on her hands, however; they were on her face, watching for her reaction. Though Kendall attempted to show no reaction to the photos, a wave of shock washed over her when she realized their significance.

The first was taken the day of her last meeting with Superintendent Daniels and Frank Howard. She knelt in the dust of the school parking lot, Brady's basket beside her and a look of utter despair on her face.

In the next picture, her mother stood at an intersection. Although nothing in the picture gave away the location, Kendall recognized it instantly as the corner in front of her father's house. She also recognized the dress her mother wore, and she knew without a doubt someone took this picture just moments before her parents died.

One word was written on the top of each. *Desperation.*

"Where did you get these, Margo?"

"They were here." Margo patted the papers spread across the desk. An envelope addressed to Kendall and postmarked from Atlanta was on top of the pile.

She looked at the photos again.

"I know that's you," Margo told her, "but who is that?"

"My mother," she said, staring into the familiar hopeless eyes in the photo.

"She looks very sad, doesn't she?" Margo observed as she began straightening the papers on the desk.

"Margo, did the postman deliver these pictures this morning?" Kendall came to stand in front of her.

Margo continued her work, though she appeared to grow a bit more frantic while Kendall waited for an answer.

"Adam will want to know what happened here," Margo lamented. "I have to clean it up before he gets home."

Kendall grabbed the envelope from the desk and shoved the pictures inside. She made the sudden decision not to show them to Luke or anyone else. She needed time to think, to sort out what Rebecca might possibly gain by sending them. She thought of Rebecca's body pressed against Luke's. Perhaps it wasn't what she stood to gain that drove her, but what she'd already lost.

"Margo, let's not tell anyone about the pictures, okay?" She placed her hand on Margo's, holding it still.

"What pictures?" Margo asked, looking at her blankly. Then, urgently, she whispered, "Will you help me clean up this mess?"

Realizing Margo was rapidly losing her grasp on reality, she nodded. Delores and Avery were at a benefit luncheon, and Luke and Adam weren't home yet. So it seemed it was up to her to keep an eye on Margo until someone else arrived.

She began straightening the papers from the filing cabinet, barely looking at them as she smoothed them out and put them away. Later, she would tell Luke what happened so he could let Adam know. She wouldn't mention the pictures, only the upended office.

****

"Adam is going to have to do something," Luke said when Kendall told him about the office. He raked his hand through his hair. "I know he hates to hospitalize her, but if she gets much worse, he's not going to have a choice."

"Could anyone else have ransacked the room?"

"Of course not. There's no doubt it was Margo. It's a typical action during one of her episodes."

"Has he hospitalized her before?"

"Yes, once, about three years ago. From what I can tell, it wasn't long before he met you. She was gone for six months."

"Adam thinks it would help if Brady and I left."

"Adam has no right to ask you to leave."

"Do you think Margo suspects the truth? Could that be what's made her so upset?"

"No. If anything about you being here upsets her, it's Brady. And I wouldn't let you take him if you did decide to leave."

His words knocked the breath out of her, and she sat back in the chair. Over the past few months, she'd almost forgotten that Luke and his family tolerated her presence only because of Brady.

"That's not what I meant, Kendall," he said as if reading her mind. "I wouldn't want you to go, even if you didn't have Brady."

"But you'd let me," she said.

He stared at her for a long time, before answering. "If that's what you wanted."

"Will you talk to Adam?" She forced herself to ignore the sharp sting of pain.

"Yes, I'll talk to him, but don't be surprised if he doesn't do anything right away."

"It must be a hard decision for him."

"It's a hard decision for everyone. We all care for Margo. We hate to see her hurt."

"Of course," Kendall murmured.

"I'm going to go find Adam and talk to him. I'll see you at supper."

****

Kendall spread the pictures on her bed in chronological order, a photographic testament to her mother's sad transition from unwed pregnant teenager to murderess, as well as her own journey to this point. As she always did when she considered her mother's plight, Kendall wondered about her father and his role in her mother's demise. All she really knew was his name. Of course, Kendall admitted, she knew little more about her mother. As far as stories went, theirs were nearly nonexistent.

She remembered asking, "Mama, why'd you name me Kendall?" Ten-year-old Kendall was on the floor doing her homework while her mother sat on the couch smoking.

Her mother slid from the couch to sit beside her. With a gentle hand, she stroked Kendall's hair. Her eyes were filled with the sadness Kendall knew so well.

"I named you after your daddy. His name is Kendall."

"Kendall what?"

"No, his last name is Kendall. They wouldn't let me give you his last name. So, I gave it to you as a first name. Kendall James. It's a nice name. Names are important, Kendall. Don't forget that. You can go far with a name like yours."

"How far, Mama?" she asked, hoping it was so far that she never had to come back to this horrid place.

"As far as you want to go, Baby," had been the wistful reply. "You go as far as you want to go."

Now tears pricked Kendall's eyes as she picked the pictures up and began to put them away. Her mother was so young in these pictures, not much older than Avery when she became pregnant, not much older than Kendall when she sat on a bar stool trying to wash away her pain. She was only thirty-four the day she killed herself. A tear rolled down Kendall's face, and she dashed it away. She couldn't remember the last time she cried over her mother's death, but as she stared at the picture of her mother crossing the street that final time, the tears came of their own free will.

On her way down to supper that night, she met Avery coming up the stairs.

"I need to talk to you," Avery said urgently and led her to Delores' study.

"Maybe we should find another place to talk," Kendall suggested, her gaze moving about the room.

"Mother won't know we were here. Did you talk

to Rebecca this afternoon?"

"Yes, we met at the café in town." Kendall barely paid her any attention as her eyes scanned the dozens of pictures that lined the bookshelves across the room. Many of them were of Delores' children, and she could definitely see a resemblance between them and Brady.

"Everything's okay, then?"

"Everything's fine."

"Really?" Avery asked doubtfully.

"Really," Kendall answered. "Are you surprised?"

She didn't wait for an answer as one picture in particular caught her eye, and she tried to step past Avery to get a better look.

Before she could move, however, the door opened and Avery grabbed her arm to pull her down behind the huge oak desk. Expecting to see Delores come into view, Kendall was shocked to see Margo appear. Even more shocking was Margo's obvious distress. As she crossed the room to stand at the window, her hands twisted nervously and low whimpering noises escaped her.

"We need to get Adam," Kendall mouthed, but Avery shook her head.

Margo pressed her face to the pane, staring out the window for several long seconds. Finally, her mouth curved into a smile and she raised a hand in greeting. Though the room remained silent, she cocked her head to one side, as if listening closely.

"No!" she suddenly cried, her head swinging back and forth in denial. "No! No! No!"

Kendall registered the sound of footsteps running down the hallway just as Margo began to slam her fists against the window. The door burst open and Adam ran in, Luke hot on his heels.

"I can't do it," Margo sobbed, paying no heed when Adam caught hold of her.

"It's okay," he soothed, pulling her tightly against him. "It's okay."

From her vantage point, Kendall could see Adam's face, the tightness about his lips, and the concern on his face. Sadness bowed his body as he bent toward Margo, trying to catch hold of her hands, which clawed wildly at her face and chest.

As if drawn by a magnet, Luke's eyes locked with Kendall's. A slight narrowing of his eyes was the only sign he might disapprove of her hiding behind his mother's desk with his teenage sister.

He turned back to Adam, who nodded curtly and stood up, his suddenly docile wife clutching his chest to keep from collapsing. A hypodermic needle lay on the table, and Luke picked it up and brought it to the waste basket beside the desk, his legs blocking Adam's view of the women crouching in the shadows.

"I don't know what in the hell you two are doing, but you both need to stay out of Margo's way. Now get out, before Mother finds out you were here," Luke ordered the moment the door shut on Adam and Margo.

Kendall walked out without speaking to him, wishing desperately for a better look at the picture on his mother's bookshelf. When she reached her room, she sank onto the bed, trying to recall every detail of the photograph. Three young women, barely more than girls, smiled into the camera. A beaming Delores Templeton stood on the left and Julianne Delacroix on the right, as beautiful then as now. It was the girl in the middle, however, who caught Kendall's attention. Joy, hope and love shone from her face, and Kendall thought even if she were in another position in the lineup, that girl would still be the center of the picture, the center of the photographer's attention. Kendall would swear that girl was her mother.

Of course, she had to be mistaken. The picture

sat high on a shelf. In black and white, she couldn't even tell if the girl had the same coloring as her mother. To be honest, the face was much too full and the mouth too soft to be her mother. She couldn't imagine that even in the bloom of youth her mother had looked so carefree and joyful. Besides, there was no explanation to link her mother to Delores Templeton and Julianne Delacroix.

Around midnight, she felt Luke slip into bed beside her. He whispered her name and reached for her, but she stayed still, her face turned away from him, remembering the cold disapproval in his eyes.

He ran a hand gently over her head and down her arm, letting it rest lightly on her waist as he leaned toward her. His lips brushed against her hair.

"I won't let them hurt you," he whispered so quietly she wasn't even certain she heard him correctly.

****

Thanksgiving dinner was a quiet, lavish affair; the polar opposite of the few boisterous Thanksgiving dinners Kendall and her mother had spent with Mary Christopher and her brood of children. While those were meager meals in a ramshackle old house, thankfulness and love compensated for whatever they had lacked. Thanksgiving dinner at The Grove was served on the finest china and linens, the decorations impeccable and the food bountiful, but the tension in the air was almost tangible.

At his mother's stern reprimands, Adam ceased his endless sniping, and a heavy silence now hung between those gathered at the dining room table.

Kendall turned from feeding Brady to find Margo's eyes burning feverishly into hers.

"My father was shot," she said.

"What?" Kendall croaked, her breath freezing in

her chest.

"Margo!" Delores barked.

"Things like that aren't easily erased," Margo continued, for once ignoring her mother-in-law's disapproval. "They destroy who we were before and shape us into what we become."

Without another word, she turned her attention fully to her plate once again.

As Kendall's gaze swung from one face to the other, she saw stark, inexplicable fear in every pair of eyes.

Chapter Twenty-Five

Kendall woke to an empty bed the next morning.

Luke had come to bed late again, after she was asleep, and although he once again reached for her, she hadn't turned toward him.

She dressed slowly, taking time to feed and bathe Brady before carrying him downstairs.

As she passed his mother's study on her way to the kitchen, she heard Luke clearly through the closed door.

"What's going on, Mother?"

"Luke, honestly, I don't know what you're talking about." Kendall imagined her stroking the ever-present pearls at her neck.

"I'm talking about Kendall. I'm finding this whole story to be more and more difficult to swallow. Of all the women on earth, why did Adam pick her?"

"How would I know?"

"You know, Mother. I don't know how or why, but..."

"What does it matter now?" Delores interrupted him. "Adam and Kendall are water under the bridge. I made certain of that."

"By using her child as a pawn? You're just lucky it worked."

"Of course it worked. Kendall has far too much of her mother in her. That's how she got in this predicament in the first place."

Kendall placed a hand on the doorknob. She'd had more than enough of the Templeton wisdom. How dare Delores act like she caused this mess?

"Mother, you're wrong about that. The way she

got in this predicament is through your son's dishonesty and conniving. Which, I might add, he learned at your knee."

"Luke!" Delores exclaimed. "How dare you say something like that to me?"

"Mother, I love you, but Kendall is my wife. You chose the path we're on, not me."

"You love her, then?" Delores asked.

"Love has nothing to do with it. Isn't that what you always say?"

Kendall's hand dropped from the door knob and she dashed up the stairs to the nursery. Fighting the tears that threatened, she placed Brady on the floor to play with his toys while she sat beside him.

Love has nothing to do with it. He'd warned her of that before she married him. He'd told her what to expect, so why had she allowed herself to believe any of them cared for her?

"Kendall," Margo hissed from the doorway. "Come here!"

Margo's eyes darted between the hallway and the nursery. Kendall hesitated, unsure whether she should encourage the woman. When Margo stepped into the nursery, however, Kendall quickly jumped up and led her back out into the hallway, away from Brady who still played happily on the floor.

"What is it?" she asked.

"Quiet. They'll find me," Margo rasped, leaning closer and curling her hands around Kendall's wrists.

"She didn't do it," Margo confided, her fevered eyes shooting back toward the stairs.

"Margo?" Delores' imperious voice came from somewhere below.

Margo stiffened and stepped away from Kendall. Without another word, she darted down the hallway.

Unnerved by the encounter, Kendall went back to the nursery and sat down beside Brady.

"You should ignore whatever she says to you," Delores said from the doorway. There was no need for her to explain who she meant. "She has no idea what she's talking about."

Kendall remained silent, and after a few minutes Delores disappeared down the hall.

****

"Mother said you never came down to breakfast," Luke told her when he appeared in the nursery door later that morning.

"I wasn't hungry," she said.

"Are you coming down to lunch?"

She shrugged. "I don't know."

"Are you ill?"

She shook her head and bent toward Brady, pushing one of his toys back and forth in front of him. He ignored it when he caught sight of Luke and began trying to scoot toward him.

Luke scooped him up, planting kisses on his cheeks before dropping down beside her to stand the baby on his outstretched legs. Brady bounced up and down, trying to get his legs to support him.

"Are you sure you're okay?"

"I'm fine, Luke. Really."

He studied her closely before he spoke.

"Kendall, please. I don't know what to say to you to make things better between us."

"Why don't you start with the truth, Luke?"

"What does that mean?"

She looked at him and wanted to demand he explain his conversation with his mother, while at the same time she was afraid to hear his answer.

Suddenly, bloodcurdling screams filled the house. Luke sprang to his feet, passing Brady to Kendall and rushing from the room.

"What's going on?" Luke demanded of Cora, who met them at the top of the staircase.

"It's Miss Margo. She's gone crazy."

Adam appeared at the bottom of the stairs, looking exhausted and unkempt. His hair was mussed and his clothes rumpled. He stared at them blankly before realization struck, and he hurried toward Luke.

"What's happened?" Luke asked, meeting him halfway.

"Margo's completely lost it, Luke." He looked toward Kendall who stood just behind Luke on the staircase. "If she sees her, she'll be uncontrollable."

"The doctor's on his way?" Luke asked.

Adam nodded and ran his hand over his head. "She tried to kill Avery."

"What?" Luke grasped his brother's arms. "Is she okay?"

"Who? Oh, Avery. Yes, I think she'll be fine."

"Kendall!" Margo, a blur of green velvet rushed up the stairs and launched herself at Kendall. Kendall handed the baby to Luke, seconds before Margo's hands closed around her arms.

"Margo!" Luke thrust the baby into Cora's arms and tried to pry her away, but she refused to loosen her grip on Kendall.

"She didn't do it! She didn't do it!" Margo sobbed out the words as she shook Kendall roughly, and Kendall fought to keep her balance on the stairs.

"Why are you doing this to me?" Margo screeched when Adam grabbed her by the waist, trying to pull her away.

Kendall saw the doctor come through the door. He was up the stairs in a second, Delores close on his heels. She closed her eyes against the sight of the needle imbedding in Margo's arm.

"No!" Margo whimpered, her hands falling away from Kendall and her body crumpling helplessly.

"Are you okay?" Luke asked as Margo was carried from the house to the waiting ambulance.

She nodded and gingerly rubbed her arms.

"Come to Mama, honey." She reached for Brady, who was sobbing in Cora's arms. Hugging him close, she took a deep breath of the baby-fresh scent of him.

"Pay no attention to her, Kendall. She's truly delusional. She beat Avery with a tennis racket. Did some serious damage to the child's nose," Delores said. "I think even Adam realizes she's out of control. He has no choice but to hospitalize her."

Chapter Twenty-Six

Exhausted and disheartened by the events of the night before, everyone seemed to avoid each other the next day.

Kendall spent the day in her room reading, but as the dinner hour approached she realized she couldn't hide there any longer.

Avery was bruised and battered, with two black eyes and a row of stitches spanning the bridge of her nose. Still, she obeyed her mother's command and came down to dinner, although she ate little and remained uncharacteristically silent.

Like his sister, Adam hardly said a word as he pushed his food around on his plate, and Kendall felt a spark of pity for him. She wondered now if Margo's insanity was partially responsible for his double life with her. Of course, she thought, his double life could just as easily be responsible for Margo's insanity.

As if he could read her mind, Adam lifted his gaze to meet hers.

"I love her, you know," he said.

"Yes, I know." What could she say to his admission?

"She was already crazy before I met you."

"Okay."

"It hasn't been easy on her having you and Brady here."

"Why? She doesn't know anything about us."

His gaze shot to Avery who ceased feeding Brady to stare at them.

"She wants a baby so badly. It breaks her heart

147

every time she looks at him."

"Because he's a baby or because he's yours?"

Avery gasped while Adam and Kendall glared at each other over the table.

"Like you said, Ken, Margo doesn't know he's Adam's." Luke's voice was tight with anger.

"That's enough from all of you," Delores said imperatively. "Avery, you keep your mouth shut about what you just heard. Do you understand me?"

Avery nodded, but her eyes darted between her brothers and sister-in-law, and Kendall knew she would be bombarded by questions the next time Avery caught her alone.

Delores continued her lecture.

"Adam, there is no one but yourself to blame for Kendall and Brady's presence in our lives. If their being here has been hard on Margo, that's just something you'll have to live with. Kendall, we made a deal. No one but the four of us was ever to know that Brady is Adam's child. The fact that you made Avery privy to that information is not something I'm pleased about. Avery knows her place in this family, and I don't doubt she'll keep quiet. However, should you ever speak of it to anyone else, you will find yourself on the street posthaste. Alone."

Before she could respond to Delores' threat, Luke spoke.

"Mother, you lost that power the day Kendall and I were married. She has as much right to be here as you. And I won't hesitate to fight you for custody of my son."

The color drained from Delores' face, but she was quick to recover.

"At least I see where I stand now," Delores said, throwing her napkin to the table. "You always did have more guts than your brother."

With that, she rose and walked out of the room, leaving them sitting in silence. Avery was the first to speak.

"You all can't spill the beans about something like that and then leave me to figure out the hows and whys of it."

"Not now, Avery," Luke barked. "You'll have to wait until later. For now, just watch Brady."

He grabbed Kendall's hand, jerked her to her feet and led her upstairs to their room.

Once inside, he pushed the door shut and pulled her into his arms. She clung to him as he kissed her so hard it left her breathless.

"You don't love him anymore." he declared, his mouth a mere breath away from hers.

"No," she whispered in agreement.

"You're mine."

"Yes."

"And Brady is my son."

"Yes."

He moved so that he could see her face, his steel gray eyes searching for the truth in her words.

"I wish I could erase your relationship with Adam. It gnaws at me that you haven't forgotten it."

"Luke, it's not something we can forget. We made a child together. Yes, in every way that counts, you're Brady's father. But physically, Adam and I were the only two involved."

Without a word, he drew her against him and lowered his mouth to hers again. She lifted herself on tiptoe and pushed her body closer to his. A low moan escaped him and the kiss deepened, acknowledging everything they felt for each other. Never breaking contact, they edged toward the bed. Their lovemaking gentled as each sought to show the other how deeply the feelings ran.

He rested his arms on each side of her head, his hands gently cupping her skull as he studied her face. His eyes darkened with emotion, and for a moment she thought he might speak the words she so longed to hear.

With each passing day and each night they spent in each other's arms, it became easier for her to believe he loved her. Still, she longed to hear the words.

The only part of her that still belonged to Adam was the one small piece of her that still heard those words; the piece of her that still *needed* to hear those words.

Please, she pleaded silently when he brought his thumb to her mouth and gently traced her lips. *Please erase his voice from my mind like you've erased everything else he left behind.*

She wanted to cry out in protest as he leaned down to kiss her again, but it took him only a moment to make her treacherous body forget her disappointment.

Chapter Twenty-Seven

With Margo gone and Avery in bed for over a week due to a terrible head cold on top of the injuries Margo had inflicted, the household settled into a rather peaceful existence. No one seemed concerned about when Margo would return home. Rather, they all seemed content with her absence.

Without the restraints of Margo's scrutiny, Adam showed more interest in Brady. Several times, Kendall walked in to check on Brady during his nap and found him wide awake, with Adam crawling around the nursery floor with him.

At those times, she felt almost sad for the lie they were perpetrating on her child. Unlike her, he would know a father. Still, he wouldn't know the man who fathered him. That Luke was a wonderful father and the closest thing possible to Adam only made it seem worse to her. Still, she saw no other way, and she had done the only thing she could, given the circumstances. It was up to her to make the best of it for Brady's sake as well as her own.

****

Two weeks after Adam admitted Margo to the hospital, Kendall was in the living room reading while Brady napped upstairs. Adam stood in the doorway staring at her for several long moments before entering the room.

"I wish I had stayed with you," he said.

She chuckled. "Your leaving was probably for the best."

"How can you say that? We have a child together. We should have been a family."

"You already had a family, Adam."

"Not children."

"You and Margo could still have children."

"No," he said walking to the window. "We won't ever have children. I don't really know if Margo will be coming back this time. Her mother and stepfather want her to live with them after they return from France. They think living here is just too stressful on her."

"Have you ever thought of moving away?" she asked.

"No," Adam said. "I don't want to live anywhere else. I like it here. And Mother likes having us all here."

"But Adam, Margo is your wife. You should do what's best for her."

"So, you're the one who filled Luke's head with the idea that he shouldn't care if he hurts Mother or not."

"I would never tell Luke any such thing. I just think a person's duty is to their children and their spouse before anyone else."

"So, you don't think your father should have left his family to take care of you and your mother?"

Although she knew that having a father would have been better for her, she had rarely taken the time to think it through to the next level. If her father had come to live with her mother and her, he would have left behind another woman and child. Now, she was rather surprised to realize how she felt.

"Yes, his duty was to stay with his wife and child. Of course, he also had a duty toward my mother and me. He was wrong to leave my mother to face the consequences of their actions all alone. No one can really know how it is for a woman who has a baby and no husband, not until they've been there themselves. Her prospects dwindle down to nothing.

No respectable establishment will hire her. No respectable man will look twice at her. I lost my job, and there wasn't another one to be found."

"You had a ring."

She shrugged. "But I didn't have a husband. They said any girl can buy a ring and stick it on her finger."

He stood there quietly and she wondered if at last the predicament he'd left her in was becoming real to him. The fact that it had taken this long didn't speak well of his character, in her opinion.

"How did you pay rent?" he asked.

"I saved a little of the money you sent me the first few months you were gone. I gave the landlord what I could, and by the time you quit sending it, I knew I was pregnant. He was kind enough to let me stay for free until after Brady was born."

"Is that why you came here?"

"I had no choice. I decided to find out what happened to you. I couldn't believe you would simply disappear on purpose."

"It was too hard, Ken. You were so sweet and trusting. I couldn't keep lying to you."

"So, you decided it would be better to never acknowledge our child?"

"Ken, you have to believe me. I never knew you were pregnant. I had no idea we had a child until the day you came here."

"I wrote the whole time I was pregnant, Adam. I wrote you when he was born. You had to have received at least one of those letters."

"I never got any of them. I swear. I thought you just gave up and went ahead with your life."

"Do you think someone intercepted them?"

"Who? Mother? Avery? Luke? Margo." Her name was more a statement than a question.

"What's going on?" Luke asked from the doorway.

"You didn't happen to intercept any letters addressed to me in the last year or so, did you?"

"Why in the world would I intercept your mail?" He looked between the two of them. "Did you ask Mother? She seems to think everything is her business."

"No, it couldn't be your mother. She was as surprised by Brady as either of you were. If she'd known I was having a child, she'd have demanded to be part of his life from day one. She wouldn't have waited for me to show up on your doorstep."

"Avery has no reason, either," Adam said to Kendall.

"That leaves Margo," Kendall said quietly, but firmly.

"Do you two mind cluing me in on what the hell you're talking about?" Luke grumbled.

"Later," Adam said and disappeared out the door.

"Well?" he said to Kendall.

"I wrote Adam when I learned I was pregnant, after every doctor's visit throughout my pregnancy, and when Brady was born. He says he never received any of those letters. Luke, he never even knew about the baby."

"So what happened to them?"

"The only logical conclusion is that someone intercepted them," she said. "And the only person it could be is Margo."

"So you're saying Margo may have known about you and Brady all this time?"

"It would seem so."

Luke looked at her. She didn't appear to be the least bit worried about the fact that Margo might know Adam fathered Brady. The wistful look in her eyes caused him a moment's panic. Did the knowledge that Adam hadn't known about Brady somehow change her feelings?

If he'd met Kendall as his brother's wife, would he still feel this overwhelming attraction for her? He knew if circumstances hadn't forced her to look at him she would never have spared him a second glance. The thought of going his whole life without feeling her in his arms left him feeling empty.

"Do you wish it had turned out differently?" he asked hollowly.

"No," she said with conviction. He let out a sigh of relief and she turned wide blue eyes to him. "That surprises you, doesn't it?"

"I know it bothers you that Brady won't know who his real father is. And I know you loved Adam."

"Of course, it bothers me a little. But in every aspect of his life except paternity, you are his father."

He couldn't help but notice she didn't say anything regarding her own feelings for Adam.

Chapter Twenty-Eight

"Kendall, wait!" Avery called from the porch before Kendall and Brady could round the curve in the drive. Kendall groaned inwardly but stopped pushing the pram and waited for Avery to catch up to them. Apparently, her luck had run out, and it was time she paid the piper for her outburst at the dinner table. She hated to admit her relief when the poor girl had ended up confined to bed for so long. The brief visits she made to Avery's sickroom weren't conducive to the interrogation she was about to endure now.

"You knew I was going to find you eventually," Avery said as she came even with them.

"Should you be up?" Kendall asked, looking over at her. She was still pale, and there was still faint bruising around her eyes and nose, but she was much less subdued than the last time Kendall saw her.

"I'm fine," Avery claimed, lifting her face to the warm mid-December sun, "and so glad to be out of the house! But enough about me. Tell me, how did you have Adam's baby and marry Luke?"

"Avery, I don't really want to talk about it," Kendall protested.

"I'm not going to let you alone until you do," Avery promised. "This really isn't something that you all should have kept from me. Mother's always telling me to grow up, but everyone still treats me like a child."

"You are a child."

"No, I'm not. Tell me, Kendall. Please."

With a sigh, Kendall gave in and told Avery about her sham marriage to Adam, Delores' threats, and her marriage to Luke.

"Mother's so horrible sometimes. I can't believe she threatened to take him away from you. She should have been pounding Adam, and instead she punished Luke. That's how it's always been."

Kendall hated to think of her marriage to Luke as punishment, as Luke paying for his brother's crime.

"When you're around them, you think Mother and Luke are closer than she and Adam are. But they aren't. Luke knows more about the estate. He and mother talk more because they have more to talk about, I guess. But Adam has always been her favorite, maybe because he's most like her. Luke will do a lot to protect the family name and keep up appearances, but it's basically for the good of all of us. Adam and mother think only of themselves, regardless of where that leaves Luke and me."

"That's not very nice, Avery," Kendall reproved her, but it was impossible for her to put any real conviction behind her words.

"It's true. My whole life, I've watched Luke clean up Adam's messes and pay for his sins. You aren't at all Adam's type, you know. I always figured Luke would marry someone just like you."

"Well, you were right," Kendall said.

"Yeah, but I always thought he'd marry for love, not out of obligation. Or maybe I just hoped he would. He deserved that."

Kendall looked straight ahead. What did she say to that? Although she knew Luke cared for her a great deal, and she felt confident the affection he showed her and Brady was real, he did deserve to marry for love instead of some misguided notion of his obligations.

"I never realized Luke was such a great actor.

He should win an academy award." Avery said.

"What do you mean?"

"I've seen you two together for months now. I never would have guessed any of this. I've never seen two people act so crazy about each other. Do you love him?"

"We've come to care for each other very deeply," Kendall said evasively.

"That's pathetic, Ken. Either you love each other or you don't."

Kendall shook her head at the girl's audacity. She smiled to herself.

"Okay, if you insist, I'll tell you the truth."

Avery leaned closer.

"I'm so in love with him, it makes my toes curl."

"I knew it!" Avery cried and hugged Kendall tightly. "And he loves you, doesn't he?"

"He says love has nothing do with anything."

"That's just Mother talking. Don't pay any attention to that."

The postman was pulling away when they rounded the last curve in the drive, and Kendall could already see the large envelope sticking out of the open mailbox. Even before Avery read her name on the front and handed it to her, her throat was dry with foreboding.

"So, you aren't going to open that one, either?" Avery eyed the envelope as Kendall stuck it in the stroller. "You are really weird, Ken."

A car horn honked behind them, and they turned to see Rebecca in a bright red convertible.

"I thought you were in Atlanta for a few more days," Avery said.

"Good Lord, no. I had to get out of there. All that excitement wears a body out. Costume balls, parades, receptions. You'd never guess there was anything wrong in the world, as excited and happy as the people in Atlanta appear to be."

"Did you see the film?"

"It's amazing! Clark Gable is dreamy and Vivien Leigh is the perfect Scarlett."

Kendall ignored their excited chatter. Was it mere coincidence that Rebecca arrived moments after she received the latest package?

"Avery, honey, what in the world happened to you?" Rebecca finally asked.

"Margo attacked me. It took ten stitches to close my nose up, but the doctor doesn't think it was broken."

"What set her off?" Rebecca asked.

Avery shrugged.

"Who knows? She was being a nut."

"And?" Rebecca prodded when Avery grew silent.

Kendall almost smiled. Rebecca knew Avery well. Avery wasn't exactly forthcoming about her own role in Margo's attack on her. Of course, by the look in Margo's eyes that night, Kendall knew Margo's state of mind had nothing to do with reality.

"I said some things I shouldn't have," Avery admitted. She was trying to sound repentant, but Kendall suspected she was far from it.

"Like what?"

Avery shrugged again.

"I told her Adam needed to send her away. She was acting crazy all day."

"And she just attacked you after that?"

Avery rolled her eyes.

"No. She was loony, I tell you, and it was scary. She went on and on and on about something she needed to show Kendall. By the time it happened, I'd just had enough. So, I told her that Kendall had better things to do than see some stupid ring. She was on me before the words were out of my mouth. I couldn't really hear what she was saying. After she whacked me a few times, I was screaming as loud as

159

she was."

"Good grief, Avery, when are you going to learn to keep your mouth shut?"

"Probably never," Avery said lightly.

"Do you think Margo knows?" Rebecca looked worriedly at Avery, who shrugged.

"Knows what?" Kendall asked Rebecca then turned toward Avery. It was high time the two of them spit out whatever it was they were keeping secret.

The look that shot between Avery and Rebecca foretold something big.

"One of you tell me what I need to know right now," she pleaded.

Rebecca laid her hand on Kendall's arm, and Kendall fought the urge to snatch it away.

"Margo is your sister," Rebecca said.

"What?" Whatever she'd expected, that certainly wasn't it.

"Julianne Delacroix was married to Thomas Kendall. Margo is their daughter."

The memory of her father coming out of his house with his beautiful blonde daughter on his arm blended with the one of Adam entering the room with his beautiful blonde wife.

"Are you sure?" She prayed it was some sort of horrid mistake, but in her heart she knew it wasn't. She was also certain it wasn't a coincidence.

"I'm sure," Rebecca said with conviction.

"I've got to go," she whispered. She felt frozen, dizzy with shock and confusion, and her breath seemed to have permanently caught somewhere in her chest. "I have to go."

"I'll drive you up to the house," Rebecca offered, a worried frown on her face.

Kendall shook her head and started walking.

"Kendall, let Rebecca drive us," Avery pleaded. She put her arm on Kendall's. "Come on."

Kendall shook her off.

"Leave me alone, Avery. Just leave me alone."

As if sensing his mother's distress, Brady began to cry.

"Don't cry, Pumpkin," she told him numbly. "We'll be okay. I promise we'll be okay. Mommy's going to take you away from here, and everything will be fine."

Avery and Rebecca were just behind her in the car, and she couldn't walk fast enough to get away from them. She knew they were worried. She also knew that she shouldn't be upset with them. Every time either of them had tried to talk to her before now, someone always stopped them somehow. Delores, Adam, and Luke had made an orchestrated effort to keep the truth from her.

Delores was waiting in the hallway when she came through the door, Rebecca and Avery right behind her.

"Kendall, Avery, come here," she commanded imperiously.

Trembling from head to toe, Kendall lifted the baby from his stroller. He was tired and needed a bath and a nap. She would settle him down before she found her husband and demanded answers.

"Kendall, let Cora do that. I need to speak to you immediately."

Kendall pointedly ignored her.

"Cora, take the child," Delores impatiently instructed the housekeeper who hovered nearby.

Cora took a step toward her, and Kendall attempted a smile in her direction.

"That won't be necessary, Cora. I'll take care of him."

"Kendall, I said I need to speak to you. Now, do as I say and give Cora the baby."

Kendall straightened with Brady in her arms. She plucked the envelope from the stroller before

161

turning to face her mother-in-law.

"I said I will take care of him. I will not be talking with you at the moment. I will be upstairs tending to my child. Then I will be speaking to your son. After that, if it is convenient for you, I'll speak with you. For now, I would appreciate it if everyone would just leave me the hell alone."

Without a backward glance, she walked away.

As she ascended the stairs, she heard Delores say, "Well! I see the two of you have finally done what you've been trying to do since Kendall arrived. I hope you're pleased with yourselves."

The study door slammed in an uncharacteristic show of emotion from Delores.

Once in her room, Kendall pushed all she now knew to the back of her mind and lost herself in the simple act of caring for Brady. Finally, she sat on her bed and opened the envelope.

Instead of the photos she expected, it contained a wedding invitation, a birth announcement, and a newspaper clipping.

The wedding invitation announced the marriage of Julianne Martin to Thomas Kendall. The birth announcement proclaimed the birth of Margo Teresa Kendall. She was surprised to see that Margo's birthday was only a month before her own.

The last item in the envelope was a newspaper clipping regarding the death of her parents. It included a grainy photo of a group of debutantes dressed in white gowns. The faces of two of the girls were circled and Kendall realized with a start that one of them was her mother and the other was Julianne Delacroix.

Beneath that photo were snapshots of Thomas and Lydia.

Soon after her parents' deaths, Kendall had read one newspaper article in their local newspaper. That article made it seem that her mother barely knew

Thomas Kendall and didn't even hint at a past relationship or her own existence. Her mother seemed like some crazed stalker instead of a scorned lover.

Now, Kendall read the words of this newspaper clipping and saw it all through a different light.

In a story that took two decades to come to a heartbreaking end, Lydia James murdered her former fiancé Thomas Kendall before killing herself. James and Kendall were childhood sweethearts before his marriage to Julianne Martin, heiress to the Carlyle Shipping Empire. Thomas Kendall is survived by wife Julianne and daughter Margo. Lydia James is survived by parents Louisa and George James and daughter Kendall.

Below the single paragraph was a picture of her father's house, and she could clearly see herself sitting on the bench, dressed in the flowered dress she had worn that day. She scanned the article for a byline or photo credits.

Leon Templeton.

The name leaped out at her, and with a muttered curse she stuffed the contents back into the envelope, along with the pictures from her drawer, and stalked from the room.

She was headed for the front door when another thought crossed her mind. Without knocking, she marched into Delores' study and crossed to the bookshelf beside the fireplace.

"What are you doing?" Delores demanded as Kendall pulled a chair over to the shelf and climbed up in it. "Get down this instant."

Kendall grabbed the picture she had noticed the night she and Avery hid here. Ignoring her mother-in-law completely, she exited the room, slamming the door as she left.

****

"You lying son of a..." She broke off as a sob escaped her.

"Have you lost your mind?" Luke asked, looking up from his desk in the stable's office.

She flung everything she carried onto his desk.

"Why didn't you tell me about Margo?"

He closed his eyes.

"Avery," he said his sister's name with certainty.

"You bet. Avery is the only one of you who cares. And if you had included her in the planning of whatever evil plot you all have, she might not have cared about me, either."

"You've got it all wrong, Sweetheart." He came around the desk and reached for her, but she sidestepped him.

"Don't touch me. You know I can't think when you touch me."

He chuckled, and she wanted to throw something at him.

"Tell me how I have it wrong, Luke. Adam, you, your mother—every one of you lied to me. What I want to know is why."

"To protect you."

"Protect me from what?"

"Margo."

"Do you honestly think she doesn't know?"

He shook his head. "If she knew, she'd have said something."

He stepped closer to her again. She wanted to turn away, wanted to refuse to listen to him, but she remained in her place. The anger gradually receded, leaving her chilled to the bone once again by shock and betrayal.

"Kendall," he said in a soft, stern voice, "When Margo comes home, I don't want you to say anything to her about this."

She would never try to force Margo to

acknowledge her. Her father was the only person she'd ever wanted to make notice her, and her mother destroyed any chance of that ever happening.

"As soon as I learned who you were, I wanted to tell you, Ken, but I didn't want to hurt you. You were already devastated by Adam's choosing her over you. I couldn't imagine telling you she was also the same girl your daddy chose."

She turned to look out the window. She wanted to believe him, needed his words to be true so badly she ached with it.

"Your father took those pictures of my mother and me."

"Yes."

He picked the pictures up from the desk and began looking through them.

"You knew?"

"I wasn't sure. I knew they looked like his work, but I couldn't be sure."

He shuffled the pictures.

"You didn't show me all of these."

"No."

"Why?"

"I wasn't sure if I could trust you."

He swore loudly, but he didn't argue with her.

"My father didn't take these recent ones of you, and he certainly didn't mail any of them."

"What about Rebecca?" she asked. "She's a photographer."

"Why would Rebecca do this?"

"I don't know. Obviously, I don't know why anyone would do it. Why would your father have taken pictures of us?"

"I don't really know. Maybe your grandparents asked him to. Maybe Thomas asked him to." He held up the invitation, birth announcement, and newspaper article. "Where did you get these?"

"They came in the mail today."

"For the life of me, I don't know what someone sending this to you means. All I know is it scares the hell out of me."

Chapter Twenty-Nine

Kendall woke alone in the dark. She missed the feel of Luke beside her. The bedside clock read three in the morning. Hoping to find him and tempt him back to bed, she tiptoed from the room.

At the top of the staircase, she stopped and listened to the voices from the hallway below. She couldn't help noticing how adept at eavesdropping she was becoming. Her list of flaws seemed to be growing each day she spent among the Templetons.

"We're leaving in the morning, Mother. Kendall deserves to know where she came from. She deserves to know the truth. Lydia was your friend. Don't you owe her anything at all?"

"I don't owe Lydia a damn thing," Delores said hoarsely. "She destroyed our friendship. She destroyed everything. Just look at her parents! Poor Louisa has never been the same since Lydia ran off. And George isn't much better. For heaven's sake, Luke, they still have her bedroom set up just as it was thirty years ago! She's dead and gone, and they know it! Still, they wait for her to return to them."

"I thought they kicked her out."

"They did! But they would have taken her back. Anytime she wanted, they would have taken her back."

"On what conditions?"

"On the condition she forget about Thomas!"

"And his child?"

Kendall's breath caught in her throat and she awaited Delores' answer.

"Well, Mother? Was giving up her child a

condition of her return?" Luke pushed.

"What does it matter now?" Delores cried. "She didn't give up the child. Although, I have no doubt Kendall would have been better off if she had. There were even people in our circle who would have taken her. You remember Hudson and Martha Graham, don't you? They begged Lydia to let them adopt her baby. They would have raised her right. Her life would have been completely different. And Lydia could have watched from a distance. But, of course, she wouldn't have it."

"Mother, how could you think that would be acceptable? Can you imagine Kendall giving Brady to someone and watching from a distance as they raise him?"

"No, but as I've said before, Kendall has far, far too much of Lydia in her. She lets her heart rule her head and doesn't even realize what she's giving up."

Luke sighed heavily, and Kendall heard him move away from his mother.

"We'll be leaving at daylight, Mother. I don't know when we'll be back."

"Luke," Delores said quietly, "do not force me to give you an ultimatum."

"Mother," he returned, equally as quiet, "don't force me to choose. I promise you, you won't be pleased."

Kendall hurried back to the bedroom when she heard Luke's footsteps on the stairs. When he reached for her, she went willingly into his arms.

He woke her early the next morning, and they left as the sun rose over the meadow.

An hour later, he pulled over at a hotel on the side of the road. Memories of the nights she'd spent on her little makeshift pallet in room twenty-nine assailed her, and she shuddered at the sight of the hotel's partially burned-out sign and the flat, one-story rooms. Though they moved when she was not much more than a toddler and she forgot exactly where it was located, she had never forgotten the place altogether.

"We can't stay here," she whispered in revulsion. "I won't stay here."

"I don't want to stay here. I just want to show you something."

She breathed a sigh of relief, and he squeezed her hand reassuringly as he pulled away.

He turned into the second road past the hotel. She vaguely remembered walking this road with her mother, feeling the enchantment of the tunnel formed by the huge live oaks that stretched their limbs across the road and seeing the huge stately mansion that stood in the center of the meadow at the end.

She told Luke this as he slowed down and turned into the drive that led up to the house.

"You never met the people who live here?"

She laughed.

"Of course not. Why?"

"Their names are Louisa and George James, and they're your grandparents."

"Louisa?" she repeated with a start. "That woman at the restaurant thought I was Louisa's daughter. She thought I was my mother. Your mother knew that."

"I would assume so, yes."

"Why wouldn't my mother tell me she lived here?" she asked, barely noticing that Luke had pulled to a stop in front of the house.

"According to my mother, her parents kicked her out when she told them she was pregnant. She was never to come back on the premises. To have told you about grandparents who wanted nothing to do with you would have been cruel."

"To have me live in the places we lived was cruel, Luke."

"You couldn't have lived here, Ken. Her parents wouldn't accept you."

He stepped out of the car, and came around to open her door. Her heart nearly stopped, then began to beat wildly in her chest when she realized he intended for her to meet her grandparents.

"What makes you think they'll accept me now?"

"Time changes things, Ken. Come on. Let me introduce you to your grandparents."

Though uncertain about the idea, she followed him onto the wide porch, Brady on her hip, and waited behind him as he knocked.

An elderly woman answered the door, her face lighting up when she saw him.

"Luke! What a nice surprise! Won't you come in? How's your mother?" the woman chattered as she led them through the foyer and into a room overflowing with flowers.

"Mother's doing well, Miss Louisa. How have you and George been?"

"Oh, fine, fine. George is about to drive me crazy with all these flowers. You know how he is. He has an unbelievable green thumb. Just keeps cutting his blooms and bringing them into the house."

"They're beautiful. Aren't they, Sweetheart?" he looked toward Kendall with an encouraging smile.

"Oh, yes." She breathed in the scent of the flowers.

"You've brought your wife!" Louisa exclaimed. "We heard you'd gotten married. It was wonderful news."

"Well, let me introduce you."

Before he could, Louisa gasped and put her hand to her heart, swaying slightly as she stared at Kendall.

Luke helped her sit just before a tall, white-haired man walked in.

"What's going on, Lou?" He rushed to her side.

"Did you have another dizzy spell?"

She shook her head and motioned toward Kendall.

"Look at her, George. Just look at her."

George James turned toward her. His face paled, and he sank into the seat beside his wife.

How could Luke think this was a good idea? Both of her grandparents looked ready to pass out from shock.

"You're her daughter, aren't you?" Louisa asked breathlessly.

Kendall nodded.

"Our granddaughter." George's voice tightened with emotion.

Standing to her feet, Louisa moved quickly to Kendall and wrapped her in a hug.

"Heard she named you after him. That true?" George boomed. He shook his head in exasperation when Kendall nodded. "Never could figure out what she saw in him. He was nothing but a namby-pamby sissy boy."

"George!" Louisa scolded. "We shouldn't speak ill of the dead."

"Why the hell not? I quit blaming Lydie long ago. Wasn't her fault he sweet-talked her into thinking he loved her, was it? She was nothing but a girl. She loved him. That's what's obvious now. She loved him more than he deserved."

"She killed him," Kendall observed.

"That she did. Can you blame her? Look at what he did to her, all he took from her."

"He couldn't have taken anything if we hadn't let him," Louisa said. "We took more than he did."

George looked away to hide his tears, but Louisa made no such effort. Tears tracked steadily down her wrinkled cheeks as she spoke.

"We cast her out in the street with nothing. Did you know she came to us a week before she died?

171

She begged us to take you in, said she was worried about you ending up alone if something happened to her."

Kendall shook her head. Of course she didn't know that. She tried to grasp the fact that her mother had once lived here and been part of this world but gave it up in order to keep her child.

"We told her she should have thought of that before she decided she could raise you all alone. We heard she was seeing Thomas again, you see, and we were so angry she hadn't learned her lesson." She shook her head, shame tingeing her voice. "We slammed the door in her face."

Brady began to fuss, and Kendall turned her attention to him, grateful for the distraction. She didn't know what to say. It was obvious they regretted the way they'd treated their daughter, but it was too late. Lydia was the one who had needed their apologies and their regret. Kendall had no idea what to do with either.

After a few moments of silence, Louisa blew her nose and got to her feet.

"I was just about to make some lunch," she said with a watery smile. "Won't you join us?"

"Oh, no, we don't want to impose," Kendall said.

"It's no imposition at all. Is it, George? We'd actually love the company. We rarely have company anymore. After all these years, we get tired of hearing only each other. So, it's nice to hear a different voice now and then. Besides, we want to get to know you, if you'll let us."

After lunch, Luke excused himself and took Brady down to the river, leaving Kendall alone with her grandparents. They'd taken seats in the large windowed room off the back of the house. Kendall stared sightlessly at the river outside the window, her mind full of questions she didn't dare ask.

"You look like you've got a lot on your mind,"

George observed. "Those Templetons are a trying bunch, aren't they?"

"Yes, sir."

"So, why don't you tell us what you want to know?"

Kendall pulled the envelope of pictures from her bag. She spread the pictures out on the coffee table between her grandparents and herself.

"I think these older ones were taken by Leon Templeton. Did either of you have him take them?"

They examined them carefully, especially those of that last fateful day. Louisa ran her finger over the image of her daughter.

"This was the day she died, you say?"

"Yes."

George placed a comforting hand on Louisa's back.

Kendall watched the gentle exchange and felt a twinge of wistfulness. Growing up with parents who loved each other so, her mother must have longed for just such a relationship.

"We loved our daughter, you know," George said.

How was she to respond to that? She always thought her mother's tears were for Thomas, but now she realized many of them were shed for the life and love she knew here in this house.

"Thomas Kendall was the golden boy of our social set. Everyone wanted to believe he could do no wrong, even Louisa and I. He and Julianne were married by the time Lydia told us. Of course, we realize now that she was pregnant before he married Julianne, but by the time we knew, everyone saw him as a married man. No one would have accepted her pregnancy or her child. We wanted her to do the right thing. We had friends who wanted to adopt you. They would have given you a good home, a good name. They would have loved you. But Lydia wouldn't hear of it. When we tried to press the issue, she left."

"She didn't go very far," Kendall said. "The Harbor Inn is the first home I remember. Certainly you could have found her there."

"We knew where she was when you lived there. Maybe she thought if we saw her there, pregnant and alone, we'd have mercy on her. Or maybe she just wanted to rub our faces in it."

He stared sightlessly at the picture of his daughter outside the hotel, lingering bitterness and hurt clouding his eyes.

"We went past that place one day. She was outside, sitting on one of those brick flowerbeds between the doors of the rooms. You were toddling around, digging the dirt out of them. No shirt, no shoes, only a diaper. You looked like a ragamuffin. Louisa cried all the way home. We didn't know what to do. We wanted her home so badly, wanted the girl we raised and loved. Maybe we were wrong, but we just couldn't accept the woman she had become."

How could they have driven past their daughter in such a condition? How could they withhold their help or demand she make such a heartbreaking choice? Kendall couldn't understand it.

"No one had any problem accepting my father and getting over what he had done," she said bitterly.

He shook his head sadly.

"No, none of them did. All those friends we thought we had, the ones we were trying to impress. None of them gave a damn about what he did, but they were quick to whisper behind their hands about Lydia. We held on for years, ignoring their whispered gossip. After your mother's death, we gave up trying to stay in their good graces. Louisa and I withdrew from society, and we've rarely seen any of them since. Delores Templeton remained a friend to us. Maybe it was because she lost her parents around the time we lost Lydia."

"But even Delores found it easy to blame Lydia and hard to hold a grudge against Thomas Kendall," her grandmother added when he stopped talking momentarily.

"In the end, all we did to keep up appearances was for nothing. What we did to Lydia has haunted us far more than the loss of our friends. Sometimes, I remember the things I said to her before she left, and I hate myself. I remember what Louisa said, and I hate her. How could we have been so cruel to our own child?" Regret and grief were thick in his voice, and Kendall touched his wrinkled hand.

"She never said an unkind word about either of you," she offered as comfort. She didn't add that Lydia had never spoken of her parents at all.

"She wouldn't have," he said. "It wasn't in her to be unkind. In a way, I think she understood our reaction. That makes it even worse. Her thinking she deserved what we did to her, what she did to herself."

"We didn't have Leon take the pictures," Louisa sniffed. "We forced ourselves to keep our distance. We didn't want to witness her self-destruction. After she left town, we never even attempted to find her."

"We didn't see her again until that day just before her death." George stood up. "If you'll excuse me, I need some air."

He left the room, and in a moment the back door slammed behind him.

"Come on," Louisa said, pushing herself up from the chair very slowly. "There are a few things I'd like to show you."

Kendall followed her grandmother up the stairs and into her mother's girlhood room. Delores claimed nothing had changed since Lydia walked out of their house for the last time, and Kendall believed it. Mementos from her mother's childhood were everywhere. Ribbons and photos decorated the walls. Kendall went to the desk as Louisa disappeared into the closet. She picked up a program for a Chadsworth graduation. She was hardly surprised to find her mother's name there, along with Julianne's.

A picture hung on the mirror. She easily picked out her mother, Delores and Julianne. A young, smiling version of her father stood behind them. Douglas Martin stood on one side of him, but his eyes were focused on Lydia instead of the camera. Behind Delores was a handsome bear of a man a few years older than the others.

With a gasp, Kendall pulled the photo closer.

"What is it, dear?" Louisa stepped from the closet, her arms full of billowing white satin.

"Who is this man?" she pointed to the picture, both expecting and dreading the answer. He resembled his children too much to hope it was someone else.

"That's Leon Templeton."

Kendall nodded. Of course, it was Leon Templeton, the photographer. She should have realized it sooner. He was the photographer with the car, the one her mother had modeled for, so long ago.

"Are you okay?" Louisa asked worriedly.

"Yes, I'm fine," Kendall assured her as she replaced the picture.

"This was the dress she wore to her last winter cotillion," Louisa said, holding it up. "I'll never forget how she looked in it."

"It's beautiful," Kendall said, not sure what other response to give.

"Of course, I didn't know she was pregnant when she wore it, but she must have been. I've often wondered if she suspected it at that time. She didn't tell us until she was five months along."

She sat on the bed, still clutching the dress to her chest.

"We were so bad to her, Kendall. She was our daughter. She should have come before anything else. We should have cared more about her and less about what people thought."

"It was a long time ago." It was little in the way of absolution, but it was all she could offer.

"Were there any good years?" Louisa asked hopefully.

"No," Kendall answered, unable to lie or even to gloss over the facts. "There were good days. There were times when she held a job and could make rent. There were more times when she couldn't."

"But you lived at the hotel for years."

Kendall hesitated. If she told the truth, it would hurt Louisa more than she wanted to, but if she lied, it seemed unfair to her mother.

"She had an arrangement with the landlord," Kendall said. Louisa's sharp intake of breath confirmed that she understood what sort of arrangement her daughter was forced to make in order to keep a roof over her child's head.

"She was a good mother, wasn't she?" Louisa asked after a few minutes of silence, her words more statement than question.

Not so long ago, Kendall's answer would have been an unequivocal "no." Having her own child had softened her heart toward her mother, however, and she no longer felt as certain in that answer. Now she looked at herself and saw what a mother would do to take care of her child. In reality, she had sold herself to the Templetons to keep her child, just as her mother sold herself to the men who traipsed in and out of their lives. She scolded herself silently. A whore was a whore no matter the price a man was willing to pay.

"She did the best she could to give me what I needed."

"Tell me about the good times," Louisa said.

"Once, we went to the zoo. It was when Mama was a waitress. A big family came in, and they gave her a really nice tip. She had the next day off, and when I got up she was packing a picnic for us. We took the bus to the zoo. It was a good day. We bought spun sugar, fed the monkeys, and rode the carousel. Mama laughed all day long. I don't remember ever seeing her like that. She lost her job not long afterward."

Kendall stopped, not needing to tell her grandmother what they both already knew. The good memories too quickly led to bad.

Louisa took a long shuddering breath, and by unspoken agreement they turned the conversation to other things.

"How did you meet Luke?" Louisa asked. "It's an amazing coincidence that you would become entangled with the Templetons."

Entangled. That was the best word Kendall knew to describe her life with the Templetons. She intended to tell Louisa the agreed-upon story, but the truth tumbled out of her mouth. When she finished, her grandmother patted her hand.

"Lydia taught you well."

Kendall laughed bitterly at the similarity between her grandmother's words and her own thoughts.

"I guess Mama would be proud of the bargain I made."

"Don't talk that way, Kendall. I meant Lydia taught you how to love. When you think what a horrid mother I turned out to be, it's amazing that I could have raised a girl who would sacrifice everything for her own child. Obviously, she taught her daughter the same thing."

Kendall knew her mother could easily have walked away from her. She might even have been tempted to at times, but she never did. Once Kendall had overheard one of her mother's lovers begging her to leave Kendall behind and run away with him. Her mother kicked him out of the house within minutes, and she'd never seen him around again.

How many other chances had her mother passed up in order to keep her?

"Kendall," her grandmother said now in an urgent voice, "I want you to be careful. Margo isn't stupid. She'll figure out what was between Adam and you. When she does, you need to be as far away from there as possible."

"Dolores still swears that she'll take Brady from me if I try to leave."

Louisa's eyes narrowed. "There is absolutely no need for you to be afraid of Delores and her threats. We may not run in her circles any longer, Kendall, but our family is just as upstanding as hers. And I assure you, George and I can afford an attorney on par with anyone Delores Templeton hires."

"I'm not asking that of you," Kendall protested.

"I know, and it hasn't come down to it yet. Delores can threaten all she wants, but Luke wouldn't let her do it and neither will we."

Kendall didn't waste her breath arguing that point.

Chapter Thirty

Christmas at The Grove was like nothing Kendall had ever seen. A huge Christmas tree stood in one corner of the parlor and another was in the dining room. Garlands and wreaths decorated every fireplace and doorway throughout the house, and candles burned in every window.

Avery grew more animated than ever, reminding Kendall of the holidays at Chadsworth. By the time Christmas break came and the girls left for home, the teachers nearly gave up any semblance of normalcy in the classrooms or anywhere else. It was a relief to sink into bed on that last night of school and wake up the next morning to the blessed silence of empty dormitories.

Despite the turmoil surrounding her, Kendall gave herself over to the celebration of the holiday. Margo was still hospitalized, no more mail had arrived since she'd learned about her relationship to Margo, and she sincerely hoped that whoever had sent the photographs was now satisfied that she knew all she needed to know. Her anxiety seemed to evaporate as she threw herself into enjoying her first Christmas as a mother.

On Christmas Eve, Luke and Kendall played Santa Claus, wrapping presents for Brady and Avery and placing them under the tree. Although Avery insisted she was too old for Santa, Kendall enjoyed the idea of surprising her anyway.

Afterwards, they stood in the door and surveyed their handiwork. Kendall sighed happily and wrapped her arms around Luke's waist.

"Merry Christmas, Santa," she said, lifting her face to his.

"Merry Christmas, Mrs. Claus." He smiled and caught her mouth with his own. "I hope we have a hundred more."

He swung her up into his arms and carried her to their room.

****

Kendall stood at the nursery window and watched her husband stride toward the stable. After a brief stretch of freezing temperatures between Christmas and New Year's Day, the sun had come out today, creating the illusion that spring waited just around the corner.

Luke exited the stable astride Bard and, with a gentle kick, sent the horse flying across the field the minute they cleared the doors.

Sometime over the last few weeks they had fallen into a morning routine in which he dressed while she nursed Brady. Before he left for his daily ride, he came in and gave them each a gentle peck on the head. When she was sure he wouldn't be coming back upstairs and catch her, she moved to the window to watch him. Once he and Bard disappeared into the woods at the edge of the meadow, she rarely saw him again until lunch time.

"Bye-bye, Daddy," she said quietly to Brady, waving at Luke's retreating form.

He gazed at her quizzically, and she gave him a quick kiss and turned away from the window. She gasped when she saw Adam watching them intently from the doorway.

"You startled me," she said with a chuckle, but he said nothing in return.

With a silent nod, he moved down the hall, leaving her to wonder why he was there at all.

Carrying Brady with her, she crossed to her own room to dress for the day. A note was lying on the bed, and she smiled when she read Luke's invitation. *Follow me.*

She dressed quickly, left Brady with Cora, and had one of the grooms saddle up the only horse she felt skilled enough to ride. The patient yellow mare she rode during her riding lessons would never match Bard's long-legged gallop, but they were soon ambling across the meadow in the same direction as Luke.

As she crested the small hill, she caught sight of Luke seated under a huge oak tree. He watched her ride toward him, standing as she drew closer and slid off the horse. Their lips met, and he lifted her against him so that her feet barely brushed the ground. His mouth held hers as he tied her horse.

He pulled her down to the grass, and they began undressing each other with frenzied movements, rarely letting their kisses end. There was no need for words as they made love in the shadow of the trees.

****

"I need to get back," Kendall said. They were dressed once more, and Luke's head lay in her lap as she ran her fingers through his dark hair.

"Me, too. I've been away much longer than I intended when I set out this morning." He smiled up at her. "Not that I didn't welcome the surprise."

"What surprise?" she bent and kissed him. "You invited me."

"I did?" his hand cupped her head, pulling her closer to deepen the kiss.

In an instant, Kendall was once again lost in the passion that arced between them Finally, with great reluctance, she forced herself to remember the world beyond the sheltering copse of trees and pulled away.

"I really need to get back to Brady."

He stood up and offered her his hand, pulling her to her feet and kissing her one last time before helping her onto her horse.

As he turned to untie Bard, a gunshot came from nowhere, the bullet hitting the oak tree and sending bits of bark flying.

"What the hell?" Luke roared, dropping Bard's reins and lunging for Kendall.

The second bullet found its mark in Kendall's chest. Searing pain burned her lungs as her breath froze, and she felt herself falling, her body's impact with the ground dulled by the icy cold seeping through her veins to meet the fire in her chest.

From a distance, she heard Luke cry out to her. She felt him fall to his knees beside her, covering her trembling body with his own. She tasted his tears on her lips as he held her, and she wished she could touch his face, wipe away his tears. She moved her mouth, fighting to tell him she loved him and beg him to take care of their son, but in the end, she couldn't even whisper good-bye.

****

"Stay with me, Ken," Luke pleaded as she grew too still beneath him, her breath too shallow.

He sat up, gathering her close to him. The horses were gone, and they were too far away for anyone to hear him call for help.

Blood seeped from the bullet hole in her chest at an alarming rate, and he frantically tore off his blood-soaked shirt and wrapped it tightly around her, praying it would staunch the flow of blood.

He talked to her as he stood and carried her back to the house. In a voice that broke, he told her how much he loved her, begged her to hang on. He could feel the life ebbing from her, feel the emptiness she was leaving in his soul.

"Luke! What happened?" Adam waved wildly, and spurred his horse into a gallop. When he reached them, he slid from its back, holding out his arms. "Give her to me."

Luke shook his head. He couldn't let her go. He needed to hold her, feel her here in his arms as long as he could.

"Luke, what the hell happened?" Adam demanded again.

"Someone shot her." His heart lurched when he spoke the words, and the world seemed to darken. He felt himself sway on his feet as he looked at his brother. "She's dying."

Adam placed a hand on his arm, pushing him toward the horse.

"Give her to me. I'll hand her up to you," he ordered.

Luke swallowed hard, forcing himself to place Kendall in Adam's outstretched arms.

As soon as Luke had Kendall, Adam gave the horse a sharp whack that sent it galloping toward home.

"Call an ambulance!" Luke cried as they burst into the yard surrounding the stables.

He slid from the horse, Kendall still firmly in his grasp, and fell to his knees. With a tortured cry, he folded his body around hers.

****

Luke sat at Kendall's bedside as he had for the last week. The bullet had broken several ribs and severed an artery. She'd lost a vast amount of blood and was so near death when she arrived at the hospital the doctors gave them almost no hope of recovery. By some miracle, they were able to stabilize her, and they now assured Luke she was healing. So far, however, the only sign he saw that she was alive was that she continued breathing.

He repeatedly relived the moment when the bullet hit her body, followed by the terror of feeling her life seeping out of her. Each time, he cursed himself for waiting until she couldn't hear him before speaking the words he knew she longed to hear. He'd read the silent pleas in her eyes when he made love to her, had seen her anxiously waiting for the words to cross his lips. But, for reason he didn't understand, he couldn't speak them. Each time he wanted to, he heard his own voice warning her, "Love only gets in the way." No matter how badly his heart wanted to say the words to her, his head won every time, and he let the moment pass.

"Luke, take a break. I'll sit here with her." Adam entered the room behind him.

"I'm fine."

"You don't look fine. You need a shave and a bath. If Kendall wakes up and sees you sitting there, she won't even know who you are."

"She'll know," Luke assured him. "How's Brady?"

Adam sat in the chair beside him.

"He's okay. He's sort of cranky, naturally. He wants his mother."

Luke nodded.

The only time he'd left the hospital was to fetch Brady and take him to his great-grandparents. He refused to let the child sleep in a house where someone tried to murder his mother. Depending on the perpetrator and the motive, Brady might not be any safer than Kendall. The thought of losing either of them chilled him to the bone.

"Go home, Luke," Adam said again. "Get some rest, or go see Brady. Get out of here for a little while. She won't wake up while you're gone."

"You don't know that."

"I do know it. She's your sleeping beauty, not mine."

Luke bent his head to Kendall's hand. He pressed a kiss there on her palm.

"Someone tried to kill her," he said.

"Possibly."

"What do you mean, 'possibly'?" Luke snarled.

"Someone shot her."

"It could have been an accident, a stray bullet," he offered. "Who would have done it on purpose, Luke? Who has any reason to want her dead?"

"I don't know." He rubbed his eyes, and then grabbed the paper from the table by the bed. "I've got a list."

"Who's your main suspect?" Adam asked and Luke knew that he knew.

"Margo."

"Margo's in the hospital."

"I know."

"What about Julianne?" Adam suggested, before Luke could tell him his was the next name on the list.

"If she was murderous, wouldn't she have killed Lydia?"

Adam shrugged. "Maybe she did."

Luke stared at him. "What does that mean?"

"I don't know. I guess I'm talking crazy."

****

Kendall opened her eyes slowly. The purples and grays of dusk through the window and the one small lamp on the bedside table were the only light in the room. Across the room, Adam sat in a chair, his head leaned back and his eyes closed.

She spared him only a cursory glance before turning toward Luke. His eyes burned holes into hers as he leaned forward, taking her hand in his.

"I love you," he vowed. Tears spilled over as he kissed her. "God help me, I love you."

Her heart soared at the words, and she smiled.

"I love you, too." Her voice was too soft, but she knew he saw the words on her lips.

Over Luke's shoulder, Adam offered Kendall a wistful smile and wave before slipping from the room.

Chapter Thirty-One

Luke sat at his desk, pen and paper in hand, trying to make sense of the past few days. He'd brought Kendall home today and confined her to bed, with Avery in charge of keeping an eye on her and reporting to him immediately if she didn't obey doctor's orders.

His list consisted of everyone in the household, and anyone outside the household who had any connection at all with Kendall. If he could come up with any reason they might want to harm Kendall, he listed the reasons and what those reasons might be.

His mother's name was the first on the list. As always, his mother was an enigma, alternately looking out for her own best interests and everyone else's until it was impossible to tell her motive for doing anything at all.

Although the hospital administrator insisted they were required to call the police about gunshot victims, she had convinced the man to make an exception. He guessed the few quick and determined conversations between them included a substantial donation to the hospital's coffers.

The question was why she was so adamant about the police not being involved. Was her determination to keep the police out of the matter due to her own involvement, or was she protecting someone else? What would her motive be for wanting Kendall dead?

She wanted to keep the truth from Margo, but at what cost?

Now that Kendall knew her grandparents, his mother's threats to take Brady from her no longer held such power. Killing Kendall would certainly prevent a custody battle.

He longed to cross her name off the list, but in the end, he left it alone and moved down the line.

Avery. He immediately crossed it off. Avery was the only person in the house he trusted completely.

Adam's name stood out in capital letters, as did Margo's. Like he'd told Adam, Margo was his main suspect, but Adam was neck and neck with her. Both of them had more than enough reason to want Kendall dead.

In his own way, Adam loved Margo. What would he do to keep from hurting her with the truth about Kendall and Brady?

There was no denying Margo was damaged tremendously by her father's murder. If she knew the truth about Kendall, it may have pushed her over the edge of sanity. If she somehow knew about Kendall and Adam, neither Kendall nor Brady was likely safe from her wrath. The niggling suspicion that Brady's choking wasn't an accident still haunted him. Yet Margo was in the hospital when Kendall was shot. Though she was an excellent marksman, that fact ruled her out.

Julianne Delacroix's name was next. Julianne was a reserved woman, adept at hiding her feelings, but he suspected her maternal instincts would kick in if she thought Kendall's presence caused her daughter distress. As far as he knew, however, Julianne was still in France, so he eliminated her, as well.

He came to Rebecca's name with a heavy heart. Except for the scene at the Citrus Ball, she seemed to handle his marriage to Kendall with her usual grace and had actually befriended Kendall. Was it all an act? He shook his head and drew a line through her name. He knew her too well to even think her capable of such deviousness.

There must be something he was missing, he thought, as he stood and paced the floor. It seemed a logical assumption that the pictures Kendall received were from the same person who shot her, but no matter how logical it seemed, he just wasn't sure it was correct. He wasn't even certain of the point behind the pictures. Was someone just trying to show her they realized who she was? Were they trying to illuminate the similarities between Kendall and Lydia? Or was it something more sinister?

For years, no one in their circle had even hinted at her existence. Most of them knew, but no one spoke of it aloud. He wasn't even sure that any of them knew where Lydia had gone when she left her parents' home. Everyone knew why she left, but no one really cared to find out where she went. No longer on their social level, she ceased to be of any importance. So, Kendall lived for years without any contact with or knowledge of the people who were once her mother's friends and family.

He had never known Lydia, and although he knew Louisa and George James' daughter had been childhood friends with his mother and Julianne Delacroix, he'd never heard his mother talk about her at all.

He knew his mother well enough to know she kept a file on Kendall. When Kendall arrived, Delores knew about her past with an ease that told him she already knew at least some of it beforehand. She would keep every bit of information she had for future use against Kendall. None of it would be carelessly cast aside just because he and Kendall were married. His mother created a file on everyone she knew. She liked to know how to deal with each and every person with whom she associated.

He needed to search those files and find out just

exactly what his mother knew about Kendall and about anyone who might want her dead. Determined to learn what he could, he left his office for his mother's.

"Luke," Kendall's voice was barely a whisper, and he rushed to her side when he saw her inching her way down the stairs.

"What are you doing down here? Where's Avery? You should be resting." He situated her on the sofa in his mother's office, lifting her feet and propping pillows behind her head.

"I've been resting. I need to talk to you. I'm sure Avery's right behind me. She should be in here any minute to scold me. I think she's enjoying getting to tell me what to do."

"I'm sure she is. You should listen to her. Now, what is so important it couldn't have waited until I came upstairs?"

"I've made a list of who might have shot me. Margo is the number one suspect, but she isn't here. I thought of Rebecca, but I just don't think she would have. Really, Luke, when I come right down to it, you, your brother and your mother are the only logical suspects."

"Me, Ken? Do you really suspect me?" He couldn't quite keep the hurt from his voice.

"I don't want to, but you have to admit you have motive. You were forced into marriage with me."

"We'll get to motive later. For now, think about it. I was with you when you were shot. How would that have worked?"

"I don't know," she admitted miserably. "I thought maybe the three of you worked out some plot to kill me. You have to admit my appearance here has caused a lot of commotion."

"I didn't shoot you or arrange to have you shot. Yes, we married under odd circumstances, but I couldn't have been forced if I hadn't thought I could stand to be married to you. Whatever the circumstances were, though, they don't matter any longer. I love you. I would never hurt you."

"What about Adam? You said he was nearby. He heard the gunshots. He doesn't want Margo to find out the truth about our marriage or about Brady."

"He has the motive. That's for sure. But he seemed genuinely worried about you. As hard as it is to believe, judging by his behavior I think Adam does care for you in some way. Still, I wasn't able to cross him off my list of suspects, either."

"That leaves your mother."

"Yes, it does. I wish I could swear it wasn't Mother. I hate thinking she'd do such a thing, but I can't help it. I just don't believe she'd risk it only to keep Margo from finding out about you. There would have to be another reason. That's what I'm looking for."

He opened the closet doors, revealing file cabinets that ran the length and width of the sizeable interior. Luke pulled one of the drawers open and quickly skimmed over the files inside.

"Here it is," he said and pulled out a file.

She stayed as she was while he leafed through the contents. The pain medication she'd taken earlier was beginning to wear off, and it suddenly seemed too much of an effort to sit up and move to the desk. A soft sigh escaped her, and Luke looked over at her, concern darkening his eyes at her obvious discomfort. She could almost see a lecture forming on his lips, before his face softened with compassion and he pulled an ottoman up beside the couch and sat down.

"Some of this is decades old," he murmured, pulling items from the file.

First, he passed her duplicates of the pictures she already had. She gave them only a passing glance as he shoved others her way.

There were pictures of Thomas and Lydia when they were teenagers. Then, to Kendall's surprise, some of them just before their deaths. Didn't her grandparents say they'd heard Lydia was seeing Thomas again at that time? It was the reason they'd turned her away.

There was another of Thomas Kendall and the pretty blonde girl Kendall remembered so well. As an adult, Kendall saw things she hadn't noticed as a child: the tightness and worry around his mouth and the same lost, hopeless look that was in her mother's eyes.

With trembling hands, she picked up the articles and pictures Luke pulled from the file. They dated back to the year her mother and Julianne were debutantes. Just as her grandmother had said, Lydia looked beautiful in her full white dress. There were pictures of cotillions and balls in which her father appeared to be quite the ladies' man. Although several showed him dancing with Delores and Julianne, most of them were of him and Lydia. Any fool could see they were in love. So, how was it he married Julianne?

The next item was a series of postcards from Europe, addressed to Delores. Kendall barely recognized her mother's girlish writing as she raved about the scenery and museums. The last line was a reminder that she would be home the following week, and she could hardly wait to see Thomas after being away for a month.

Clipped to the postcard was a photo of Thomas and Julianne sitting side by side at a bonfire. Her hand was splayed on his thigh and the camera caught a moment of playful flirting.

A duplicate of Margo's birth announcement followed. Kendall looked at the postcards again before flipping over the photo to search for a date. The photo of Julianne and Thomas was taken

Delores asked Kendall after Adam told her about Margo's escape.

Before Luke or Kendall could answer, the phone began to ring, and Adam leapt up.

"Maybe they've found her," he said.

Luke followed him into the living room, and Kendall sank into the chair Adam had vacated. From there, she could see and hear both men.

"Yes, yes, this is Adam Templeton."

A long silence followed, ending only when Adam gave a low moan and sank to his knees.

"Jesus, Adam, what is it?" Luke demanded, bending down to him.

"She's dead," Adam groaned.

Luke grabbed the phone from him, barking questions until he finally hung up and turned back to Adam.

Kendall lifted her eyes to Avery's shocked gaze. Tears pooled in the girl's eyes, and Kendall motioned her to take the chair beside her. When Avery sat down clutching Brady to her chest, Kendall wrapped her arms around her.

Without a word to any of them, Delores disappeared into her own office, shutting the door behind her.

exactly a week before the last postcard was written. Kendall found it hard to believe that the whole sordid mess of her birth was so simple. One boy, two pregnant girls. Someone was destined to have their heart broken. It was fate that made Lydia the one who was destroyed.

Feeling heartsick for her mother, she dropped the clipping to the desk and scooped up a few that followed her father's career.

The last one regarded his death and was clipped to a photo of Kendall the day of her parents' death. The handwritten caption read, "Lydia's daughter."

"Your mother knew who I was before Adam met me," she said looking up at him.

"Yes," he said and handed her the last item from the file. Another picture taken without her knowledge: Adam and her in front of the house they shared.

It had always seemed too much of a coincidence that his brother found and married Kendall of all people, but now it was obvious his mother had plotted to get Kendall here. Why she had done so and how deeply involved Adam was in the plot were what Luke wanted to know. None of the answers he thought of made him feel better about Kendall's safety.

"Kendall, listen to me. I want you to take Brady and leave here." He crouched in front of her and cupped her face in his hand. "I don't know what the hell's going on, but I don't like it, and I want to know you're both safe and away from here before I start asking questions."

"Do you think Adam found me on purpose?" she asked.

"Yes," he said, giving voice to his suspicions.

"Why?" Her voice trembled, and he kissed her gently.

He didn't want to think about why. He would

figure it all out once Kendall and Brady were safely away. He lifted her in his arms.

"What are you doing?"

"I'm carrying you up the stairs. You aren't well enough to be traipsing all over the place. I would just leave you here, but I don't know what you need to take with you."

The fact that she didn't argue with him spoke volumes about how frail she was at the moment. She seemed to grow paler by the minute, and her eyes were shadowed with worry. He longed to hold her close to him and comfort her. But he was afraid to take the time. He felt certain it was only a matter of time before whoever shot her tried again.

Adam burst through the front door as they left the office.

"Margo's gone," he told them, his voice harried.

"What do you mean, 'gone'?" Luke asked, his arms tightening around Kendall.

"The hospital called. They said she escaped last night."

"Is she with her mother?"

Adam shook his head. "She and her husband are on the ship heading home. They should be here tomorrow."

"What about Douglas?"

"I haven't been able to reach him."

"How did she get away from the hospital?" Luke demanded.

"They don't know." Adam looked away.

"What else?" Luke asked, and when Adam would have shaken his head, Luke stopped him, "You're hiding something. What is it?"

"It isn't the first time she's left. They say she was out another day."

"What day?"

"The day Kendall was shot."

Luke swore softly.

"They didn't call because they found he don't think she was gone but an hour or couldn't have made it here and back in that time."

"But they aren't certain?"

"No."

"Avery!" Luke roared.

The girl appeared at the top of the sta eyes wide.

"I want you to pack Brady a bag. He diapers and clothes. He'll need enough for a He was already halfway up the stairs with I in his arms. "When you're done, take him a bag downstairs and wait for us."

"What's happening?" she cried, fear maki sound much more like a child than usual.

"Margo's escaped from the hospital, and Kendall and Brady away from here immediate

Avery nodded and hurried into the nurser

Once in the room, he put Kendall on th grabbed a suitcase from the closet, and began her things from her drawers. He filled the su and then slammed it shut. Kendall noticed his shook slightly as he fought with the latch.

Once it clicked into place, he bent to lift he

"I'll walk," she said and pushed herself up.

"You don't need to," he argued.

"Yes, I do. You carry the suitcase. I'll be fin

Avery waited at the bottom of the stairs, and two bags in her arms. Adam sat in a behind her, his face buried in his hands.

The front door opened, and Kendall caugh breath, half expecting to see Margo. She beg breathe again when Delores appeared.

"What in heaven's name is going on l Delores demanded, her eyes flying from Aver Adam to Kendall and Luke.

"Are you going to your grandparents' he

Chapter Thirty-Two

Luke stared down at Kendall and Brady as they slept. Brady's tiny hand clutched the neckline of her gown and her arm lay loosely around him. He, Adam and their mother had been at the police station and then the hospital for hours. Relieved to be home with Kendall and Brady, he sat down on the bed and ran his finger down the tracks of her tears.

She turned her face toward his hand and opened her eyes.

"Hi," she said.

"Hi."

"How's Adam?"

"Not good."

"What happened?" She pushed herself to a sitting position, careful not to wake Brady.

"She was hit by a car."

"What? How?"

"She ran out in front of it. The driver didn't have time to stop. She was killed instantly." He was still as shocked by the news as Kendall appeared to be.

"Where?"

"In front of the house where she lived with your father. No one knows why she went there or what made her dash out into the street."

"Oh, Luke. How sad."

"We called Julianne. She's on her way home."

"Avery's in a really bad way," she told him. "I'm worried about her."

"I'll talk to her in the morning."

He showered and returned in a pair of pajama pants. Leaving Brady where he lay between them, he climbed into bed. He needed to feel the warmth of them both beside him tonight. In the darkness his hand found Kendall's, and he held tightly to it as he drifted to sleep.

Kendall found it more difficult to get back to sleep.

She didn't have a doubt as to what had driven Margo to that house, but she wondered what drove her away. Had she been overcome by memories of the day her father died? Had she realized Kendall's mother pulled the trigger?

She didn't do it. Margo's words seemed to echo in the silence of the room.

Kendall sat up quickly, hoping not to wake either Brady or Luke. Was it possible Margo was there the day her parents were shot? The screams began just seconds after the gunshot. Kendall had never known or cared who screamed. Now, suddenly, it seemed imperative that she know.

Unable to settle back down, she slipped from the bed.

"What are you doing?" Luke mumbled.

"Nothing," she assured him. "I'm just going downstairs to get a drink of ice water."

He sat up. "I'll get it."

"No, Luke. Lie back down. I'll be fine."

He started to protest, and she sighed.

"I'll just get one out of the bathroom, you silly man." She leaned over and kissed him.

He sank back on the pillow and was asleep again almost immediately.

Kendall got a glass of lukewarm tap water from the bathroom, suddenly not wanting to venture too far from either Luke or Brady.

She fell asleep with Margo's whispered words ringing in her ears. *She didn't do it.*

****

In her dream, Kendall stood on the street in

front of her father's house. Inside, her mother and father lay dead, and as she stood reeling with horror, a car flew around the corner, heading straight for her. She could see the driver's face through the windshield.

A man grabbed her from behind, pulling her out of the street, as the car came to a screeching halt where she'd been standing.

"Shush, Kendall," the man behind her said and pushed her into the back seat of the car.

Through the back window, she saw Margo's lifeless body lying in the street.

****

Kendall woke with a start. Though she had always remembered the horror of hearing the gunshots that ended her parents' lives, the ensuing moments were a blur. She knew she had run across the street, calling out for her mother, and a passerby had grabbed her around the waist. Until now, she'd never heard his familiar voice saying her name. Was he really more than just an innocent passerby?

Beside her, Brady whimpered and rooted closer. At the soft sound, Luke turned toward them in his sleep, his hand coming to rest on her hip as Brady began to nurse.

As the two of them slept, Kendall stared into the darkness, juxtaposing memories and dream until she knew what was real and what wasn't. A shiver of foreboding rushed down her spine as she accepted what she must have known all along.

The man who grabbed her and pushed her into the car was Leon Templeton. The man behind the wheel was Douglas Martin.

Chapter Thirty-Three

Julianne Delacroix arrived the next afternoon. Pale and drawn, she leaned heavily on her husband as he led her into the house.

Her eyes narrowed when she saw Kendall standing at Luke's side. She quickly hid her ire, however, and turned toward Adam.

"I want to know exactly how this could happen."

"We were at the hospital last night, Julianne. Why don't you come into my office, and we'll talk about what we know?" Delores motioned toward her office, and Julianne and Jacques did as she requested.

"I need to be in there," Luke told Kendall, with a quick kiss, before following his mother and brother into the room.

She and Avery wandered out to the patio and sat at the table.

"I shouldn't have been so cruel to her," Avery sniffed.

"No, you shouldn't have," Kendall agreed. "But there's nothing to be done about it now."

"Why do you think she was at that house?"

"I don't know. Maybe she was trying to find her father."

"Maybe. I know if I could, I'd forget mine was gone and look for him."

"Did you know your father knew my mother?"

"Sure. I used to go with him to take pictures of her. I think we took some of you, too. He always told me he was keeping track of an old friend."

Avery would have been four the day Lydia and

Thomas died. Was it possible she was there, too?

"Were you ever with him on the street where my father lived?"

"Not to take pictures. Our families visited each other pretty often."

Luke came out of the house and sank into the chair beside her.

"Are you okay, Ave?" he asked.

"I feel terrible about how mean I was to her."

"Margo knew you loved her. Sisters are cruel to each other at times. And that's how Margo saw you. As a sister."

Avery nodded, tears spilling down her cheeks.

****

Margo's funeral was a rather elaborate affair, with hundreds of people in attendance. Kendall wondered where they had been in all the months she knew Margo. She never saw any of them visit her at the house, and she was certain none of them would have visited the hospital.

Standing at Margo's grave, she thought of the only other funeral she'd ever attended. Her mother's funeral was kept short and quiet, attended only by a few neighbors and a handful of curiosity seekers who had read the story in the newspaper and came to witness the burial.

Feeling eyes upon her, Kendall lifted her head and met the burning blue gaze of Douglas Martin. Once again she felt a sense of déjà vu, and she gasped. As Margo's uncle, he stood near the grave with the rest of the family. At her mother's funeral, he had stood on the periphery of the mourners, but he had been the only person there whose grief mirrored her own.

After Margo's funeral, the mourners gathered at the Delacroix mansion. If Kendall had felt awkward at the Citrus Ball, she felt even more so now.

Adam and the rest of his family were

surrounded by people extending their condolences, but somehow Kendall became dislodged from Luke's side.

Obviously everyone now knew who she was. She was openly snubbed by the majority of the people in attendance, proving they valued Julianne's approval far more than that of the Templetons.

At last she found an out-of-the-way corner in which to stand, hoping not to call any more attention to herself than absolutely necessary.

She didn't realize Douglas Martin stood beside her until he spoke.

"I can't believe you're here."

"Delores thought it would be inappropriate if I stayed home."

"That's Delores. Appearances matter more than anything else. Including any pain keeping them up may cause."

Kendall flushed. "I wasn't sure your sister would appreciate my being here. I didn't want to hurt her."

"So, you've figured it all out, have you? Did your husband tell you?"

"If you mean that Margo and I were sisters, then yes, I know that."

"What else would I be referring to?" he said.

"The other secrets," she said.

"The other secrets?" he repeated, but she thought she detected a slight tremor in his voice.

"Your secrets."

"I have no idea what you're talking about." Oh, yes, definitely a tremor of uncertainty. He knew exactly what she was talking about.

"Your relationship to my mother. I know you were at her funeral. I know you were there the day she died. I know you came to the place we lived at least once. You knew exactly where to take me that day."

"You don't know anything," he muttered and

stalked away.

Her grandparents were crossing the room, and she hurried toward them, surprised and grateful to see them here. They were at the funeral, of course, but she hadn't expected them to face the people they'd avoided for so long.

Whispers followed them as they made their way through the room and came to stand on either side of her.

"This might not be the most appropriate time and place to do this, but we couldn't let you face them alone," her grandfather murmured to her.

"Thank you," she whispered, tears threatening to choke her.

Julianne separated herself from the small group of people surrounding her and walked slowly toward them, her eyes burning with grief and fury.

"Louisa, George," she said tightly when she stood before them.

"Julianne, we're so sorry about Margo," Louisa offered.

"I'm sure you are," Julianne said sarcastically.

"Of course we are," Louisa assured her, placing a hand on her arm.

Julianne stepped back, dislodging the gentle hand. "I want you to leave." Her voice cracked. "All of you."

"Julianne," Delores moved to Julianne's side. "Don't do this here."

"Shut up, Delores. Margo was my daughter. I have every right to decide who is welcome here and who isn't."

She glared at Kendall. "I can't believe you would show your face here. You have no business being here at all."

"I'm sorry," Kendall said. "I truly liked Margo. She was very kind to me."

"Get out," the woman said showing no sign that

she heard Kendall's words.

Luke pushed through the crowd gathered around them. He moved to Kendall's side, between her and her grandmother, and wrapped a steadying arm around her.

"She came as my wife, Julianne. We're sorry if it upset you."

He led Kendall back through the crowd. Shaking from head to toe, it was all she could do to make herself walk toward the doors. Once outside, her knees seemed to give way and she stumbled. Luke's arm tightened, holding her against his side.

Her grandparents were just behind them.

"Are you okay, dear?" Louisa asked, studying her closely. "You've had a very trying few weeks."

Kendall nodded, not trusting herself to speak. Her stomach joined the rest of her body in trembling, and she was afraid she would be sick if she attempted to talk.

"I'm afraid we all rode together," Luke said. "Would you two mind giving us a ride home?"

"Of course not," George said while they waited for the valet to bring his car around. "It will give us a chance to make sure Kendall is okay and see that son of yours for a minute or two."

Once they were home, both Luke and Louisa insisted that Kendall go to bed. She argued adamantly that she wasn't an invalid, but in the end her own exhaustion won out, and she fell asleep almost instantly.

She woke hours later to a room in semi-darkness. She went down the hall to the nursery, where she found Cora knitting while Brady slept soundly in his crib. Although she offered to let Cora leave, the woman refused to budge until Kendall went downstairs and had supper. Kendall was surprised and moved by the usually amenable housekeeper's stubborn refusal to give up her duties until Kendall had taken care of herself.

Before going downstairs, she straightened her clothes and brushed her hair, choosing to wear the same thing she'd worn to the funeral instead of changing. Surely Delores had more important things to worry about tonight than Kendall's wardrobe.

"Well, this was a most unpleasant day," she heard Delores saying as she neared the parlor.

"A most unpleasant day?" Adam repeated, and Kendall cringed at the raw anguish in his voice. "That is quite the understatement, Mother."

"Well, of course, it was more difficult for you," she amended, with little emotion.

Silence followed Delores' statement. Adam nearly ran into Kendall as he stalked from the room.

"Mother, he buried his wife today," Luke reprimanded her.

"Yes, I understand that, Luke. But Margo became completely unstable, dangerous to herself and others. Adam will realize that in time."

"Mother!" Avery sounded horrified.

Witnessing Delores' cold dismissal of Margo's death, Kendall was tempted to run back up the stairs. Delores had known Margo her entire life and had been her mother-in-law for years. Yet, instead of mourning her death, she credited it as an end to her problems. *Love has nothing to do with anything here.* She found herself more inclined to believe Luke's words every day, or at least to understand his certainty they were true.

"Avery, it is past time you grew up enough to get hold of your emotions. Margo's death is a horrid tragedy, yes. But in the end, it's for the best."

Righteous anger forced Kendall into the room.

"What is wrong with you?" she demanded of her mother-in-law. She went to Avery and wrapped an arm around her shoulder. "Your children are hurting, and all you can say is that Margo's death is a good thing?"

Delores stared at her coldly.

"You of all people should understand what I'm saying, Kendall. Several of your largest problems were buried today."

Since Kendall didn't trust herself to speak, she remained silent, hoping every bit of her contempt showed on her face.

"Maybe I shouldn't expect you to understand," Delores said after a moment. Her lips curled in disgust. "Your mother was ruled by her emotions, and although you obviously witnessed what little good it did her, you continue to let yourself be ruled by yours."

"That's enough, Mother," Luke said harshly.

Delores gave a nonchalant shrug.

"Of course it is."

Without another word or a backward glance, she walked from the room.

"I'm going up to check on Adam. You two should try to get some sleep," Luke told Kendall and Avery.

"He's right, Avery, you should try to get some sleep."

"I don't know if I can sleep or not."

Kendall hugged her tightly. "I think you'll be surprised just how tired you are."

"Sometimes I'm afraid I'll grow up to be just like my mother," Avery confided as she leaned her head against Kendall's shoulder.

Kendall smiled despite herself. She couldn't imagine Avery ever being able to contain all the emotion she possessed.

"I don't think so, sweetheart. Just remember that it's never a mistake to love people. It's never a mistake to feel anything."

Avery hugged her. "Do you think Adam is okay?"

"No. But I think he will be." She took Avery's hand in her own and pulled the girl to her feet, leading her out of the room toward the stairs.

"Kendall, could I see you, please?" Delores asked. She stood at the doorway of her office, and Kendall had no desire to follow her inside.

"I'm very tired, Delores, can't it wait until tomorrow?"

"No, it can't."

"Yes, Mother, it can," Luke said from the stairs. "My wife is coming to bed now. She is still recuperating from her injuries, and it has been an exhausting few days."

"How are you feeling?" Luke asked when they were in bed.

"I'll be okay. How is Adam?" She nestled close to him, her head on his chest.

"Not well. Of course, Mother's making it worse."

"Do you really think she believes what she says?"

"Yes. I know it's hard for you to understand, but she truly believes that giving in to emotion is a weakness."

"I don't know how to control my emotions," she confessed.

He kissed her on the forehead. "Thank God."

"I wonder if she's right, sometimes. What if my mother had used her head instead of her heart? Would our lives have been better?"

"Who knows? It seems to me that even through the bad times you knew your mother loved you."

"Yes, I guess I did."

"I never did."

"Oh, Luke," she murmured. "Of course, your mother loves you."

"I don't know if any of us ever knew we were loved. Mother cared for us. But we were raised knowing that The Grove and the Templeton name came first and foremost. Before us, before Dad, before anything."

"She just wanted you all to have the best."

"No, Kendall. Her devotion came before we were born. Of all of them, your mother's family, my mother's family, the Kendalls, the Martins, my father's family had the most money and power. He belonged to the most established family, while Mother's family was the least established. They were rich but hadn't been that way long. Her father made his money from good land investments and smart financial decisions. Dad's money was centuries old. He could trace his family all the way back to the Renaissance. Mother married him because he had more to offer than anyone else."

"That doesn't mean she didn't love you."

"I guess she loves us as much as she can love anyone."

"I never really thought about whether I was loved or not. Maybe that's a sign that I knew I was. I've only just begun to realize how much my mother must have loved me."

"God, Ken, your whole life was an act of love. Ours was just an assurance that Dad wouldn't leave her. Avery's was a total accident. Mother was devastated when she found out she was pregnant. Luckily, Dad wasn't. She was his princess from the moment she was born. I never knew if Mother's indulgence of Avery was because she adored her or because she didn't want to bother with her."

"What was Margo's life like, Luke? I mean, did she know she was loved?"

"I think so. Julianne spoiled her rotten, but she was an only child, so that was to be expected."

"What about our father? Did he love her?"

Luke touched her hair gently, his voice full of compassion. "Why do you want to do this?"

"Because I need to know. Was he a good father?"

"He was a good father to her. He loved her. But there was something missing in his relationship with Julianne. We all knew it, even as children. Sometimes, they seemed to love each other passionately. At other times, their hatred was a palpable thing."

"But they stayed married?"

"He didn't have a choice. After Thomas' father died, he inherited the Kendall estate. He squandered it on gambling and bad business deals, and he was flat broke within five years. After that, he was only rich because of his wife."

"So what happened to Margo?"

He seemed to be debating what to say. "Margo was there the day your parents died, Ken. She was supposed to be in school, but for some reason she came home. She's the one who found their bodies."

"She was there when it happened, wasn't she?" The screams echoed in Kendall's memory.

"No. I don't think so. She came home just after."

"But she screamed just after the gunshots. Not even a minute passed."

"How do you know?" There was no mistaking the concern in his voice.

"It was my sixteenth birthday. I was across the street, waiting for my father to come out of the house. I was finally going to speak to him."

With a groan of sympathy, he drew her close to him.

"When I think of how he hurt you, I can hardly blame your mother for what she did."

Kendall lightly ran her fingers across his chest.

"You know, when you're a child living on the fringes of society, you tend to focus more on what you don't have than on what you do. My mother made choices based on love, yes. But her last choice, the choice to kill my father and herself, how could that have anything at all to do with love? I don't understand how she gave up everything to raise me, loved him for years, but in one split second she could kill him and leave me all alone. It seems as if she had suddenly decided it was all a waste, as if neither her love for me nor her love for my father was worth it any longer."

"Maybe she felt it was an act of love. Look at you. She could never have given you the education you received after her death. How did you end up with Frank and Connie Howard, anyway?"

"I stayed with our neighbor, Mary Christopher, for a week or so before Frank and Connie showed up at the door. I had never seen them before, but I went to live with them that day. I was their ward through the Christian Children's Society. It was as simple as that."

"How little you knew." He paused momentarily before continuing, "Connie and your mother were cousins. Her mother and Louisa were sisters."

She couldn't believe it. Never once in all the years with Frank and Connie did they mention they were related.

Her mother definitely took many secrets to the grave, and Kendall wondered if she would ever unravel all of them. Haunted by Margo's words as well as her own shooting, she knew she had to try.

Although everyone else seemed to be certain Margo had shot her the day she escaped from the hospital, Kendall felt uneasy with that assumption. She didn't know who else would want her dead, but she needed to know if there was someone else out there who wanted her permanently removed. The longer she was here in this house, the more determined she became that Delores Templeton would not raise her child. If she wanted to stay alive long enough to raise him, she needed to know who wanted her dead and why.

Chapter Thirty-Four

A week later, Kendall stood on Frank and Connie Howard's porch. Connie's wide blue eyes stared at her through the screen door. For the first time, Kendall noticed how much they looked like her mother's.

"May I come in?" she asked when Connie continued to stare.

"Kendall? You look so different." Connie held open the door. "Yes, yes, come in. Wow. You look like you should attend Chadsworth instead of teach there."

Connie blushed furiously and tried to correct herself.

"I mean you don't teach there, of course. Not now." She motioned for Kendall to sit on the sofa. "What are you doing here?"

"I came to see you and Frank. Is he here?" She removed her hat and gloves, placing them beside her as she sat back on the sofa and crossed her legs.

"He should be down in a few minutes. He just finished mowing the grass. He's in the shower."

"Why didn't you ever tell me we were cousins?" Kendall didn't even try to couch the question between small talk.

Connie twisted her hands in her lap, and Kendall wondered why she seemed so jittery. Connie was often scatterbrained, but not usually nervous.

"I didn't think it was wise at the time. How did you find out?"

"My husband told me."

"Oh. Your husband! How wonderful! You found

him then?"

Kendall smiled and inclined her head slightly. "Of course I found him. Did you think I wouldn't?"

"Well, you know, there was talk. Especially with your mother being like she was." Connie's voice lowered to a stage whisper, and she blushed furiously.

Kendall took a deep breath, willing herself not to give in to the anger that shot through her.

"You'd be amazed to know just how like my mother I am, Connie," she said quietly.

Connie looked away, her face still aflame, her eyes worried.

"Kendall?" Frank said from the doorway before Connie could speak. "How are you? My goodness, you look beautiful. Where's the baby?"

She gave a bitter chuckle.

"Do you really care, Frank? For all you care, both of us could have starved to death. That would have been fine so long as you didn't have to stick your neck out."

"That's not fair, Kendall. I did stick my neck out for you. I got you that job. Connie and I took you in when no one else would have. You were lucky we came for you. At least it gave you some sort of past to be proud of."

"You're right. You and Connie did give me a home after my mother died, and you did get me a position at Chadsworth. But let me ask you something, Frank." She paused for a moment while he waited expectantly. "Why?"

He ran his hand across his head.

"Your mother came to us a few days before she died. She told us she was ill and said she didn't have much time left. She begged us to take care of you after her death. We agreed because she was Connie's cousin. She gave us five thousand dollars to help take care of you."

"Five thousand dollars! Where did my mother get that kind of money?"

"I don't know. I always thought Thomas might have given it to her."

"Douglas Martin gave it to her," Connie said calmly. She stood up and went to the writing desk in the hallway. She unlocked it and pulled out an envelope. "She gave me these in case I ever needed more. She said they were money in the bank."

She tossed it on the coffee table, and Kendall pulled the pictures from inside. Lydia and Douglas lost in a kiss. Lydia trying to walk away while Douglas held her arm and pulled her around to face him. Did anyone else notice the desolation on her mother's face? Lydia half dressed and pressed against a wall, as Douglas nuzzled her neck, and she looked into the distance with broken eyes.

Sadness welled up inside her, and Kendall quickly thrust them back in the envelope. "Did you ever show these to anyone?"

Connie shook her head. "No, of course not. I may not have agreed with the choices Lydia made, but she was family. I never wanted anyone to see her like that."

"Thank you," Kendall said in a trembling voice. She stood up, taking the pictures with her. Before she left, she needed one more answer. "Do you know who I married?"

Both of them looked away, and she had the sinking feeling that another secret was about to be dropped on her.

"We always knew who you married, or at least who you thought you married," Frank said.

"Delores came to us after your parents died," Connie added. "She was and still is on the board at Chadsworth. She promised that if we kept her informed of your whereabouts and well-being, she would help Frank get the principal's position at the school."

Kendall gasped. "Why?"

Connie shrugged. "I don't know. I think for some reason she set her sights on you as a wife for her son."

They were silent for a moment before Connie offered more information.

"She was always a bit jealous of Lydia and Julianne. They were friends forever. Delores was somewhat new. Their families were old money, and Delores' father was a self-made millionaire. They were so graceful and beautiful. Delores was just a tad crass and not quite as pretty. They epitomized all she wanted to achieve. Maybe she wanted to give that epitome to her sons."

Kendall stood again, feeling more than a little dazed. "I need to leave."

"Ken, I'm really sorry for the way everything turned out," Frank said, and she knew he was thinking of the last time they saw each other. "I knew you'd be taken care of."

****

Kendall walked slowly past the last house she and her mother had lived in. She could still feel the swell of hope that beat in her chest when she'd kissed her mother good-bye and walked down those rickety steps for the last time. She rarely kissed her mother, but that day she was so excited, so buoyant, she wanted to impart just a little of that hopefulness to her mother's tired frame. So she kissed her on the cheek and hurried down the steps, hoping beyond hope that this was the day her life would change.

Mary Christopher's house was directly across from theirs, and she looked at it now. Other than having recently been whitewashed, it looked exactly the same. Barefoot children still bounded across the yard chasing each other and a litter of mixed-breed pups. As always, Mary sat watching the mayhem from an old cane-back rocking chair on the sagging porch.

The gate squeaked on its hinges, and Mary looked toward the noise, shading her eyes against the setting sun.

"Lord have mercy, is that you, Kendall?" she cried, lumbering to her feet.

"Yes, ma'am," Kendall said.

No other words were needed as Kendall threw herself into the woman's open arms. Mary was heavier now, and her hair was completely gray, but she still felt as comforting as she had after Lydia's death.

"I heard you were married," Mary said, standing back and surveying Kendall's black-and-red polka-dotted dress and matching shoes. "It looks like you did good for yourself."

"I had a baby, too," Kendall told her.

"I heard that, too. Is he with you?"

"No. He's at home."

"Who is that, Gram?" a tall blond boy asked. He looked to be about ten but eyed Kendall with a suspicion beyond his years.

"She's a friend, Jess. Now, you just go back out and play with the others."

Kendall watched him lope into the yard. He moved just like his father.

"That one's Layton's, as if you can't tell. The little blonde girl, too. The others are all Amelia's. Beth's expecting one in March, and Carry's got three at home with the chicken pox. I told her she should bring 'em on over and expose 'em all. Best to get it over with when they're young, but she's afraid Beth will catch it."

Kendall surveyed the children, thinking of her childhood playmates. After her husband died, Mary had raised them all alone right here in this ramshackle wooden house. At times, they barely had enough to feed all of them, but they loved each other fiercely. From the day Kendall and her mother moved into the shack across the street, they were welcomed into their midst.

"I'll be right out," Mary excused herself.

In a moment, she returned carrying two bottled sodas. She proudly held one out to Kendall.

"Feel how cold that is? Layton bought me a refrigerator for Christmas. Amazing, ain't it? Layton's managing the supermarket now. He's done real good for himself, married a good girl from across town. My girls have done good, too. Beth's a receptionist for a doctor downtown. Carry don't work. Her husband Guy owns his own car lot, so they've got plenty. Amelia writes magazine articles sometimes. Her husband works out at the paper mill."

"I'm so happy for them."

Mary beamed at her.

"You were always a good girl, Kendall." Mary studied her worriedly. "So, what are you doing visiting the past?"

"The past keeps visiting me, so I thought I'd pay it back."

"Ah," Mary breathed knowingly and motioned for Kendall to sit in the empty rocker. "Your mama's secrets are finally catching up, eh?"

"Did you know her secrets?"

"I knew some of 'em. But your mama had her share and more. I don't know if anyone ever knew 'em all."

"Did you know where she came from?"

"She told me. Of course, any fool could see she didn't come from around here. She was always different from the rest of us. Even at the end, after years of being here and even worse places, she still moved different, talked different. Her polish was rusted by then, but it was still there if you looked for it." Mary shook her head sadly. "She was a sweet, loving girl, and no one could help but like her. She kept a lot to herself, but after a while she shared some of her secrets with me."

"I met her parents. They're sorry for the way they treated her."

"They should be."

"They've been very kind to me. I like them."

"If you're wondering if you're disrespecting your mama's memory by that, then I'll tell you what she would if she were here. They're good people who made a bad mistake. She loved them until the day she died, and she never seemed to blame them for what they did to her. She understood it more than I did."

"Did you know my father?"

"No, and I thank God for that, because I don't know what I'd have said or done to him if I ever met him. He caused your poor mama more misery than anyone should have to suffer. He strung her along for years."

"It didn't end after he married?"

"Oh, I think it ended for about five years after you were born. Then he found her, and it started back up again. He'd let her be for a while. She wouldn't hear a thing for months, sometimes years, and then he'd call. And no matter how long it was, she ran to him like no time had passed at all."

"Do you think they were seeing each other again before they died?"

"Oh, I know it. She came to me a few months before and said a gentleman had asked her to marry him. One of the boys she knew way back before she came here. He wanted to take care of both of you. She said she could never love him like she loved your daddy, but I think she was real tempted. She was getting older and so were you. She asked for my advice, and I told her she should marry the one who was asking and forget the one who wasn't. Love don't do to people what your daddy did to her."

"Do you know who asked her?"

"No, she didn't tell me. I didn't know none of her gentlemen friends. I knew the men she ran with from here. Like Marty. He'd have married her, too, and taken fine care of her. Not like the other, of course, but good as he was able. But when he asked, you were still young and so was she. She still had hopes that everything would turn out right for her and your daddy."

"I guess she said no to getting married."

"Oh, no! She agreed to marry her gentleman friend. He gave her a diamond ring you wouldn't believe. None of us had ever seen the likes of it. But then one day she came to me crying. Your daddy had called. He heard she was getting married. She said he was so upset, he told her to give the ring back and break off the engagement. He promised he would leave his wife and marry her."

"And she believed him." Kendall's heart broke for her mother.

"Of course. She went to the other man that day and gave him back his ring. Then she started seeing your daddy again. That lasted about six weeks and he was off again, gone off for two months with his wife and daughter. He didn't even tell her he was leaving."

Mary looked at her sadly. "She wasn't the same after that. It seemed like she finally realized it wasn't ever going to change. Her heart was broken, and I think that's what made her do what she did."

"Did you know she was going to do it?"

Mary shook her head. "I never dreamed it, or I would have tried to stop her. I saw you leave that morning, all dressed up. I knew it was your birthday, and I knew exactly where you was going. She did, too, I guess. She stood on the steps while you got on the bus. When she came back out of the house a little bit later, she was fixed up pretty as a picture. She came by and spoke to me and the girls. I won't ever forget how she looked. I guess she'd made up her mind and wasn't worried anymore. She looked ten years younger and more at peace than I'd ever seen her. She had on that big old red ring of his. Do you remember it?"

Kendall nodded. She'd looked for it after her mother died, but she never found it. She assumed Lydia had pawned it at some point. Had she been wrong? Was her mother wearing it the day she died?

"Gram!" one of the children in the yard wailed, and Mary pushed herself up from the chair. She waddled toward the spot where the wailer, his brother, and his cousin were in a pile, pummeling each other. Kendall smiled to herself when she realized Layton's daughter was getting the best of both of her male cousins.

"You young'uns better cut it out right now," Mary scolded. "Can't you see we've got company?"

When they continued their squabble, Mary got hold of two of them and pulled them up by their shirts with practiced ease. The third followed, based solely on the glare Mary leveled at her.

"It was his fault!" one of the boys cried.

"No, it was not! It was yours!"

Mary's eyes rolled merrily at Kendall.

"I've got to be going, Mary," Kendall said. "My own family is probably wondering if I've gotten lost."

"You come back anytime. You're always welcome here." Mary reached past the still quarreling children and gave Kendall a hug. "You remember that no matter what else you find out about your mama, she loved you. That's one thing that she never kept a secret."

****

It was well after dark when Juan pulled the car

to a stop in front of the house, and Kendall could see Luke's silhouette at the parlor window. He moved away quickly, meeting her just inside the door.

"Where in the hell have you been?" he yelled.

"Jacksonville. I told you I was going." She removed her gloves and hat, bristling at his demanding question and obvious anger.

"You didn't tell me you were going to be gone all day and half the night."

A hint of fear lingered in his voice, and her resentment evaporated as she realized he was more worried than angry. She leaned toward him, her lips meeting his in a soft, sweet kiss before she spoke again.

"I took the bus, Luke. It takes a while to get there and back. I told Juan what time he should be at the station to pick me up. You should have asked him. He knew I'd be gone this late."

"He did try to tell me, but I wouldn't listen and sent him to the station hours ago," Luke admitted sheepishly. "Did you have a nice trip?"

"Yes. After I saw Frank and Connie, I stopped to visit my mother's friend, Mary Christopher."

"What on earth were you doing there?" Delores entered the room at that moment, her voice mirroring the horror on her face.

"I was visiting old friends."

Though not quite ready to confront Delores with what she'd learned today, she had certainly done all the cowering she intended to do as far as her mother-in-law was concerned.

"It's best if you forget those years, Kendall. You have a new life now, a new family, and new friends. Those old ones can't offer you a thing."

"Forgetting the past doesn't make it untrue, Delores," she snapped.

Delores stepped back, a hand on her chest. "There's no reason for you to speak to me in that tone, my dear. I've done more for you than any of those people ever could."

"Then you shouldn't feel so threatened by my visiting them." She turned back to Luke. "I'm going to see Brady and get ready for bed. It was a long day, and I'm quite tired."

She kissed Luke gently on the cheek, and he turned his head, catching her mouth with his.

"I'll be up in a few minutes," he promised softly, sending a tremor of excitement through her.

She walked past his mother without another word.

"Luke, you've got to do something about her."

"That's funny, Mother, you used to tell Adam the same thing."

"Luke!" Delores cried, but his only answer was the sound of his footsteps moving away from her.

Kendall smiled to herself at the sound of the back door slamming behind him.

"I hope you're happy!" Delores called up to her. "You've turned both my sons against me."

Kendall turned and faced her. "You didn't need my help to do that."

Delores said nothing else as Kendall continued up the stairs and went into the nursery.

She ran a hand over Brady's soft hair.

"He's gorgeous," Adam said from the rocking chair in the corner, making her jump.

"Oh, Adam, you scared me."

"Sorry."

"How are you?" she asked, feeling stupid. How would he be? His wife had been dead only a few weeks.

"I'll be okay, I guess." He shrugged, but then his face crumpled. "I miss her."

"I know you do," Kendall said.

"How can you be so kind to me after what I did to you?"

She shrugged. "I care about you. I always will. You're my brother-in-law now."

"Mother's right. You are ruled by emotions."

"Maybe, but I don't think that's a bad thing. At the end of the day, I just don't want anyone I've known to doubt how I felt about them."

He came to stand beside the crib with her.

"I want to claim him as mine."

"Absolutely not." Kendall was surprised how adamant she now felt about that.

"I knew you'd say that. I couldn't do that to him or to Luke. Regardless of what you think of me, I'm not a monster. I couldn't put Luke through that ridicule, and I certainly couldn't open Brady up to it."

"Thank you."

"You're welcome."

Luke came to stand on the other side of her, and the three of them stared down at the baby they shared.

"You'll never be sorry you let him be mine," Luke said quietly to his brother.

"If I thought otherwise for a moment, I'd claim him. But you and Kendall will do right by him, and I couldn't ask for more. Lord knows I'm not fit to be a parent."

Kendall swallowed back her tears. It had proven to be an emotional day, and she was ready for it to end. She leaned closer to Luke, and he wrapped an arm around her.

"Good night," Luke said, and patted Adam's shoulder before leading Kendall down the hall to their bedroom.

As if sensing her fragile mood, Luke's kisses were slow and gentle, his lovemaking a luxurious adoration that left her completely spent and relaxed.

When he lay beside her afterward, his hand stroking her hair gently, he asked her about her trip.

"Let's not talk tonight," she whispered. "Let's just *be*."

Without a word, his mouth covered hers again, coaxing her back into an easy passion.

****

The next day, she woke early, the euphoria of the night before making her that much more determined to find the answers she needed to put the past to rest. She slipped from their bed, careful not to wake Luke, and started a bath.

She no longer had a doubt in her mind that she wanted to spend the rest of her life with Luke. But they couldn't possibly move ahead until she linked all her mother's secrets together.

As if a dam had broken, the secrets were suddenly being revealed at such a fast pace she barely comprehended them all.

With a sigh, she slipped into the warm, lavender-scented bath water and leaned her head back. As her body relaxed, she closed her eyes and went through everything she'd learned about her parents, piece by piece.

Obviously, Lydia kept in touch with the men, if not the women, she'd known as a girl, and at some point, she and Thomas began to see each other in an erratically pathetic attempt at a relationship. Kendall didn't doubt what Mary told her. She knew the first time she saw her father that Lydia loved him deeply and would do whatever he asked, even if it meant a lifetime of misery.

She hadn't thought of her mother's ring for years. It was a man's ring, a large ruby with two small diamonds on each side. When Kendall was small, her mother had sometimes let her slip it on her own finger. Kendall loved the weight of it on her tiny hand. But as the years passed, the ring went from her mother's finger to a chain around her neck. As far as Kendall knew, Lydia never took it off or put it away. She only moved it out of sight.

****

"Mama, can I wear your forever ring?"

Lydia slid the ring onto Kendall's finger.

"Tell me about it, Mama." Kendall begged. She'd heard the story a dozen times, but still loved it.

"Once long ago, there was a princess, and she was in love with the most handsome prince in the world."

"And he gave her the forever ring?"

"Yes, Ken. He gave her the ring, and he promised he would always, always love her. He knew they had to wait to get married, so he asked her to promise him that she would wait. He put the ring on her finger and she promised him she would wait however long she had to before she was his wife. Even if that meant forever."

"And then what happened?"

Lydia looked away, catching her lip between her teeth, and Kendall held her breath.

"They both lived happily ever after," her mother said, and only now did the thickness in her voice register with Kendall.

****

Not old enough then to understand her mother's heartache, she never realized exactly where the lies left off and the truth began. As she got older, her questions came more frequently, and maybe her mother hoped hiding the ring against her heart would shield her from them. Maybe it did. Kendall eventually lost interest in the fairy tales her mother spun and gave up asking questions at all.

Now, Mary swore the ring was on her mother's finger the day she died. It didn't make sense that she would take it off before killing herself. Unless she gave it back to Thomas.

She hated the thought of confronting Julianne. It seemed cruel to ask her to dig up more painful memories at such a time. Besides, she couldn't imagine Julianne being willing to help her. The woman hated her and had every reason to feel that way.

Would Douglas know? He was Julianne's brother. It was probable that he was with her during the days following Thomas' death.

Although begging Avery to tell her where Douglas Martin lived led to a barrage of questions she refused to answer, Kendall was soon on her way to the car, his address in hand.

A few miles away from The Grove, Juan pulled to the side of the road.

"What are you doing?" she asked him.

"Mr. Luke is behind us," Juan said. "I think he wants me to stop."

She turned and looked out the rear window. Luke was behind them, motioning for them to pull over. With an aggravated growl, she faced forward while Juan got out.

"What are you doing?" she demanded when he slid behind the wheel.

"I'm driving." He started the car, but didn't pull away.

"What about your truck?"

"Juan's taking it home.

"What is wrong with you?"

"If you're hell-bent on visiting everyone who ever knew your mother, then I intend to be with you."

"I don't need you to be with me, Luke. I just have some questions."

He swiveled his body to look at her. "Can you really be so naïve that you don't realize what a dangerous game you're playing?"

She shrugged, and looked out the side window.

"So, where are you headed right now?" he asked.

"I was going to see Douglas Martin. I thought

maybe he would know if a ring was given to Thomas' family." She quickly filled him in on what Mary had told her and what the ring had meant to her mother.

"So, you were just going to go to his house, knock on his door and ask him that?"

"Yes."

"And what if he is the person who shot you?"

"Why would he be?" She thought of the pictures Connie had shown her. Had her mother been blackmailing Doug? Was that where she got the money she left behind? She waited for Luke's answer.

Luke shrugged. "I don't know, but at this point we can't rule anyone out."

"I'm going to see him, Luke. If you don't want to go, get out of the car. If you do want to go, drive."

"I could drive you right back to the house and leave you there," he observed.

"You couldn't keep me there forever. Eventually I would sneak away while you weren't looking." She leaned forward and placed a beseeching hand on his arm. "I need this, Luke. I need to know everything about my mother. I need to know why she did what she did."

He studied her while he ran his fingers through her hair. His lips touched hers gently, then more hungrily.

"I'm worried about you."

He kissed her once more before turning again to the steering wheel. She breathed a sigh of relief when he finally pulled back onto the road and headed toward Douglas Martin's house.

Douglas himself answered the door and, looking more than a little surprised, showed them in.

"What can I do for you, Luke?" he asked when they were seated in the parlor.

"I'm here with my wife, Doug. She's the one with the questions."

Douglas turned his bright blue gaze on her.

"I guess I should thank you for not taking your questions to my sister. She's in no shape to have to answer them."

Kendall inclined her head slightly in silent acknowledgement.

"Well, before we embark on our journey down memory lane, what say we have a drink? Luke? Kendall?"

Without waiting for an answer, he went to the bar in the corner and pulled out three glasses. His and Luke's were the same, but he handed a different one to Kendall, who studied it dubiously. He chuckled.

"Never had a mixed drink, have you?"

"No." She sipped it cautiously and gasped. "Oh, my goodness."

"Bad or good?" He watched her take another experimental sip.

"Delicious," she said with a blush.

"That was your mother's favorite." He spoke softly, and took a long sip of his own drink.

"You saw her after I was born?"

"Oh, yes. I saw her plenty after you were born. I loved your mother. And I hated Thomas and Julianne for what they did to her."

Kendall lifted the glass to her mouth, letting the slow burn of the alcohol work its way into her belly. She already felt herself relaxing and suddenly understood why her mother dulled her senses with liquor.

"You look so much like her it's unnerving."

"Did she love you?"

"Of course not. She only loved Thomas. She cared for me, I guess. She let me come around, and she slept with me when I asked, but she certainly didn't love me."

Kendall remembered Mary's words. "Did you

ask her to marry you?"

"At least a dozen times over the years. She always said no. Then one day she surprised the hell out of me. I asked, and she said yes."

"You were willing to marry her even though she didn't love you?"

"I thought I could love her enough for both of us. I thought if I was a good enough husband to her and a good enough father to you, eventually she would learn to love me. If not, that was okay. We had been friends for a long time, and our lovemaking was fine without the passion she felt for Thomas."

"But you didn't marry her," she said.

"No, I didn't. She chose Thomas again, of course. Even though she could only have bits and pieces of him, she chose that over having all of me."

"I'm sorry," she said sympathetically.

He shrugged, but she could see the sadness in his eyes.

"It was a long time ago. Lynette and I were married by the time your parents died. I was in New York City when it happened."

Their eyes met, and his widened just a bit, as if he could tell she knew the truth and was surprised by it.

"Were you?" she asked. She had no idea why he lied, but she recognized the unease that clouded his eyes once the surprise dissipated.

"I hurried home as soon as I heard the news."

"Do you know if Julianne was given any of Thomas' personal effects?"

"Yes, of course. I was with her when the officer gave them to her. Why?"

"My mother always wore a ruby ring, and it wasn't returned to me. I wondered if it was given to Julianne by mistake."

"It was Thomas' ring," he stated with certainty.

"Then it was given to her?" Relief snaked

through her.

"No, I don't remember seeing it with his wallet and other things. But I remember it clearly. She wore it on a chain around her neck. She never took it off."

His voice trailed away, still thick with emotion, and she instinctively knew what he didn't say. Her mother made love to other men, including him, with Thomas' ring around her neck. Even in her most intimate moments, Thomas was always there, closest to her heart.

"Did you give my mother five thousand dollars just before she died?"

He almost choked on his drink. Luke, too, made a sound of surprise. Douglas stood up, a fake smile pasted on his face.

"Well, I must say, it's been a lovely visit, Kendall, Luke, but Lynette should be home any minute, and I really don't want to explain to her what you were doing here."

"Does she know who I am?"

"Everyone knows who you are, Kendall. She never knew your mother, but she's my wife, so she knows our family history. She knows about Thomas and your mother."

"Does she know about you and my mother?"

The smile slipped from his face, and he took a step toward her.

"No, and she won't find out."

Luke cleared his throat and moved closer to her.

"Is that a threat?" he asked quietly.

"Of course not, Luke. I just want your wife to realize that she's playing with people's lives."

"She realizes it, Douglas. It's her life, too."

Luke's hand closed around her arm, and he led her away.

"Thank you," she said sincerely to Douglas at the door. "I know that this has been a painful conversation for you, and I'm sorry."

He looked at her solemnly. "Your coming on the scene set things back in motion. Now, they just have to play out to the bitter end. Nothing good can come of it."

"What does that mean?" she asked, but he shook his head and closed the door.

A cacophony of questions played in her head on the ride home, but she was sure of two things. Douglas Martin loved her mother, and he was hiding something that scared the hell out of him.

Why would he allow her mother to blackmail him? Would Lynette care who he loved before their marriage? Or was it more an emotional blackmail, a reminder of his feelings for her?

What did he say? *Your coming on the scene set things back in motion.* That seemed to mean that they were in motion before. When? Why did her coming make them start again? And if that was so, why did Delores purposely manipulate her life to get her here?

She had yet to tell Luke what she'd learned about his mother. She tried to tell herself it was because she just hadn't found the time, but she couldn't deny it was mainly because she feared he already knew, or worse, helped her.

Chapter Thirty-Five

The clock in the hall struck two o'clock in the morning as Kendall walked the floor with Brady. He was teething, and so far nothing she tried soothed him.

"You should rub some brandy on his gums," Adam said from the doorway. He looked haggard, and his eyes were red-rimmed and swollen.

"Will that hurt him?" Kendall asked.

"I wouldn't advise it if it would hurt him," he snapped in an injured tone.

"I know. I'm sorry. I'm so tired, I'm not thinking clearly. Did we wake you?"

"No, I can't sleep. I've barely slept since Margo died." His voice cracked, and he motioned toward the hall. "I'll go down and get the brandy."

"We'll go with you. We could use the change of scenery. I've been trying to stay in here in hopes of not waking the household."

"If Luke was going to wake up, he'd already be awake. Mother takes sleeping pills, so she's dead to the world. And Avery snuck out of the house around midnight."

"Shouldn't you have stopped her?" She followed him down the stairs, Brady whimpering on her hip.

"Nah, she'll be fine. She told me where she was going, and who she was going with. The Carnes boy picked her up out on the driveway."

"That's not sneaking out."

"No, but it makes it seem like it to her. She likes to pretend Mother cares what she does."

Kendall was surprised at his perception. Adam

rarely showed what she believed was his real personality. From what Rebecca and Avery had told her, he kept it well hidden. She wondered now if his insistence on appearing the sometimes detached, sometimes belligerent playboy was an act he'd perfected to garner his mother's attention.

At Chadsworth, she had taught girls who acted out just to get their parents there, to get some reaction from a mother or father with too many irons in the fire to pay much attention to the child. Then there were the girls who excelled at their studies, never misbehaved, were obedient to a fault, and never got the acknowledgement they longed for from their parents. It had broken her heart to watch them wait so patiently for something they were never going to have. Delores Templeton seemed to have created one of each type of child.

Kendall went into the living room, and Adam followed with the brandy, which he placed on the table.

"I'll be right back." When he came back, he carried a handful of cotton swabs. He carefully poured brandy in the bottle lid and dabbed the cotton swab in it.

"Here you go, big man," he said as he popped it into Brady's mouth, making sure it touched the part of his gums where the tooth was ready to emerge.

Brady turned his head away grumpily, before curiosity got the best of him and he took the swab from Adam's hand. He studied it before sticking it back in his mouth. Kendall watched closely, fearing he would swallow the whole thing. He held it up to her mouth, and she laughed softly.

"No, thank you. Mommy doesn't want any. Put it in your mouth." She felt Adam studying them, and she looked at him with a smile.

"I never dreamed it would all turn out this way," Adam said, a bemused expression on his face.

"What way?" she asked, making smacking noises as if she were eating the swab as Brady touched it to her lips.

"You being here. Brady. You married to Luke."

"It turned out better than you and your mother expected, didn't it?"

She looked down at Brady, whose eyes were already beginning to droop. He held the swab firmly in his hand as he moved up and laid his head on her shoulder.

"How did you know?" Adam asked, not bothering to deny it.

"I visited Connie and Frank Howard. They told me your mother contacted them after they took me in. I know that you found me on purpose."

"It was a mistake, Kendall. I shouldn't have gone along with it."

Brady slept soundly on her shoulder now, and she kissed his cheek. How could she regret anything? If Adam had never come into her life, she wouldn't have this precious child. She wouldn't have Luke. She wouldn't even know what she was missing.

"I need to know why, Adam."

"You would have to ask my mother. I've never been a hundred percent clear on her motives. I never could tell if it was money, jealousy, or just plain craziness. All she ever told me was to find you, tell you I was Luke, which I never did, and marry you. I was to come back here, and she would take care of the rest. She never gave me a reason."

Too tired to push him for his own reasons, Kendall stood up carefully, adjusting Brady as she did. "I better get him into bed. Maybe he'll be able to sleep. Thank you."

"No problem," he said, grabbing the liquor and swabs and following her out of the room.

She placed Brady gently in his crib and covered

him. Adam set everything he carried on a chest of drawers. He kissed her softly on the cheek.

"It's hard to regret bringing you here."

"I was thinking the same thing. I almost feel like thanking you when I think about it. I can't imagine my life without Brady and Luke."

He smiled. "You and Luke were made for each other."

"Good night, Adam," she said as she flipped out the light, casting the nursery in the pale glow of the nightlight on the bookshelf.

His hand trembled slightly as he touched her arm, and she wished she could discern the emotions tinting his softly spoken admonition.

"Take Luke with you when you question Mother."

****

When she slid into bed beside Luke, he wrapped his arms around her and pulled her against him.

"Is everything okay?" he mumbled.

"It's fine."

"Mmm," he said as he nuzzled her hair sleepily.

As had become her habit, Kendall found it more difficult to drift off to sleep. When she did, she slept fitfully, worried she might not hear Brady if he began to cry and haunted by all she had learned over the last few days.

Just before dawn, sleep finally claimed her, but the shrill ring of the telephone jarred her awake a few hours later. She reached for it on the second ring.

"Tell me what you were doing there," Douglas Martin insisted before she could say anything.

Kendall covered the mouthpiece, hoping her breathing wasn't heard in the silence that met his demand. She could almost feel his impatience coming through the line.

After what seemed an eternity, Delores spoke.

"The hospital called early, before anyone else was up. As soon as I heard, I knew exactly where she was. She's been insisting on discussing her father's death since Kendall arrived in this house. I knew she'd go back there eventually. She had barely gotten into the house when I arrived. As soon as she heard me, she ran."

"It's a shame she didn't see that car."

"I'm surprised you feel that way, Douglas."

The conversation came to an abrupt end, and Kendall quickly replaced the receiver.

"Are you okay?" Luke asked from the bathroom door. A towel was wrapped around his waist, and his hair was damp from the shower.

"Yes, I'm fine."

"Who was on the phone?"

"It was for your mother. She picked it up downstairs."

"I checked on Brady before I got in the shower. He was still asleep. I guessed that meant he exhausted himself last night."

"He exhausted me, too."

"I'm very worried about him," he warned solemnly.

"Why?"

He grinned.

"I think he has a drinking problem. There's a bottle of brandy in the nursery."

She laughed. "I put some on his gums to quiet him. It worked like a charm."

He sat down next to her on the bed, his eyes roaming over her bare shoulders and the pale skin visible above her bias-cut nightgown.

"You look beautiful this morning."

She laughed. "Oh, I'm sure I do. I was up half the night."

"You do." His finger traced the line of her collarbone, stopping just short of the silk straps of her gown, and the smoldering fire in his gray eyes sent her pulse skittering beneath her skin.

"I've got to get dressed, Luke."

He sighed heavily and stood up.

"Yes, I suppose we both do. Who are you going to harass today?" he teased.

"I might give everyone a break today."

He looked at her skeptically. "Well, if you change your mind, I expect you to find me."

"Where will you be?"

"I'll be around. Josef and I will be working on the gazebo Mother wants at the other end of the lake."

****

Kendall let Brady attempt to feed himself while she ate her own breakfast. She intended to find Delores the moment they were done.

"Good morning," Avery sang as she came into the room.

"Did you enjoy yourself last night?" Kendall asked, and the girl's face flushed.

"How did you know?"

"I was up with Brady." She didn't want Avery to think she couldn't trust Adam. The child needed someone she could trust.

"Oh. Yes, I had a good time. We met everyone down by the river."

"You need to be careful. Don't do anything foolish."

"I'm not foolish, Kendall. I won't do anything dangerous or wrong."

"That's what everyone says."

"Oh, fiddle. I don't want to argue with you this morning."

Brady banged a toy on the high chair, smiling broadly at Avery.

"Hey, kiddo," Avery said, bending down and giving his messy face a kiss. "He looks like he's feeling better this morning. He was in a bad mood yesterday."

"He's teething. He was up most of the night."

"Do you want me to take him for a walk?" Avery asked.

"He needs to be cleaned up first."

"I'll clean him up. He's so funny in the bathtub now. He splashes like crazy."

"Wear your raincoat or you'll be as wet as he is," Kendall warned. "His stroller is in the kitchen."

As soon as the door closed behind Avery and Brady, Kendall hurried to Delores' office. Her mother-in-law didn't look a bit surprised when Kendall walked in. She actually looked as if she expected her.

"I hear you've had quite the time playing amateur detective the past few days," Delores informed her. "I suppose you have questions?"

"Yes."

"So, what did they tell you?" She leaned back in her chair, folding her hands carefully in her lap.

"Your husband followed my mother," Kendall blurted out. It wasn't at all what she'd intended to say first.

"Oh, Kendall, darling, Leon did much more than follow your mother. I believe he screwed her every chance he got."

Taken aback by the venom in Delores' voice, Kendall was even more disturbed by the fact that Delores hadn't moved a muscle. Her hands were still folded demurely, her face as unlined as ever. It was as if the vitriolic words came from someone else.

"Why did he take so many pictures of her?"

"Thomas asked him to. Thomas couldn't let their relationship go. I don't know why. Even after she became nothing, he acted as if she was everything."

"Did you help Frank Howard get his position at Chadsworth in return for information on me?"

"Yes."

"Why?"

"I wanted to prepare you." She offered no further explanation, and Kendall stood up and began to pace the floor.

"For what?"

"To marry Luke."

"What?" Her heart skipped a beat.

"I was preparing you to marry Luke."

"Did he know that?" She prayed silently that he hadn't.

"Of course not. Luke would never have cooperated with such a plan."

"Adam knew," Kendall stated.

"Yes."

"Did he know about Brady?"

"No. He knew I wanted you here. He was supposed to locate you, court you, and marry you as Luke. After a few months, he'd send for you. By that time, your memory of his face would have been hazy enough for you to think Luke was the man you married."

"And you thought Luke would go along with me just showing up as his wife?"

"Luke would do what I told him was best for us. He is very loyal. Besides which, he always wants to make everything right. He would have stayed married to you out of some sense of justice because of what Adam and I did." Cold steel gray eyes gleamed with maliciousness. "Of course, I'm sure you've realized that about him by now."

Kendall chose to ignore the barbed reminder of why Luke married her.

"So, Adam was to find me, trick me into marrying his brother? Then what?"

"Then, Adam would be married to Margo, Julianne and Thomas' daughter, and Luke would be married to you, Lydia and Thomas' daughter."

If that was all she hoped to accomplish, Delores was obviously insane. Who would go to such measures to assure her son married her friend's child? Kendall listened carefully as Delores continued talking.

"It's all a moot point though, isn't it? Adam flubbed up the deal and let you know his real name, so you weren't very well going to come here looking for Luke. To be honest, I wasn't even sure you'd come looking for Adam once he abandoned you."

"But you made sure I couldn't go back to Chadsworth, didn't you?"

Delores shrugged in answer to Kendall's question. "If it's any consolation, Adam never knew about the baby. I could tell he had feelings for you. Luke and Avery always bucked against my demands, but Adam always saw the benefits of what I said. He could see more easily than the others that some things were worth going against his feelings. But when he came back from Jacksonville, he was different. He was torn between you and Margo. He actually told me he wanted to leave Margo and marry you. I threatened to disown him, and, for a moment, I could see that he actually thought about going through with it anyway. But in the end he agreed that he was better off here. I began to watch the mail for your letters. I intercepted the letter in which you told him you were pregnant. After that, I burned them all. I knew eventually you would come looking for him. Having lived without a father, you would think it imperative for your child to have one."

"I still don't understand why you chose me."

"I chose you simply because of who your parents were."

She decided to try another line of questioning.

"Did you ever talk to my mother after she left home?"

"Never," Delores said with disdain.

"But you stayed in contact with my grandparents?"

"Yes."

"How do you know your husband was with my mother?"

Delores shrugged, "He was giving her money. He swore it was only a gift because he cared for her. He said it wasn't payment for sexual favors, but I never believed him. He said we could afford to help her. That she needed it. He felt sorry for her."

"I don't remember ever seeing them together," Kendall lied.

"Yes, you do." Delores took out a stack of photographs and slid them toward her. "You were there that day."

She gazed at them, remembering how beautiful her mother had looked, how she had asked Lydia if the man could be her daddy.

"Leon said he took them to try to help her get a job as a model. He wanted to show them to Dave Houston, Rebecca's father. Leon felt sure that he could connect her to the right people."

"Why didn't he?" Kendall asked.

"Because the last thing I wanted was a whore feeling that she was indebted to my husband." Delores' hands were still, but Kendall could see the whiteness around her knuckles. "I burned the pictures and told him I destroyed the negatives. Of course, I had a copy made for my own file."

"File?"

"Don't act like you don't know what I'm talking about, Kendall. I can tell you've looked through my file on you."

"Those weren't in there," Kendall said, her eyes meeting Delores'.

"Of course not. They were really nothing about you. I kept these in my file on Leon."

Kendall watched in fascination as Delores stuck

them into a file. She kept a file on her own husband?

"Kendall, I can understand that you aren't happy about how I got you here. You feel you were tricked and manipulated. But once you get over that, you'll thank me. You'll have a much better life as Luke's wife than any you could have created on your own."

"That choice should have been mine, Delores."

"It was, dear. I distinctly remember giving you the choice."

"You used my son as a bargaining tool."

Delores let loose a harsh, ugly-sounding laugh. "I couldn't have done that if some part of you weren't tempted by this." She waved her hand around her. "If it were totally repugnant to you, you'd have told me to go to hell and walked away."

"You and your son made perfectly sure that wasn't an option. I had no place to go and no money."

"Well, yes, I suppose that is true, to an extent," Delores agreed without remorse. "But think of your mother, Kendall. The choices each of you were given were basically the same. She could have improved both your life and her own if she had married Douglas. But she wouldn't. She held out for a dream that was never going to come true. Just look where that got her."

Kendall spoke without thinking, her voice rising in anger and frustration as she voiced a growing suspicion. "It got her murdered."

Delores remained haughtily composed as she stood up from the desk and walked to the door. "This conversation is over. We won't speak of it again. Do you understand me?"

"Perfectly," Kendall said and left the room.

Kendall rushed up the stairs and into her room, sinking onto the bed before her legs could give out. Even though Delores had never raised her voice, never shown the slightest emotion through most of their conversation, Kendall knew it had disturbed her. Kendall was still surprised at her own veiled accusation and even more surprised at how thoroughly she believed Delores capable of murder.

Luke burst into the room, out of breath and flushed.

"What's wrong?" she cried, her mind conjuring up several horrible scenarios.

"Mother sent Cora for me. She said you were hysterical, and she was worried about you."

"Worried about me?" Kendall repeated dubiously.

"She said you accused her of all sorts of atrocious things. I've never seen Mother so upset. What did you say to her?"

"Oh, for goodness' sake, Luke. I didn't say anything that upset her that badly. When I left her office, she was fine."

"Did you accuse her of murdering your mother?"

"No."

"Did you accuse her of anything else?"

"Yes."

"I need more than one-word answers, Kendall."

"Okay. Fine."

An exasperated sigh met her answer.

"What did you accuse her of?"

"Manipulating my life so that I would show up here, broke and desperate enough to marry you. She wanted Adam to marry me as you, so that when I got here, we'd already be married. She admitted it. If you don't believe me, just ask Adam. He was in on it too."

"Don't worry, I will," he promised angrily.

"Adam told me to make sure I took you with me to talk to your mother. Now I know why."

"I wish you had told me you intended to talk to her today. I would have gone with you. I could have helped straighten out what is obviously a misunderstanding."

Her temper skyrocketed and she jumped up. "Get out."

"What?"

"Get out! Just go away! Tell yourself whatever you need to tell yourself about how I got here, but do it away from me!"

"Calm down," he said in a soothing voice, trying to reach for her.

"No, I won't calm down. Don't touch me!" She twisted away and moved toward her closet.

"What is wrong with you? Have you completely lost your mind?"

She stopped her rampage suddenly as a thought struck her.

"No," she said quietly. "I haven't lost my mind. It's funny, though, that you should think so. Maybe if Margo hadn't had to live here with your mother, she wouldn't have seemed so crazy, either."

"So, you think my mother drove Margo crazy?"

"As a matter of fact, I think she did. Or maybe she just worked hard at making it appear Margo was crazy."

Kendall remembered all the times that Delores implored Adam "to do something" about his wife. Was her concern because Margo needed help, or because she was too close to the truth for Delores' comfort?

She went into the closet and took out her suitcase.

"What are you doing?" he demanded angrily.

"Brady and I are leaving."

She steeled herself against the pull of pain-filled silver eyes and stalked to her dresser.

"You aren't leaving," he vowed, forcing the drawer shut.

"I'm not staying here."

"Brady is." His voice was ice cold, and his words

and tone sent her reeling with horror.

She wanted to tell him to go to hell. She wanted to say she would see him in court, take her baby and walk away. At least those were the things she told herself she wanted to do. What she really wanted, however, was to throw herself against him and beg him to take her away from here.

She sat heavily on the bed, the fight suddenly gone out of her. As if they were both mortally wounded opponents, he dropped to his knees beside her.

"I'm sorry," he whispered, his voice thick with emotion.

Without warning, a sob came from deep inside her, and he gathered her close.

"I won't stop you from leaving if that's what you want to do. And I wouldn't try to keep Brady from you," he promised as he held her against him.

"I don't want to leave, but I don't know where to go from here," she told him. "I have all these loose ends and can't seem to join them together."

"We'll figure it out together, but that means you have to include me in everything." He sat beside her on the edge of the bed. "If what you're saying is true, the implications are huge. Thinking my brother would seduce you, lie to you and then leave you pregnant and broke was bad enough. To have to accept that my mother intended for it to happen, that it was all planned so that you would come here, desperate enough to marry me, is unbearable."

"It worked like a charm," she said bitterly.

"I'm sorry," he said again.

"There's no need for you to apologize. You were as manipulated as I was."

He stood up and began to pace the room. He stopped in mid-stride and turned toward her.

"Did she know you were pregnant?" he asked in a voice gone deathly quiet.

Kendall nodded. "Yes."

"When did she find out?"

"I wrote him when I was three months pregnant. That was the first letter she intercepted. After that, she intercepted them all."

He shook his head, obviously finding it difficult to believe his mother could do such a thing.

After a few minutes, he resumed pacing, stopping every now and then to ask her a question as he pieced together what she knew from her recent conversations with the Howards, with Douglas, and with Delores.

He had stopped again, his next question obviously on the tip of his tongue, when the door flew open, and Avery rushed inside.

"Kendall!" she cried. "Do you have Brady?"

"Avery, that's not funny," Kendall scolded.

"I'm not joking! Cora had a bottle ready when we came in from our walk. He was sleepy, so I gave it to him and put him to bed. I went to my room after he fell asleep. When I came back, he was gone."

"Someone must have him," Luke assured them, remembering Kendall's panicked flight her first morning here. "Is Mother home?"

"No. She was leaving when I came in with Brady. She seemed really upset."

"Adam?"

"He's in his office, but he says he hasn't seen him."

"What about Cora or the maids?"

"No one has him!" Avery insisted, nearly hysterical. "I've asked everyone."

Kendall remained frozen on the bed, her face devoid of color.

"It's okay," he assured them. "I'm sure he's fine. He's here somewhere. Avery, you go tell Cora to round all the household staff up and have everyone meet me in the hallway, please. Ken, you and I will go down and talk to Adam."

They found a bleary-eyed Adam sitting behind his desk. Kendall spared a single second to deduce he hadn't slept at all last night. His hand shook so badly the whiskey in his glass threatened to slosh over the side.

"Avery's already been here. I don't have Brady, and I'm pretty sure he didn't escape on his own," Adam snapped.

Kendall made a small mew of distress, and Luke put an arm around her. Adam glared at her for a second before her terror seemed to register, and he set the glass down with a thump.

"What's going on?" He turned his eyes to Luke.

"Avery's checked with everyone. No one has him."

"What about Mother?" Adam staggered around the desk.

"Mother is gone." Luke stared at him. "And just so you know, the four of us have a lot to discuss once we've found Brady."

Luke turned and strode from the room, barking orders to the already assembled household staff.

****

Kendall stared sightlessly out the window in the foyer, listening through a haze of disbelief to each person's account. None of them knew anything, and not one of them had seen anyone or anything that might lead them to him.

Luke quietly thanked each of them and asked them to stay close.

"I still think it's possible Mother has him," Adam assured her for what seemed to be the hundredth time.

"She's here. You can ask her yourself," Kendall said when she caught sight of Delores' car pulling up the drive.

Luke and Adam were at the car before it came to

a full stop. Delores took her time getting out of the car and stood stroking her pearls as they began to speak. Then the color leached from her face, and she shook her head.

Kendall regarded her mother-in-law skeptically. Did she know where he was? Had she finally made good on her threat to take him away from Kendall? Quick on the heels of that thought came the question of whether Delores was the person who had tried to kill her. Of course, then she wouldn't need to steal him. He would belong solely to the Templetons. Had failing at murder led her to hide him? What would that help? Unless she intended to kill Kendall and then return to wherever she'd left him. With Kendall out of the way, she could raise him to her own specifications.

Kendall was tired of the pretense and questions, the secrets and lies. She just wanted Brady safely returned to her, to live a normal life with him and Luke.

As Delores came through the door, Kendall stepped in front of her, blocking her passage down the hallway.

"Do you have him?"

Her mother-in-law burst into tears as she pushed past Kendall and dashed into her office.

Luke, Adam, and Avery stared at the door that slammed behind her, obviously shocked at her emotional display.

"Kendall?" Her grandfather's booming voice came through the open door behind Luke.

She rushed outside. When George opened his arms to her, it felt right to fall against his broad chest and be held there while she cried.

"Oh, honey, it's going to be okay. They'll find him. Don't you worry now," her grandmother soothed, running a hand up and down Kendall's back.

"Who would have done this?" Kendall sobbed.

"Where's your mother, Luke?" Louisa demanded in a voice that brooked no argument. For the first time Kendall saw the unflinching woman who had cast her pregnant daughter into the street.

When he motioned toward the study, Louisa marched in without knocking. The rest of them followed her.

"Delores Templeton, I want you to tell me what's going on, this very second," Louisa demanded.

"I'll thank you to remember that I'm a grown woman, Louisa," Delores said haughtily, attempting to gain some composure.

Louisa's laughter was a hard, bitter sound.

"Don't you get an attitude with me. I know you as well as I knew my own daughter. You think just because you want something it should become yours. Lydia learned the hard way that it doesn't always happen that way. You've been blessed with a lot of years before having to learn that. This time, your scheme got out of hand, and it's Kendall and Brady who are paying for it. Now, you tell me what's going on, right now."

"I wanted Thomas, too," Delores said miserably.

The answer hardly helped them locate Brady, but it confirmed what Connie and Frank had told Kendall.

"You girls all wanted Thomas," Louisa retorted before slamming her hand down on the desk with a frustrated curse. "Damn it, Delores! In the end, he wasn't worth a moment of your time. Not yours, not Lydia's, not even Julianne's, though he did the right thing by her. Your Leon was a good man, a good husband, and a good father. You should be ashamed that he wasn't enough."

"Thomas got them both pregnant, Louisa. Except for a few dances that he was forced into out of politeness, he never gave me the time of day. And as if that wasn't enough, Lydia took Leon, too."

What in the world did any of this matter? Kendall wondered. Who cared if Thomas Kendall had impregnated every girl in the state? Who cared if her mother deserved the life she got, or Julianne deserved the one she got? Brady was all she cared about. Kendall listened to the trivial exchange of information from the past for only a few moments before exploding.

"None of that matters!" she cried. She leaned across the desk toward her mother-in-law. "I don't care why you did any of it. Just tell me where my child is!"

"I don't know where he is," Delores swore.

Delores' desk phone rang at that moment, and Kendall dove toward it.

"Hello?" she cried.

"Is this you, Kendall?" Douglas Martin asked stridently.

"Yes."

"I have something that belongs to you. Can you meet me?"

Kendall's heart dropped. The room seemed to close in around her, and her knees went weak. Luke's strong arms slid around her from behind, and she leaned back against him to steady herself.

"Where?" she asked.

"There's a bar called Bailey's between Larrimore and Jacksonville. You'll know it when you see it. Come alone. There will be too many questions if anyone else is involved."

He disconnected, and she stood still for a moment, certain that without Luke's support, she would simply fall to the floor.

"Who was it?"

"Douglas Martin. He says he has something that belongs to me. He's at a bar called Bailey's."

She pushed herself away from Luke.

"I have to go."

"You're not going alone, Kendall," he growled.

"Yes, I am. I have to do what he says."

"She's right. If he wants to meet in a public place, he doesn't intend to hurt either of them," George said. "You and Adam can follow at a safe distance, just to make sure."

****

Rain was coming down in torrents when Juan pulled the car into the parking lot of the bar an hour later. As she dashed through the parking lot without an umbrella, she didn't notice the rain anymore than she noticed how incongruous Douglas' Bentley looked in front of the ratty wooden exterior of the buildings.

Soaked to the skin, she stood inside the door, her eyes searching the darkened interior until she saw Douglas in a back booth. She went toward him quickly, scanning the space around him for Brady.

He motioned for her to sit down, and she did as he wanted. Several empty glasses sat in front of him. Where in the world had he left her child while he sat here drinking?

"Where is he?" she demanded.

"Who?" He appeared totally bewildered.

"My son."

"Why would I have your son?" he cried.

Hysteria bubbled up inside her when she realized Douglas hadn't called her regarding Brady.

"I've got to go," she cried, but he grasped her arm.

"Wait," he said. He turned her palm up and dropped something into it.

The blood-red stone winked up at her. Questions raced through her head, but she shoved them away. She didn't have time for this now.

"You were right," he said. "I was there that day, and I was at your mother's funeral."

"I don't care," she cried. She jerked her hand out of his grasp and rushed out of the bar. The past no longer mattered. The only thing that mattered was finding Brady.

Adam's sports car spun into the parking lot and Luke jumped out and hurried toward her with an umbrella. He held it over her head as she ran back to their car. The rain was coming down harder by the minute, and she had to yell to be heard.

"He doesn't have him! He didn't even know Brady was missing."

"Kendall!" Douglas called from the door of the bar. "Maybe you'll find what you're looking for in the place you lost what you never had."

He slid back inside, leaving her standing in the rain, wondering why he was talking in riddles.

"Son of a—" Luke shoved the umbrella into her hands and turned to the bar, his fists clenched.

She grasped his arm, forcing him to stop. "We have to get to Brady. He's at my father's house."

Chapter Thirty-Six

The house no longer seemed as grand as it once did. Years of emptiness had leached it of life and color, leaving it a corpse of its former self. She wondered if Margo and her mother had lived here at all after that day.

Luke began to get out of the car.

"I need to go in alone."

A chorus of protests greeted her words.

"I'll be fine. It could be that it's completely empty."

"Hello?" she called, once she stood in the foyer of her father's home. The house was shrouded in shadows. Dark stains marred the paneling and the floors. It appeared someone had tried to clean but given up the idea of completely wiping away the past. Things still stood in the places they must have been when her mother arrived. A pen lay atop a tablet by the telephone in the hallway. The coat rack still held several coats and shawls. A cup sat on the end table near the door of the living room, a long-dry circle of water staining the wood surface.

Upstairs, Brady began to cry, and Kendall hurried in that direction, her heart pounding.

She found Julianne Delacroix in what must once have been her bedroom. She stood facing a dresser with Brady in her arms. Her eyes met Kendall's in the mirror.

"We were a happy little family at times," she said waving toward the framed photos that lined the length of the dresser.

"This was our wedding day." She tossed one of

the pictures onto the bed. "You can't even tell I was pregnant, can you?"

"Here's one of my bridesmaids and me. I never could bear to look at it. I'm sure you can understand."

This picture landed closer to Kendall, but she spared it only a glance as she walked around the bed. This photograph was quite similar to the one Delores kept in her study, but the joy on Lydia's face was already beginning to vanish.

"I don't know how she stood there and watched me marry him," Julianne continued. "Her parents must have insisted she show grace under pressure. And I have to admit she did. She held the flowers and smiled for the camera and never once mentioned the fact that I stole him away from her. Delores said she realized she was pregnant at the wedding reception."

"Give him to me," Kendall pleaded, reaching for her sobbing child.

Julianne stepped back, and Brady wailed louder and tried to wiggle free. The grip on him tightened, and Kendall feared it would break his bones. At the harsher touch, he stilled, but tears filled his wide gray eyes and his mouth quivered as he stared at his mother.

"Please don't hurt him. He's just a baby."

"I'm not going to hurt him," she assured Kendall impatiently. She caressed Brady's face gently. "It's funny, isn't it, that Delores ended up with Thomas' grandchild? Margo wanted a baby so badly."

Her face clouded at mention of her daughter.

"My poor baby. After Thomas died, peace just seemed to elude her."

"Is that why you're doing this?"

"I'm not doing anything, Kendall. I'm just holding your baby, and telling you all the secrets you've been dying to know." She walked past

Kendall and pulled the curtain back from the window. As Julianne continued talking, Kendall realized she could see the bench across the street.

"Once, I dragged Thomas to this very window and demanded he tell me who you were. I knew, of course, but I wanted to hear him say it. I wanted to make him acknowledge your existence to me. He started to cry. Can you believe that? He knew exactly who you were, but he never spoke your name to me. He never said anything at all about you. Anytime I mentioned it, he would fall apart, and I would end up dropping the subject just so I didn't have to witness his theatrics, and so Margo wouldn't see her father that way. If your mother had married him, she would have realized what a groveling coward he really was."

"Over the years I heard several times that he was seeing your mother again. By the time Margo started school, I realized I didn't love him anymore. Maybe I never did. Either way, no one wants to be humiliated. If it was anyone else he was sleeping with, I might not even have minded. Every moment he spent with another woman would have been one I wasn't subjected to his company. But I couldn't bear for it to be *her*. All those years, your mother was the only one he ever wanted. If his relationship with her came to light, it would prove he never wanted me and had married me just because I was pregnant. A few months before he died, Douglas saw him and your mother sneaking out of this house at dawn while Margo and I were in New York. Thomas and I had a huge fight, and I told him to quit seeing your mother or leave. Thomas had nothing. His family lost everything years before, but he never had to worry about money because he was married to me. I knew what his choice would be. He liked this kind of life and the things money can buy. So, he chose to stop seeing your mother and stay with me. Your mother shot him a month later, a few days after we returned from a vacation in Italy."

Kendall couldn't help but feel a wave of pity for Julianne. How painful it must have been for her to know her husband loved someone else. But did she kill him and his lover? Or did she truly believe Lydia killed him?

"My mother had a hard life after she got pregnant," Kendall said in defense of her mother. Her hands itched to hold her child, but she tried to humor the woman for fear of what she would do. "Her family turned their backs on her, her lover turned his back on her, the world in general washed its collective hands of her and her child. She was forced to do things I don't believe she would have ever done if she'd had any other choice."

"She killed my husband."

"Did she?" Kendall said quietly.

Julianne's eyes widened. "Of course. That's what the police said."

"Were you here?"

"No."

"Margo saw what happened."

The woman shook her head, obviously distressed by the thought. "No, she didn't. She came in after. She wasn't here when it happened."

"I was across the street, Julianne. I remember it clearly. I saw my mother come up the walk. Thomas came to the door and let her in. Perhaps fifteen minutes passed before the first shot. Seconds later there was a second shot, and Margo began to scream immediately. Not one minute passed between the two shots and her screams."

"Oh, my God," Julianne sank onto the dusty bed, rocking Brady back and forth. She began to cry softly. "My poor, poor baby."

Kendall walked toward them. Very calmly she reached her arms out to Brady, and, to her surprise,

Julianne let him go without argument. Once he was back in her arms, Kendall went to the other side of the room. She took a deep breath, savoring the sweet baby smell of him, the soft, smoothness of his skin, the feel of his cheek against her lips.

"Julianne, before she died, Margo kept coming to me and saying, 'She didn't do it.' I think she meant my mother didn't kill herself and your husband."

"Margo was ill. She didn't always know what she was saying."

"But she was here that day."

"Who would have killed them?"

"You're a good girl, Sis," Douglas said from the doorway. "I knew you'd get the baby and bring him for me. It was the surest way I could think of to get Kendall here."

He calmly lifted his gun and pointed it at Kendall.

"Douglas?" Julianne sounded terrified. "Why do you have that gun? I thought you just wanted to talk to her, blackmail her like her mother did you."

"Do you remember that last summer we were all together, Jules?" he said. "Remember our plan? You would end up with Thomas and I would get Lydia?"

"Yes."

"It failed."

"I got Thomas," she said.

"Did you?" he chuckled harshly. "It didn't appear to me that he was ever completely yours. The best part of him still belonged to Lydia."

"He was mine for years."

"Only the part that could be bought. He stayed only because he was too weak to live without your money."

He waved the gun toward the bed.

"Get over here," he said to Kendall. "Get up, Jules."

Both women did as they were told.

"Give her the baby and sit down."

"No," Kendall said.

"Do as I say!" he roared. Then quietly, "I'll shoot you both if you don't."

Her heart pounding in her chest, Kendall passed Brady to Julianne and sat down.

"Why are you doing this, Dougie?" Julianne asked.

"Go downstairs, Jules," he said sadly. "I don't want them to think you had anything to do with this."

"I'm not leaving you here with her. None of this is her fault."

"I don't want to kill you," he told his sister, "but I will if I have to."

Julianne stepped back, clutching Brady to her. Kendall nodded encouragingly when their eyes met.

"Go," Kendall said shakily. Brady whimpered for her, holding his chubby little hands out. She turned away from the heartbreaking sight.

"Dougie, please," Julianne pleaded once more.

He turned the gun on her, cocking it, before moving it slightly so that it was trained on Brady. "Get the hell out of here. Now."

Kendall listened to Julianne's retreating steps mingled with Brady's cries.

"I tried to warn you, didn't I? From the first time we met, I tried to tell you that you needed to stop meddling."

"You said you loved my mother. Why did you kill her?"

"I put her out of her misery. I watched her suffer for years. I couldn't stand it anymore."

"Everyone will know you killed me."

He ignored her statement. "Do you know what your mother was doing here that day?"

Kendall shook her head. Every moment he talked was another moment she was alive.

"She came here with a gun. A gun I gave her years before. I worried about her being at the mercy of those men she saw. I wanted her to be able to protect herself."

He picked up the picture of Julianne and her bridesmaids. "God, she was a beautiful woman. When we were together, I pretended she loved me the way she loved Thomas. I imagined that it was me she longed for, me she cried for. But even though she never mentioned him when we were together, and she gave me her full attention, there was always some piece of her that wasn't with me. That piece was always with Thomas."

He gave himself a little shake and put the picture down.

"I was telling you about that last day, wasn't I? She came here with the gun. Maybe Thomas called her. I don't know. I followed her. I saw you there on the bench. There was a difference in both of you that day. Both of you seemed more decisive and determined. I knew something was going to happen. Maybe it was brotherly love that made me follow her into the house. Maybe I wanted to make sure nothing would happen to hurt Julianne or Margo. Or maybe I was a jealous lover who needed to protect what he held dear. Either way, I stood just outside the study while they talked."

"She begged him to acknowledge you. She took the gun out of her purse. She threatened to kill herself so he wouldn't have a choice. She thought he would take you in if there was nowhere else for you to go. But even then he couldn't do it. He put the gun to his own head and begged her to pull the trigger. Told her there was an insurance policy and he was worth more dead than alive."

"It was a pity to watch. They were so broken, so injured. I cared about them. She couldn't kill him, and he knew it. She left the gun on the couch, and they held each other as they cried. I guess they both realized it was never going to get better. There was no hope for them. Their pain would go on until they died."

Kendall could imagine her mother begging Thomas to acknowledge her. She'd sacrificed so much to keep her and was willing to sacrifice her very life in order to give her a better future.

"I don't know what came over me," Douglas continued. "I just knew what I needed to do. I shot Thomas first. Inside, she was dead the moment he was. She didn't fight me at all when I wrapped her fingers around the gun. She seemed eager for it. I'll never forget the way she looked when we pulled the trigger. After all the years happiness eluded her, it found her in that moment."

Kendall couldn't control the tears that coursed down her cheeks.

"I ran through the door that led straight onto the side street. Margo began to scream, and I realized she was in the house, but I couldn't go back. She was my niece, and I left her alone with the horror I created. I was pulling onto the street when I saw you rushing toward the house. Leon grabbed you to keep you from going inside. Thomas had asked him to take pictures because it was your sixteenth birthday. I slowed down, and he shoved you in. We both knew it was best for you to be as far away from here as possible."

"How did you get her ring?" She'd slipped her father's ring on her finger when she left the bar, and she looked at it now. It felt foreign on her finger, heavy with the weight of unfulfilled dreams and broken promises. Regardless of the way her mother ended the fairy tales she told, no one who wore it lived happily ever after.

"Margo found it. It must have fallen off your mother's finger. It was always too big for her."

"Did Margo know who I was?"

"I told her. I thought it would feed her illness and the violent tendencies it caused. I knew you recognized me from your mother's funeral. Although you didn't seem to realize I'd been there the day she and Thomas died, as well, I thought eventually you'd put the pieces together. I hoped Margo might kill you, but she was nothing if not unpredictable. When I told her who you were, she was ecstatic. She was actually glad you were her sister."

"Why did you kill her?"

"I didn't kill Margo. Not on purpose anyway. She really did run out in front of a car. I didn't force her to, but I'll admit I was relieved it happened. Over the years, I've come here often. I sit on the sofa in Thomas' study and I ponder how everything went so wrong. Margo had given me the ring years ago, and she came that day to retrieve it. For some reason she believed it should be yours since Thomas gave it to your mother."

Harsh laughter escaped him.

"I hate that damn ring. I wish I'd destroyed it when I destroyed everything else that reminded me of Lydia. But for some reason I kept it. All these years, I kept two things. Thomas' ring and a letter she wrote you. The letter fell out of her purse and landed at my feet when I shot her. It seemed as if she wanted me to pick it up, to make sure you got it."

"I never received a letter from my mother."

"You would have in a day or so. I dropped it in the mail last week. I hoped an actual suicide note would make you stop digging. Of course, that was before you and Luke came to visit me."

He shrugged nonchalantly. "I think we've talked enough now."

Terror careened through her when he took a step closer, the gun aimed at her head.

"The first time I saw you, it was almost like seeing a ghost," he said, resting the barrel squarely on her forehead and wrapping the fingers of his other hand through her hair.

She grew lightheaded with fear as he scraped the barrel down her face and throat. She listed to the side but his hand tightened in her hair, keeping her upright. When at last the gun finished its descent and rested against her belly, his hand fell away from her hair and he laid his head in her lap, his hand still curled around its butt, ready to shoot her at any second. His whole body shook with sobs, and she stiffened, fearing the gun would go off with any movement.

"I'm sorry," he whispered. "Lydie, I'm so sorry."

"It's okay," Kendall said, making her voice softer, huskier, the way she remembered her mother's. She ran a shaking hand over his head. "It's what I wanted, Douglas."

"I just wanted to make you happy."

"You did," she said. "You made me very happy."

He nodded, making the gun move against her. She pursed her lips, praying it didn't discharge.

"I loved you," he said. "I would have given you a better life, Lydie. Why wouldn't you take it?"

Kendall took a ragged breath, tears spilling over again.

"I was wrong, Douglas. I should have chosen you."

"What?" he whispered in disbelief.

"You loved me the most. I should have chosen you."

To her surprise, he stood up and moved away from her, his eyes completely clear of delusion.

When he reached the doorway, he turned. Clear blue eyes met hers across the room, and he smiled sadly as he lifted the gun once more.

"You're a sweet girl, Kendall. Lydia would be

proud of you. But she would never choose anyone over Thomas."

"Don't!" Regardless of her plea, the blast echoed through the house and Douglas fell dead at her feet.

Dazed, Kendall stood and made her way to the stairs, stepping over Douglas' body as she went. Police officers burst through the front door and rushed up the stairs.

"Mrs. Templeton, are you okay?" one of the police officers grabbed her hand as they passed on the stairs.

"Where's my baby?" she entreated him.

"He's outside with your husband," he said gently. Even as he spoke she pulled away from him to go to her family.

The sunlight hit her eyes, blinding her for a moment before she scanned the crowd gathered across the street.

A cry escaped her when she saw Luke striding towards her, Brady in his arms. Her eyes locked with his and she ran to meet him. He grabbed her with his free arm, pulling her against him.

Turning away from her father's house, Kendall saw Julianne Delacroix huddled on the park bench where she herself had spent so many days of her childhood. With Luke and Brady in tow, she walked over to the woman.

"I'm so sorry, Mrs. Delacroix," Kendall offered.

Julianne lifted her tearstained face.

"I'm glad you're okay, Kendall."

Chapter Thirty-Seven

Kendall and Luke were finally in bed, Brady snuggled between them. She was exhausted but found it impossible to sleep.

She thought of poor Margo witnessing the murders of her father and Lydia, and of herself, sitting innocently across the street, waiting for life to change. She remembered Margo's words regarding her father's murder.

Things like that aren't easily erased. They destroy who we were before and shape us into what we become.

She and Margo were both shaped into new beings the moment those gunshots echoed down that quiet, tree-lined street.

It amazed her that in a split second a life could be created, ended, changed. So many lives had been changed by the stolen moments between her mother and father. Or were the stolen moments really those between Julianne and her father? Which woman did he love, and which one did he use? She found it nearly impossible to tell.

"Are you okay?" Luke leaned up on his elbow.

"I'm fine. I thought you were asleep."

"Not yet, but I'm trying. You try to." With their joined hands resting below Brady, Kendall finally drifted off to sleep.

****

"There couldn't possibly be a reason that justified it, Mother," Luke said the next morning.

He, Adam, and Kendall sat in her office, listening to her rambling, nonsensical explanation

263

for the scheme she'd concocted.

"But look what came of it," Adam protested. "All's well that ends well."

"Did it really end well, Adam? Your wife is dead and you can say something so flippant?" Luke shook his head in disbelief.

"It wasn't supposed to end that way," Adam admitted regretfully.

"It should never have started. Don't either of you understand that? You can't rearrange people's lives just to suit yourselves."

He looked at his mother.

"Are you going to give me a reason why you did this?" he asked her.

"Julianne and Lydia both had his children. I couldn't have that. So, I wanted what they couldn't have. I wanted his grandchild. Margo and Adam weren't able to give it to me, so that left you and Kendall."

"Mother, that is the craziest thing I ever heard."

She shrugged, her hand going to her pearls.

"Perhaps," she agreed. "Perhaps we were all a little crazy."

"That's the only reason?"

"I wanted what was best for you, Luke. Kendall is gorgeous, and regardless of how she was raised, she has the breeding to match yours. Once Louisa and George are gone, she'll have the money, as well. They never changed their wills. They wanted Lydia and her child taken care of. They just didn't want to face what she'd done." She looked at Kendall with approval. "I knew Kendall would make you an absolutely wonderful wife."

Brady wiggled restlessly on Kendall's lap, and she turned her attention to him. She could have let Cora or Avery watch him for the few minutes they would be in Delores' office, but she couldn't yet bring herself to let him out of her sight.

"What if she hadn't?" Luke asked. "What if we hated each other? You would have sentenced us to a lifetime of misery?"

"Luke, I'm your mother. I know you better than you think. I chose Margo for Adam and Kendall for you years ago. I knew exactly what I was doing."

"Fine, Mother, I'll admit you've had success as a matchmaker, but that doesn't mean I can forgive you. Kendall, Brady and I are leaving. When you are ready to apologize and stop acting as if you had the right to play God with our lives, Kendall and I might listen."

Within moments, he had their luggage loaded. Delores remained in her study, refusing to watch them drive away. Adam stood on the steps watching Avery hug each of them.

As they pulled out of the drive, Kendall touched Luke's hand. "We don't have to do this."

"Of course we do," he said.

The postman was at the mailbox, and he waved them down.

"Mrs. Templeton, you are a very popular lady."

"This should be the last one," she said with a smile as he handed her the small envelope.

Tears blurred her vision, making it difficult to read the note her mother had penned the day she died.

My Dearest Kendall, You've always been so full of questions, begging me for answers about my past, as if in learning them you could improve your future. One day, you may unravel the secrets I carry. You will find the things I sacrificed—my home, my family, my sanity, my soul—and you will wonder why I chose to give them up. My darling, every reward requires a sacrifice, and the sweetest blessings require the bitterest sacrifices. You are my sweetest

blessing, the one that makes every sacrifice worthwhile. Love, Mama
****

Luke remained silent until they were well away from the house. Rows of citrus trees stretched for miles on either side, and Kendall realized they were in the same spot where he'd picked her up the night she arrived at The Grove. He pulled to a stop and turned toward her. "Remember when I told you that being a Templeton is the only thing that's important and love has nothing to do with anything here?"

"You know I do," she said, her heart in her throat.

"I was wrong." He caught a strand of her hair in his hand, gently smoothing it between his fingers. "I love you, and I love Brady, and if I have to sacrifice being a Templeton to make you believe it, that's what I'll do."

As Kendall leaned forward and caught his mouth with her own, her mother's words echoed in her heart.

Marrying Luke Templeton was the bitterest sacrifice she'd ever made. Loving him was the sweetest blessing.

You've got to get it together, Kendall,"
Luke said when she opened her bedroom door to his
knock later that night. "You can't freeze up every
time someone asks you a question about us."

"I'm sorry, Luke. I've never been any good at
lying."

"Then you'd better get good at it, Sweetheart,
because you're going to be lying for a long, long
time."

She went cold at the realization that she had
agreed to a never-ending lie. She hadn't let herself
think about how long the lies would continue. Brady
would grow up with Luke as his father, and she
would go to her grave with the secret she harbored.
If the truth ever came out, Luke would look like a
fool, cuckolded by his twin brother and his own wife.
The magnitude of what she'd done hit her hard, and
she dropped to the edge of the bed.

"You never even thought of that, did you?" Luke
asked. "What did you think, Kendall? That this
would be a convenient solution to all your woes? Did
you think it was a temporary thing?"

"I didn't really think about it. I mean, I realized
it would be a lie, but I didn't think about it being
forever."

He knelt in front of her, his eyes boring into
hers.

"Don't think I'll let you leave, Kendall. You're
my wife. I've accepted your child as mine. That
means, in the eyes of the law, you're entitled to a
part of everything I own if we divorce. So hear this,
Sweetheart. If you ever leave me, if you ever even
attempt to divorce me, I'll make damn sure you
won't leave with *our* son."

A word about the author...

Gloria Davidson Marlow is the author of several romantic suspense novels. Married to her high school sweetheart, Gloria resides with her family in a small town in Northeast Florida. When she isn't working with ESE students in the local school district or writing her next novel, Gloria loves to read, cook, sew, and travel the back roads of her home state.

Thank you for purchasing
this Wild Rose Press publication.
For other wonderful stories of romance,
please visit our on-line bookstore at
www.thewildrosepress.com

For questions or more information,
contact us at
info@thewildrosepress.com

The Wild Rose Press
www.TheWildRosePress.com